CARDS FROM KHLOE'S FLOWER SHOP

Isabella Louise Anderson

Chick Lit Goddess, LLC.

Cover design by Scarlett Rugers.
Formatting by Polgarus Studio.

Cards From Khloe's Flower Shop

Copyright © 2017 Isabella Louise Anderson/Chick Lit Goddess, LLC.

ISBN: 978-0-9914167-2-1 (ebook)
ISBN: 978-0-9914167-3-8 (print)

To my Band-Aid—my Georgia Peach—
I love you, Mom.

CHAPTER ONE

Khloe Harper

It was a perfect kind of day. The rising sun warmed the chill in the air, there wasn't a cloud in the sky, and a light breeze tousled Khloe's long auburn hair. After sliding her key in the lock of her flower shop, she inhaled the intoxicating scents of gardenias, sweet peas, magnolias, along with her personal favorite—roses—and they tickled her nose. She smiled, thinking how the aroma of flowers made for a great start to the day.

Six days a week, at eight in the morning, Khloe sat in her office at the back of the store to return emails and process online orders. While it wasn't a big office, it had turned out just as she'd designed it. Three walls were painted starfish orange, and various posters of flowers, including several Georgia O'Keeffe prints (gifts from her parents after opening her store) scattered the walls. Her cherry wood desk sat in front of a floor-to-ceiling window, which overlooked a row of rose bushes that she'd planted to make the gray slate building across the street less of an offense to look at, especially when she brought customers back to her office for meetings. Across the room was a square glass coffee table, which was made to look like a table at a dinner party with four place settings. In the center lay a large floral arrangement with fall-like colors of oranges and red roses, along with mini pine cones dispersed throughout, which Khloe had designed herself. Customers always praised the beautiful seasonal arrangements she created for the table, and these often helped make a sale for weddings, birthday parties, anniversaries, and even funerals.

After working for three florists during high school and college, Khloe knew she wanted to work in the floral business. Soon after graduating college with a degree in business, her then-boss promoted her to store manager. After six years, she felt she'd gained enough knowledge about the to open her own shop. She gave her two weeks' notice, secured a loan, and opened Khloe's Flower Shop. While it took time for things to get started and run smoothly, sales finally picked up, and just before Christmas, her store flourished. That was last year, and she had high expectations for the upcoming holiday season. Owning her shop meant everything to her, especially because it distracted her from her non-existent love life.

Right then, her phone rang.

"Hi, Mom," Khloe said, after checking the caller-ID on her cell phone, plopping herself down, and taking a seat at her desk.

"You sound perky," Linda joked, commenting on Khloe's monotonous tone.

After toggling the mouse to wake up her computer, Khloe observed the numerous overnight orders that had come in. "It's just going to be another crazy and busy day at the shop."

"That's great, honey. I'm very happy your store is doing so well, but maybe it's time to focus your efforts on finding yourself a man. Like I've told you, I had a lot of trouble conceiving you because I was in my early forties, and don't forget, you're not getting any younger. I'd love to be able to play with my grandchildren."

At thirty-one, the only child of Linda and Kyle Harper, Khloe was never pushed to be perfect or meet her parents' desires, but just as she had when she was a young girl, on occasion, she still felt the need to please her parents.

"Mom, we've gone over this a hundred times, and right now, my shop takes up all of my time." In truth, it didn't, but Khloe wasn't ready to have her heart broken again.

"I know, I know, and I'm sorry to hound you about it, but I want you to be happy—really happy." She paused, then added in a softer tone, "I just wish you wouldn't be afraid to get back out there. I mean, after Josh hurt you…"

Just the mention of Josh's name was enough. "Mom, I know you and Dad thought I'd marry Josh, but he really hurt me." She covered half of her face with her hand and tried to shake the memory away, but like a strong wind, the memory of his betrayal swooped in, causing her to relive the pain.

"I appreciate your sentiment and know you want only the best for me, but I'm doing okay."

"If you say so, dear, but if those bells on your door chime, and Mr. Right walks through, take him by the hand, marry him, and give me grandchildren." Her mother's over-excitement stung Khloe's ears. She loved her mother, but sometimes she was too brash.

"Mom, please—"

Her mother sighed. "Okay, I'm sorry. I'll try not to dig into your love life, but know I'm always here to listen. Anyway," she began with enthusiasm as she changed the subject, "your father and I went to the Mumm winery over the weekend, and we shipped you two more cases. You should be expecting them within the next few days."

"Thanks," Khloe said, trying to sound thrilled as she leaned back in her chair and saw the five wooden cases she'd received last week, having taken only one home. "It's definitely a perk when I pull out a bottle meeting with my customers, and, as you know, it's my favorite. Oh, and how's Dad, by the way?" she asked, changing the topic.

"As a matter of fact, right now, for the third time this week, he's out with his golf buddies. One would've never known he's a cancer survivor."

Khloe laughed, feeling her heart warm, thankful that her dad was well taken care of by his doctors. "Well, I'm glad to hear things haven't changed and he's doing well." At the sound of a ding, her computer signaled another order had come in. "Well, Mom, I have to go, but give Dad my best and tell him I love him." After they said their goodbyes, Khloe hung up with her mother and got to work.

She took two copies each of the morning's fifteen orders off the printer, and then placed a set in Sharon Stewart's inbox. At that moment, her childhood best friend and only employee entered the store.

"Hey, Sharon. How you doing this morning?" she asked, giving her a small hug, their typical morning routine.

While Sharon was originally only supposed to have helped Khloe during her opening week, she'd told Khloe she enjoyed it so much she wanted to stay on and work for her. This was fine by Khloe because her store was small, and she welcomed the help. Although money was tight, Khloe insisted she pay Sharon, but Sharon only agreed if she'd be paid on a part-time salary. Since she'd come from a wealthy family, Sharon had no plans to take any amount of money Khloe could use for the store. Another thing Khloe loved was that Sharon wasn't shy and was always friendly with the customers—even when they were in the wrong. Khloe was also thankful for Sharon because she was punctual and always willing to work overtime.

Sharon took a sip of her Starbucks coffee. "I'm good," she replied. Then with a roll of her eyes, added, "Though, my date last night wasn't. It was terrible."

"Why?" Khloe asked, wondering what Sharon's story was now, as she thumbed through a pile of catalogs. It seemed like every other day there was some kind of trouble in Sharon's romantic life, which almost always involved someone new. Having been friends for over twenty years, Khloe was used to the drama in Sharon's "soap opera-like" world, just like the day they'd met. It was the first day of fourth grade, and they were both in music class. Everyone was taking turns playing a solo for their teacher. During Sharon's performance, Khloe sat in her chair with her eyes bugged out and holding her breath, feeling pretty sure that Sharon wasn't playing her instrument right. After two minutes of loud screeches, the instructor simply smiled at Sharon and said, "Well, um, Sharon, you can come up for air now." Thinking that was a compliment, Sharon bowed before her fellow classmates before she reclaimed her seat next to Khloe.

"Well, how'd I do?" was the first thing Sharon had ever said to her.

"Excellent." Khloe nodded, trying not only to convince Sharon she did good, but that her ears hadn't been abused by the hideous sounds that had come from Sharon's flute.

"Thank you." She beamed and then, in a whisper, as another classmate walked up to do a solo, she added, "I overheard my mom and her friends say if you put your lips to it and blow really hard, boys will like you." She then pointed at a brown-haired boy in front of her and flashed a bright grin. From then on, they were best friends.

Now, a grown woman, Sharon was like a six-foot Barbie doll, with long blond hair and a chest that men never failed to notice. She had stunning green eyes and a bubbly personality—the kind that you would hate to be locked in a room with on a Monday morning if you were recovering from a killer weekend hangover. Khloe never understood why such a beautiful, sweet, and funny woman like Sharon hadn't found the right guy yet.

"Oh, you know, it was the typical date that involved a nice dinner and great conversation, leading to mediocre sex, ending with a kiss goodbye."

Khloe laughed. "And you call that a 'terrible' date?" she asked with a smirk, leaning against the counter and crossing her arms.

"It's not funny," Sharon replied defensively. "There just wasn't any chemistry between me and Joel. He's a nice guy and all, but I need fireworks, along with *great* sex."

"Ah, I see," Khloe said, trying to sound serious, as if having no "chemistry" on a first date was the end of the world. After Khloe's break-up with Josh, she'd done some serious soul-searching and realized every couple's love story is different. Her parents had been friends for two years before they got together, and there was no chemistry between them—until her mother made the first move to kiss her father. When Khloe was ready to jump back into the dating scene, she planned not to worry about chemistry, not rush anything, and to just go with the flow. If it happened, it happened. If not, no harm done, and she would have less of a chance of getting hurt.

"Oh, come on, you know how I feel. I'm sure you do, too."

Khloe tilted her head. "And how is that?"

"We all want a handsome guy who's charming and has all the goods…you know, the guy who looks good on paper. I want that, but I also want more. I want someone who makes me feel alive, whose touch makes me tingle, no matter how old we are. That's what I want."

"Yeah, you have a point," Khloe replied, watching Sharon tie the store's purple uniform apron over her red sweater and skinny jeans. "I want someone like that, too, but after the whole thing with Josh, it makes me wonder, does love like that really exist? After all, real-life love isn't the way it is in the movies."

Sharon shook her head, saying, "I think it's time you stop with all the Josh talk."

"Hey, we had a lot of good times."

When she met Josh Peters at a coffee shop during her last year of college, with one look, she knew she'd found "the one." When Josh finally kissed her—a kiss Khloe had been waiting for since the day they'd met—everything changed, and they became inseparable.

During her time with Josh, night after night, giddiness blossomed inside her. Khloe would go to sleep dreaming of what their life together would be like: him working at his dad's law firm, her at her flower shop, and on weekends, they'd host occasional dinners with friends. More than anything, not only would she have a wedding ring on her finger, she'd have the title of being Josh's wife, which was what she'd always wanted. Josh was the love of her life, and even when they had their silly fights, her heart still raced, because he was hers. "I love how our life will be when we're married," she once whispered to him as he slept next to her, and that's exactly how she felt every single day.

"Yeah, until he hurt you."

"He sure did," Khloe replied somberly, remembering the beginning of the end. One random night of ordering in Mexican food and drinking beer while snuggling on the couch and catching up on recorded TV shows, she furtively glanced at his phone he held in his hand. Curious as to what was up with the slight grin on his face, she caught a glimpse of miscellaneous texts, which included a very suggestive photo. When she questioned him, Josh quickly defended himself, saying it was just a prank from his buddies, and then put the phone on the table, acting as if it were nothing. Khloe was tempted to search his phone for more details, but she trusted him so she dismissed it, but the texts kept coming, and that's when she started to think something was going on. After that first night, Khloe noticed that Josh held her more, kissed her more, called her in the middle of the day just to say hello, so she tried not to let the texts and pictures bother her, but her intuition ate at her.

In an encouraging voice, Sharon said, "You have to believe in love, Khloe, and just maybe, it's time to try again."

"I don't know," she replied, sounding weary, still thinking of Josh's betrayal.

After seeing the first round of texts, two weeks later, on Valentine's Day, she'd decided to put it all aside. *What better way than to surprise him at one of our favorite splurge restaurants?*

After he got home from work, she watched him start to take off his dress shirt, only after he begged her to shower with him. She didn't want to lose the reservation she'd worked hard to get because it was a holiday, though, catching a glance of his tanned bare skin as he made his way to the shower, she decided to take him up on his offer for a quickie. However, all desire for him halted, and she stopped in her tracks when she saw a red bra strap peeking out from under the couch.

There's no way would he ever cheat on me. Then, Khloe felt Josh's phone glaring at her from where it was placed on the entryway table. Reaching for it, she inhaled, and then entered a four-digit passcode she thought would work. She had no luck on the first two tries, but the third time was the charm. With a clenched her jaw, she nervously chewed her lip, and with a shaky finger she pressed on the email app. Instantly, her eyes widened and her heart sank. Email after email, the name Cande McLove took over Josh's screen, each one with an extremely racy and sexual subject line, with attached images—things her mind had never imagined, nor her eyes had ever seen. She could barely stomach the sight of the most recent email, which consisted of two breasts covered in whipped cream—one drizzled with chocolate sauce, the other with a cherry on the nipple.

Suddenly, it was too much for her to handle, and she felt like she might faint. Khloe forced bile back down her throat as his phone dropped out of her hands and fell to the floor. She was more than disappointed that his new and expensive device didn't shatter into tiny pieces like her heart. That night, instead of going to a fancy dinner and coming home to make love, Khloe went to bed with a broken heart, positive she'd never have anyone to grow old with.

"Babe, you just gotta stay positive. One day at a time," Sharon told Khloe, patting her shoulder.

Khloe nodded, doing her best to shake away her heartache, hoping Sharon was right. "I'm sure everything will work out in the end." Though their break-up was eight months ago, Khloe was still hesitant about trusting men.

"That being said, I have another date tonight, so he might be the one," Sharon said, using air quotes around the words *the one*.

"Of course you do," Khloe said, shaking her head and reaching for a stack of cards to use for the flower arrangements.

Sharon took one last sip of her coffee and threw the cup in the trashcan. "Okay, let's see what pretty arrangements I'll make today." She reached for the orders from her inbox and then headed to the workroom.

"Don't forget that we're the best in the business, and we make a great team!" Khloe hollered after her.

"That we do, indeed!" Sharon shouted from the back room, as Khloe took a seat on one of the two high-back brown swivel stools behind her dark purple counter. The smooth countertop had the appearance of shattered glass and covered almost the entire length of the store. Next to the cooler for the flowers, it had been the most expensive purchase. It had always been in Khloe's dream to have a countertop like it, so for her birthday, right before the store opened, her parents gave her a financial gift so she could buy it.

After about an hour and a half of writing messages for the orders she'd received online, helping walk-in customers, and answering the phone to take a few more orders, Khloe hopped off her stool to stretch, just as Sharon came back in the front of the store.

"Are you finished with the messages? If so, I can start delivering the morning arrangements."

"Yeah, here you go." Khloe handed her the cards, and Sharon attached each one to its designated arrangement. Khloe then double-checked each one, just to be sure there weren't any mistakes, then one by one, they carried the various arrangements—some with balloons, chocolates, or stuffed animals added—out to the shop's delivery van. "Great, I think you're all set," she said, wiping her forehead with the back of her hand, amazed at the workout she'd managed to get in thanks to some vases acting as weights.

"Wonderful. I'll be back later," Sharon said. She hopped in the truck and drove away.

When Khloe walked back into her store, there were five customers waiting for her. "Good morning. Can I help you?" she asked two women who stood before her and proceeded to place their order. *It's going to be a busy day*, thought Khloe, happily taking a platinum card from one of the women and swiping it through the machine. Even though she was alone in the store with so many customers, she felt confident she could manage just fine. After all, she was living her dream and she wouldn't trade it for anything in the world.

Later that day, Khloe yawned as she stretched her arms above her head, feeling the usual afternoon lull. She got up from her desk, walked to the mini-kitchen's fridge, pulled out an energy drink, and put it to her lips right when Sharon came in.

She shook her head, giving Khloe a disappointed expression. "You and those energy drinks. How many times do I have to tell you they're not good for you?"

"Yeah, yeah, I know, but when I can barely keep my eyes open in the middle of the day, this is the only thing that seems to help," she replied, watching Sharon re-fill her water bottle and take a large gulp.

"At least water doesn't have any calories."

"Speaking of calories, I know you have a date tonight, but how about meeting me at the gym before, for an early evening spin class?"

It'd been a few weeks since Khloe had been to the gym, and with the holidays coming up, she thought it would be good to get started on a workout routine.

"Nope, not going to happen, babe."

"Come on, please! It'll be fun! You love tight clothes, so this is your perfect opportunity to wear Spandex," she joked.

"Hardy, har, har," Sharon responded, taking a sip of her water.

When the chimes on the door sounded, Sharon turned to go help the customer, but Khloe stopped her and whispered, "They say that a good spin workout can be like a good orgasm."

With that, Sharon turned around, and without showing any kind of expression on her face, she asked, "Where and when?"

Khloe grinned and bear-hugged her friend. "I'll text you."

"Can't wait," Sharon said, her voice filled with enthusiasm.

CHAPTER TWO

Gabriella Lewis

Finding Charlie splayed across the kitchen floor was the most horrifying thing Gabriella had ever experienced. After an ambulance rushed her husband to the hospital, she sat by his side day and night, trying to be strong, hoping for a miracle that he'd recover. Four days later, the machines he'd been hooked up to loudly shrieked, and Gabby quickly ran to get a nurse. In what seemed like seconds, her life of forty-five years was over, and Charlie was dead. Having no other family, Gabby was alone. Though, thanks to her friends and a lot of prayers, she was growing stronger each day.

Before leaving to meet her Scrabble group for the second-to-last game of the year, she put on her black wool coat and checked herself in the mirror. She hadn't worn the coat in years, but it was no longer snug, due to her weight loss, while grieving Charlie. *Not too shabby*, she thought, admiring her thin figure. Then, with her purse over her shoulder and a sweet potato bourbon Bundt cake in her hands, she headed out.

After making the fifteen-minute drive to the nearby church where the group met every other Tuesday, Gabby parked the car and looked at the white brick building, hit by the memories she had there. Aside from Charlie's funeral, getting married and signing up to be part of the Scrabble group were two of the great ones. She'd made so many wonderful friends within the church, too. Gabby didn't know how she would have made it these past few months without the church services or her friends by her side; somehow she was surviving, which she took to be a blessing. Without allowing her eyes to get misty, she turned off the car, reached for the cake, walked up the small pathway to the church, and entered through the light blue double doors. It was time to play Scrabble.

"The cake is served," she told her friends as they each took a slice. Gabriella, the last one to sit at the square table, joined her friends Clara, Wilma, and Fern. "Well, what all did I miss?" she asked, reaching her hand into the silver bag that held the lettered Scrabble tiles.

"I was telling Clara and Wilma about my grandchildren coming to visit over the holidays. Apparently, my grandson wants me to meet his new girlfriend," Fern said. At sixty-five, the same age as Gabby, Fern was a retired teacher. Her curly white hair was cut short, and she wore gold-rimmed glasses, which she donned as more of a fashion statement than a tool to see. She'd been married to her husband, Bob, for thirty-four years, and had one son and two grandchildren. Fern's family was her life. While at times she could be overly dramatic when she told stories, she was also one of the most honest friends Gabby had.

"That should be fun," Clara replied, taking the bag from Gabby.

"Yes...I'm sure it will be," she began, sounding hesitant. She placed her hands over her heart, adding, "I just don't want him to get hurt again."

"We know you don't," Gabby said. "How did they meet?" Gabby looked at her tiles, switching them around to see if she could make any words with them, but all Gabby could spell with what she had was a four-letter word: *l-o-v-e.*

When Fern didn't reply after a few moments, Gabby, Clara, and Wilma looked at her quizzically.

"Oh, in a quite scandalous way," Fern finally said in a whisper as she leaned in. "They met on the internet," she said in a whisper, and then she shook her head. "I just can't believe what this world's coming to."

"Oh, it can't be that bad," Wilma said with a laugh. "After all, like I told y'all, that's how Frank met his new wife, on one of those dating websites." Like Fern and Clara, Gabby widened her eyes, and Wilma continued. "Oh, don't be so shocked. After all, he worked in the computer industry. While our marriage failed, our friendship didn't. Besides, I've gained another friend in his new wife, Lady Bell…"

"You told us this before, but I forget. Is Lady Bell her real name?" Clara asked.

"It sure is," Wilma said with a nod as she placed the letters *c-o-u-p-l-e* on the board. "That'll be twenty-two points," she said to Gabby, who was keeping score.

Wilma was in her late fifties, worked part-time at a women's clothing store, and had been married to Frank, her second husband, for eleven years. Two years ago, on a random day when Wilma took him his forgotten lunch to a construction site where he worked, she found him kissing a young brunette in the trailer. Instead of confronting him, she furiously drove home, thinking about how she would conduct herself that evening, and if she would confront him.

"The day I found out, I had Frank's favorite dinner—chicken-fried steak and mashed potatoes—ready for him on their dining room table, then asked, 'Have a good day, dear?' and that's when he placed his fork down and admitted everything, which explained what he'd been doing on the computer when he should've been in bed with me." Gasps echoed around the table, but she shook her head.

"Believe me, I know how bad it sounds." Wilma raised her shoulders, shrugging it off. "Anyway, a few weeks later, we parted ways on friendly terms, and when Frank introduced me to Lady Bell, surprisingly, we became friends." She held up her hands, as all three of the other women began to speak. "And yes, while to some, my relationship with my ex-husband and his new wife might seem odd, I don't care what people think. All three of us are very happy." She laughed.

It was finally Gabby's turn to play. "*L-o-v-e*, and I get eleven points," she said, writing down her score. She took the bag from Wilma, reached for four more tiles, and looked up at her friends. "Would any of you try online dating?" When more gasps came from around the table, she chuckled, raising her hands in defense. "Okay, I'll take that as a no."

She sat back in her chair and looked at the word she just played. Since the love of her life was gone, it saddened her to think about not experiencing that feeling anymore. For the past few weeks, Gabby had started to wonder if there was more to life than sitting at home alone each night, studying the Scrabble dictionary and watching *The Tonight Show*.

"What about you, would you do it, Gabby?" asked Clara. The youngest of the group at thirty-three, Clara was also the quietest one of the bunch. After meeting her at a church service, Gabby invited Clara into the Scrabble group. At first Clara was hesitant, but Gabby promised her it was just about a few girls getting together to have fun, build their vocabularies, and indulge in a dessert or two. Clara said she'd think about it, and to Gabby's surprise she showed up the following Tuesday. Fern and Wilma instantly took a liking to her, accepting her with open arms.

Still, during each game, Clara remained quiet, and nobody besides Gabby really knew anything about her. A few months back, one night when she and Gabby were cleaning up together, Clara divulged that her husband of four months had recently died of brain cancer. As the words escaped her, Clara fell into Gabby's arms, telling her she was the first person Clara told since she moved to Dallas. Though there was a distinct age difference between the two women, Clara had become one of Gabby's most treasured friends.

Gabby crossed her arms, holding them tightly to her chest, and gave a faint smile. "I don't know. I'm a sixty-five-year-old woman, and I doubt they have a dating website for seniors," she joked. "Right now, I just don't think I—"

"I bet they do," Wilma interjected, wiggling her brows.

"Yeah, and if they do, you could fall in love again," Clara said in a hopeful voice, clasping her hands together as a wide grin spread across her face.

"Oh, it would be so wonderful for you," said Fern, pushing her Scrabble tiles away from her, resting her elbows on the table. "While I'm not too keen on the idea of people meeting on the Internet, I can see if my grandson can find a legit dating website for you."

Waving her hand in the air, Gabby shook her head. "No, but thank you. There's no need to do that."

"Well, let us know if you change your mind," Wilma said. "I'm sure we'd all love to hear about your dating adventures."

Gabby straightened in her chair, changing the subject. "Okay, it's Fern's turn," she said. As she turned the board toward Fern, she looked at Clara who was sitting across from her. Though she still wore a smile, Gabby could sense what Clara was thinking. While they shared something heartbreaking, having lost their husbands, they were both trying to learn how to live again, and wondered if love would ever be in their futures.

*****

16

Later that evening, Gabby heated a pot of store-bought cauliflower soup, her thoughts still on the main topic at the Scrabble group. *Could I really do online dating?*

"It's so unlike me," she said, shaking her head and ladling the soup into a bowl, wondering where all the absurd thoughts were coming from.

She knew she hadn't been the same after the love of her life died. It was like a part of her died, too. Gabby was certain that she could never love anyone like Charlie, but while she felt guilty about even considering it, she wasn't ready to give up on love completely. *What if...?*

She shoveled a steaming spoonful of soup in her mouth, still not convinced that she wouldn't do it. Gabby believed in love and wanted to be in love again, so the thought of online dating—or, even dating in general—made her curious and gave her a glint of excitement, which led her to start a list of positives and negatives in her head.

After finishing her soup and taking a hot shower, Gabby crawled into bed. She picked up her book from the nightstand, but after reading only a few pages, she put it down and tried to sleep. Hours later, after tossing and turning from her side, on to her stomach, her back, and even trying to sleep on Charlie's side of the bed, her mind raced. Giving up on sleep, she put on a robe, tied the belt around her waist and headed downstairs to make a cup of hot tea. While she waited for it to brew, she took a seat at the kitchen table and listened to the second hand of the clock above the sink. *Tick, tick, tick...*

Charlie would want me to be happy!

In an instant, she turned off the stove, headed into the living room, sat down at her computer, and began typing into a search engine. She took a deep breath and clicked the link for "Second Chances." After reading how the site matched-up couples, along with reading numerous success stories, Gabby was comforted by the fact that if a love connection wasn't made, she'd be fully refunded.

She spent close to an hour on the site, creating a profile, which included a recent picture of herself. After she re-read her profile, she clicked the submit button, and let out a breath she didn't know she'd been holding in. Gabby's hands shook when she heard a ding a few minutes later, signaling she'd received an email.

"Oh, my," she said as she brought her hand to her lips, a combination of nervousness and excitement rushing over her. When she saw it was a message from the dating website, she eagerly clicked it open, feeling her heart thump out of her chest. Her excitement faded when she realized that it was merely to congratulate her for signing up to find love. After reading the lengthy email that assured her they would be doing their best to pair her up with someone who can "make your dreams a reality," she put her computer on sleep mode, and then retired back to her bedroom.

When she climbed into bed just after midnight, she was sleepy, but a sense of giddiness buzzed through her, too, which almost kept her awake. However, within minutes, Gabby was sleeping soundly with her hand resting on Charlie's pillow—just like it had every night since he'd been gone.

*****

The next morning, Gabby lay in bed and listened to the birds chirp outside her window. Stretching, she suddenly remembered that she'd signed up for online dating.

After a few minutes of feeling guilty, she tossed off the covers, pulled on her plush white robe, and headed downstairs. After she made herself a cup of coffee, she sat down in front of her computer.

At first she was disappointed because she didn't see any new emails from the dating website. Then, as she scrolled through her inbox, filled with retail coupons, forwarded messages from friends, and her daily Scrabble word and its definition, an email caught her eye, with the subject line that read: *We've found your match!* A wide grin crossed her face as Gabby took a nervous sip of her coffee, and her heart began to flutter.

"What am I doing?" she asked herself aloud, hesitant to open the email, guilt eating at her heart again. "I can't do this."

She leaned back into her chair. Her eyes wandered around the room, landing on a picture of Charlie. The way his eyes looked back at her, she sensed he was trying to send her a message, telling her she should get back out there. "I just don't know if I can," she said to Charlie's picture. "Okay," she said, finally giving the frame a nod, with a feeling he'd given his permission.

Moments later Gabby clicked to open the email. In it was a link to a message from a man named Harry Hoffman.

CHAPTER THREE

Connie Albright

Connie typed anxiously on her keyboard, looking up from her cubicle every few seconds, waiting for Sharon from Khloe's Flower Shop to come through the glass entryway doors. She had checked her email first thing that morning, and like always, once a week, there was a confirmation about her order.

> *Dear Connie Albright,*
>
> *Your order to CONNIE ALBRIGHT has been created by one of our team members and is on its way to the recipient.*
>
> *If you have any questions, comments, or complaints, please call Khloe Harper at 1-800-555-1212.*
>
> *As always, I wish you a bouquet of happiness!*
>
> *Khloe Harper*
>
> *Owner of Khloe's Flower Shop*

With a sigh, Connie looked back down at her keyboard and continued entering patients' data into the Excel spreadsheet. Six years ago, to pay for her college education, she had started the medical data entry job, where she found mundane tasks enjoyable, and had been looking forward to making new friends. However, these days, she was now a college graduate with a degree in marketing who hated her job, finding it boring and repetitive, nor had she made friends with any of her co-workers. In fact, they barely noticed her.

Compared to the thin, sexy bombshells she worked with, Connie wasn't anyone to be desired. She was tall, frumpy, wore glasses, and, thanks to a conversation she overheard, was known in the office as "the ugly girl who wore tacky sweaters." With the exception of a few that her grandmother had sent her for her birthday, having crocheted each one, Connie didn't think the sweaters were tacky.

So, after hearing enough of what was being said behind her back, and after complaining to her best friend—her diary—she came up with an idea to change things, and, so far, it seemed to have worked like magic.

"Connie!" Mia, the office receptionist, squealed. "They're here!"

With a slight pause to get ready for the weekly act she performed, Connie popped up from her chair and watched Sharon approach. After signing her name to the page on the clipboard, she gave Sharon, the only other person besides Khloe who knew her secret, a quick nod.

Suddenly, Connie found herself in the center of a circle of women hovering over her desk, eagerly waiting for her to read the card that came with the bouquet.

"Well, what does it say?" asked a co-worker.

"Yeah, come on. Tell us," begged another.

She took in the moment, wishing she had a real man who would say the things she had written to herself. "Your beauty captures me more each day, and my love for you grows each time I touch you. I'm looking forward to this weekend…in bed! Walt."

Holding the card close to her chest, Connie forced tears from her eyes, forcing herself to blush in front of her co-workers. "Oh, I love that man so very much."

"Seriously, that has to be the most romantic thing I've ever heard," Mia said, dramatizing her voice and placing her hands on her chest. "Oh, Connie, you're so lucky to have a man like him."

"Yeah, Con, that's cute," began Nicola, the bitchiest of them all. "But the last time I got flowers, just yesterday as a matter of fact, they certainly weren't carnations," she joked, motioning her hand like she was shooing the flowers away from her. All the co-workers joined in her laughter, and then shuffled back to their desks.

Connie looked at her flowers and smiled, her feathers not ruffled by Nicola's comment. She felt accomplished and desired. For a few moments, she'd been the center of attention of a group of women who she knew despised her. Even back in high school, she had been a female nerd, which crossed her out from being friends with the beautiful and popular girls, and in college it was pretty much the same story. It's not that she didn't try to make an effort, because she did, but after failing time and time again, whether it be at orientation, working together in groups for school projects, or the few times Connie went to a pub near the university in hopes of meeting up with a few girls who she thought she could be friends with, it never worked. They either laughed in her face, said that the empty seat next to them was already taken (when it really wasn't), or simply ignored her.

Though it was beginning to get expensive and difficult to keep the lies about Walt straight, Connie had no other choice but to continue the weekly charade.

It's just the right thing to do!, she told herself, taking a seat in her chair before continuing to enter the endless data, while thinking of what Walt's card would say the following week.

*****

Several hours later when Connie got home, she put down her ten-year-old brown and green crocheted purse and slumped onto the couch. Her cats, Buttercup and Tillman, jumped up and rubbed their faces to hers. "At least you two love me," she said, smiling down at her fur babies and scratching their ears.

Glad her grueling day was over, she reached for the remote, turned on the TV, and scrolled through the guide. The only good thing about her day was that *The Bachelor* would soon be on, and she'd be able to gawk at the blond hunk with a very sexy chiseled jaw for a full two hours.

"Time to get relaxed." She stood up and headed to her bedroom, replacing her corduroy burgundy skirt and mustard-colored turtleneck for oversized sweatpants and a long-sleeved T-shirt. With a relaxed sigh, Connie allowed herself to feel like she could be herself, letting her plump belly stick out. She knew she'd gained weight, but her self-made sweaters covered up her imperfections, allowing her to feel that she could at least be seen in public. After scrubbing off the little amount of make-up she'd put on for appearance's sake, she looked in the mirror and smiled, already feeling better.

While she waited for her Lean Cuisine to heat up in the microwave, she took a seat on her couch and watched the recap of the previous week's episode, imagining what it would be like if she were as beautiful as the girls on the show. *If I were pretty, could I be on the show, too, and find love? Could it be that easy?*

On nights like this, Connie curled into a ball on her bed, wishing that she'd disappear from the world, but every morning, she was woke-up to another day. She did her best to take it as a sign to keep treading through life, without any tears and with hope—no matter how little she had—to keep as positive as she could.

When the microwave beeped, she returned minutes later with her less than gourmet dinner. She slumped over her TV tray, stirring the tasteless so-called fettuccine with a fork to cool it, while thinking, *You're never going to be pretty like them, so stop wishing for something you can't have. This is why you have Walt, someone who's imaginary.*

Later that night, after downing three diet sodas, two large snickers bars, and a Weight Watchers string cheese, Connie felt disgusted with herself. For years she tried to eat well, picking fruit bowls over potato salad, and water over sodas, but when she was feeling miserable about herself and where her life was headed, she wanted to give the world a big middle finger, and say, "I give up!"

After all the roses were handed out and the show was over, she made her way to the kitchen to throw away the evidence, when something caught her eye on the kitchen table. She tossed the junk in the trashcan and picked up the paper, which advertised early holiday specials of champagne and chocolates. With a smirk, she began formulating the next part of her plan.

CHAPTER FOUR

Khloe

"So, how'd you like your first spin class?" Khloe asked Sharon as they dabbed their foreheads with towels.

"You know, it wasn't too bad," she replied. "I actually enjoyed it and might take a few more classes."

They made their way to the juice bar, which was located in a secluded corner of the enormous gym. "Oh, come on, you don't have to lie about it. I know how much you hate working out. Remember that time in college when we both went to a Zumba class and you were dying like five minutes into it and told me you'd never be caught in a gym again?" She thought she'd at least get a chuckle out of her friend, but she didn't, seeing that Sharon was focused on the juice bar's menu, and then made and purchased her order, with Khloe following suit, still in curious disbelief that her friend seemed to be enjoying a place she said she'd never go to again.

With a glass table between them, they sat at a booth. "You do know I'm serious, right?" Sharon asked after taking a sip of her Kale Sunset, the "drink of the day."

"About what?" Khloe asked, with her arms crossed in front of her. She suddenly felt a chill with the AC vent above her blowing through her sweat-soaked clothes, and her cold drink wasn't helping the situation.

"Spin classes, silly," Sharon replied, lifting her hands up in the air with wide eyes. "Seriously, I can't remember when I've had this much energy." She giggled and then took a long sip of her juice from her straw. "In a way, I feel euphoric. My legs still feel like jelly, but the rest of my body cannot wait to do it again."

Khloe couldn't believe what she'd just heard, but was ecstatic at the news. "Yay!" she cheered. "I'm so glad you enjoyed it that much. What about it did you like the most?" she asked, before taking a sip of her own drink, but then stopped short. "Wait, don't tell me…it was at the end when the instructor was encouraging us to go as fast as we could." When she saw a slight glimmer of embarrassment, Khloe asked, already knowing the answer. "You had an orgasm, didn't you?" After Sharon looked around the empty juice bar, she nodded. "I see why you liked it so much," and then they both burst into boisterous laughter.

Just as they quieted down, a tall, well-built man walked into the juice bar. He wore neon-yellow tennis shoes, black running socks and shorts along with a white T-shirt, and he carried a bright green gym bag. When Sharon looked up, they locked eyes. The man smiled at her, keeping his gaze on her as he walked to the counter.

"Hello, Earth to Sharon," said Khloe, waving her hands in the air, trying to get Sharon's attention.

"Sorry, I, uh, just got a little distracted," she said, turning back to Khloe, blushing, as she bowed her head and chewed on her straw.

"A *little*?" Khloe laughed. "Come on, it was like watching you two get it on right in front of me."

"Oh, please, it wasn't that bad," she said. "He's hot!"

Khloe laughed. "Well, I guess you'll be coming to the gym more often." She paused and then added, "I figured if I ever ran into Josh, it was best that if I looked all tight and trim, it would make him suffer. After all, a great body makes for the best revenge."

"And you haven't seen him since, have you?" she asked.

"No, but I remember how determined I was to get more fit. Not that I had a bad body to begin with, but I was hell-bent on thinking that having a great—an even better—figure would somehow change things, and that maybe one day we'd get back together. Though, one day—after a long day at the flower shop—I really didn't want to go to the gym, I forced myself, and I'm glad I did, because I realized that I was bettering myself for me, not Josh."

Sharon whistled. "Whoa, that must've been quite a revelation."

Taking her last sip of her drink, Khloe nodded. "Oh, most definitely. Working out the anger, hurt, and loss of our relationship really helped me see clearly, and once I knew I was working out for myself, my psyche changed completely, and for that I'm grateful."

"Well, one thing's for sure, you seem more like your fun and spunky self, and like I said, maybe it's time for you to get back out there."

Khloe leaned her head back and looked at the ceiling, laughing. "I promise you that I'll think about it."

"Deal," Sharon replied, and then ever-so-slightly twisted in her chair to see the handsome man walking toward them. Quickly, she turned back to Khloe and mouthed, "Oh my gosh!"

When he reached their table, he gave Khloe a quick hello, then focused his full attention on Sharon. "I couldn't help notice you when I walked in. I was wondering if you'd like to take a private spin class with me today—actually, in about ten minutes?"

"I'd love to," Sharon told him, "but I don't even know your name yet."

"My name's Leonard." He reached out his hand to her.

She placed her hand in his, jumped up, and introduced herself. "Now that we know each other, yes, I'd love to take a spin class with you. Just give me a second with my friend, and I'll meet you in the lobby. Sound good?"

After Leonard waved goodbye to Khloe, she casually waved back. When she made sure he was out of the juice bar, Khloe looked at Sharon. "What the hell are you doing? You don't even know this man, *and* you have a date later tonight."

"Yes I do," she fired back. "His name is Leonard, and I'm going to take a spin class with him." She reached into her bag and pulled out her phone, and began typing away. "And, as for my date, it's cancelled. Besides, Leonard is way hotter." She winked at Khloe, then, standing, said, "I'll call you later."

"Be sure your legs don't turn to Jell-O," Khloe said, quietly laughing.

"Oh, honey, I hope they do, and not just from my second spin class."

*****

A few days later, Khloe was in the front of her shop reviewing sales reports, which, thankfully, had improved from the previous month. She looked up when she heard the chimes on the door sound.

"Good morning, my friend," Sharon said, sounding upbeat as she tied her apron around her waist, over black leggings and a white, silk, long-sleeved shirt.

Khloe thought Sharon's smile looked a little too bright—even for the bubbly woman she was. "You look like you're in a good mood, not to mention you're dressed overly nice today."

Sharon's cheeks turned pink, then she clasped her hands together and began bouncing on her tiptoes. "I am so happy!"

Here we go again, thought Khloe, reaching for her coffee and taking a sip. "Oh? And why is that?" She held up her hand, adding, "Wait, let me guess, you had another great date with Leonard?"

Sharon sat down on the stool next to Khloe and started yapping away. "Yes!" she exclaimed. "Oh, Khloe, Leonard is just *so* amazing!

Like I told you, after our spin class we went to dinner, but decided to cut it short because our hormones were raging and we couldn't keep our hands off each other. Our chemistry is ah-mah-zing," she said in three slow syllables. She reached for Khloe's arm and held it. "Seriously, have you ever had an orgasm that makes you feel as if you're the doctor in *Doctor Who*, in a TARDIS, traveling somewhere in time, but when you get there, you know that the rest of your life will never be the same?" Sharon's eyes were wide with anticipation, awaiting Khloe's response.

Khloe didn't know what to say and tried to keep herself from laughing. If she hadn't seen the most recent cast of *Doctor Who* on the cover of her *TV Guide*, she would have thought the TARDIS was some wacky sex toy, or even some kind of kinky position. She thought back to the few really good orgasms she'd had, but there wasn't one she could compare to traveling through time. She shook her head. "Um, no, I don't think I have."

Sharon gasped. "Well, everyone needs to have an orgasm like that sometime in their life. But be warned, your cheeks might hurt from smiling because that's how awesome the lingering feeling is." She winked at Khloe. "Well, I'm going to work."

"You crack me up," Khloe said with a small giggle. "I already put the orders in your inbox, and I'll bring you the messages when I'm finished."

"Great," Sharon said, bounding for the workroom.

Dismissing the thought of trying to imagine how "ah-mah-zing" TARDIS sex could be, Khloe reached for her pen and began writing her first card, which was for Connie. Though, this time, to go along with the usual bouquet of the week, she was including a bottle of champagne and a box of chocolate-covered strawberries. "Well, it's good to see that Connie hasn't lost her touch," she said out loud, observing the card.

"What's that?" Sharon asked, pausing in her steps, and coming up from behind Khloe.

Khloe waved her hand and said, "Oh, I was just commenting on Connie's message this week. I feel so sorry for her."

"I know, and I do, too," said Sharon in a soft voice. "It's sad that she feels the need to send herself flowers, but there's only so much you or I can do."

"Yeah, I know you're right, but I wish I could help her." She ran her hand through her hair, then leaned her elbow on her counter, tilting her head in her hand. "I guess I want her to know we've all been there." She then chuckled, adding, "Do you remember back in college when I once sent flowers to myself to feel better? You remember why, don't you?"

Sharon laughed. "Oh, yes, I remember that Valentine's Day." She stretched her arms over her head and yawned.

"Yep, and I was all alone." Grinning, Khloe added, "Besides, my best friend didn't have time for me that night. She was too busy hooking up with the captain of the football team."

"First of all, I wasn't hooking up with him. It was just dinner at a semi-romantic Italian restaurant, followed by a simple blow job that took what, like, about a minute and a half, which was before he kissed me on the cheek and bolted to go meet his girlfriend two cities away." Shaking her head, Sharon giggled. "I wonder what ever happened to those two." Her face turned serious. "Anyway, the way I see it, it's all about self-confidence and taking it one day at a time. That's what Connie needs to do. As much as we want to, we can't help her. She's the only one who can make the change to help herself."

Khloe tugged at her purple apron, which lay over her green sweater, and then dusted a speck of fuzz from her skinny jeans. She knew Sharon was right as she watched her best friend reach for the message cards and walk to the back of the store, the heels of her leather, knee-high brown boots echoing away.

A bit later, while Khloe was finishing up with a customer, Sharon wheeled a cart containing a colorful array of flowers and plants to the front of the store: oranges, reds, whites, and pinks sorted among tall and short vases and basket arrangements. "Okay, I'm off to make deliveries."

After observing the cart and waving goodbye, Khloe said, "Great, see you later." Just as Sharon left, the chimes on the front door started ringing, and they didn't stop all morning.

The shop was busier than it had been in months and Khloe felt overwhelmed, but if she stayed focused, she knew it was nothing she couldn't handle. *What great timing for the shop to be full!* Maybe it really was time to hire more help, especially since the holidays were approaching, but she pushed that thought away, saying, "Thanks so much and have a great rest of your day," sliding a small vase filled with yellow and white roses across the counter.

"You, too, Khloe." The woman picked up the vase and gave Khloe a quick wave before heading out the front door.

Khloe smiled at the next customers. "Hello, and how may I help you two?" Darting her eyes between an elderly woman, who walked with a cane, and a young woman in her early twenties, who plopped her sparkly blue clutch on the counter and dramatically piped in a high-pitched tone.

"Yes, I need to speak to the owner of the store, please," the young woman said, batting her round, green eyes, and tousled her mid-length platinum hair to one side as her lips spread into a fake grin, flashing whiter-than-white teeth.

"I'm the owner," said Khloe, hoping there hadn't been a mistake with an order.

She reached her right hand out to Khloe. "I'm Millicent Mosby," she said.

"Hello, Millicent, it's nice to meet you."

She took her phone out of her clutch and tapped it twice to open the correct application. "You see, I'm getting married in late January—I just got engaged—and I need flowers, but they *must* be along the lines of something like this." She looked at the screen, adding, "Now, of course, I wouldn't want to copy any celeb, or anything like that, but I do want something grand." Millicent turned to the older woman beside her, then said, "My granny says I can have anything I want 'because I'm the bride,'" using air quotes for emphasis, adding in a chuckle.

Though Millicent's name sounded familiar, Khloe couldn't pinpoint why.

"Anyway, this is what I was thinking." Millicent handed Khloe her phone, which was set nicely into a crystal bedazzled case.

Khloe looked at numerous photos of bushels of white roses, bunched together and embellished with sequins, of course, for the bride, her bridesmaids, the decorations for the back of the chairs, and the reception. If Khloe had understood what Millicent wanted, she knew it would be a large order, one she didn't know if she could complete. While the wedding was in late January, with the holidays coming up, she'd already received many Thanksgiving and Christmas orders, and having little storage, she couldn't possibly accommodate a job so large. It simply wasn't possible. *Nope, absolutely not*, Khloe thought. "Um, unfortunately..." Just as she was about to complete her sentence and say she couldn't fulfill the order, Millicent continued on. Khloe hadn't been able to hear the first few requests, because she was distracted by the number of customers that were scattered around her store.

"And last but not least, since I'm a Texas girl, I'd love if the roses could be *locally* grown. While it would be nice if they were flown in from Paris, the city of love—that's where my fiancé proposed,"

Millicent giggled, holding her left hand up to the light and looking at the massive marquis-cut diamond that was placed perfectly on her finger, "I just don't want to be one of *those* brides you hear about, you know?" Giggling again, she added, "After all, I'm not Kim Kardashian-West."

Hiding her eye-roll about the Kardashian-West reference, Khloe nodded, saying, "I know exacly what you mean," pretty sure that she was talking about bridezillas, who more than often were her oh-so-not-favorite customers. Khloe would never forget the first bride she'd worked with, Brenda Flangford, who was now Brenda Flangford-Schwartz. From the day Brenda walked into Khloe's Flower Shop, wearing a black pantsuit, carrying a black Michael Kors purse, and flaunting a black diamond engagement ring. The entire time Khloe did her best to help satisfy Brenda's wants, Khloe felt defeated. Despite snapping at Khloe, being late for all their appointments, and constantly telling Khloe that she'd be contacting the Better Business Bureau—for what exactly, Khloe didn't know—Brenda kept coming back. They'd had over ten meetings—*ten*—and after each one, Khloe would get a call from Brenda's assistant saying that she'd changed her mind on the flowers, only to set up another meeting, which would then run way over the scheduled time. Finally, at their last meeting, still unable to make up her mind, Brenda was once again wearing black, so Khloe jokingly suggested black and gray roses. "Of course! Why didn't I even think of that? After all, the wedding is on Halloween." So, it was to Khloe's surprise that six weeks after Brenda's wedding, she'd received a thank you note, saying how she couldn't have done it without her, and that she'd never forget how much she helped her, and how beautiful the arrangements and bouquets had been. Overall, no matter how bad it had been, Khloe was proud of the work she'd done, and with each bride-to-be, it not only challenged her to do better, but encouraged her to keep doing the best she could.

"Since it's a rustic country wedding, I think local flowers will be ideal for the grand event, and I know they'll look beautiful at Daddy's mansion—that's where the wedding and reception will be." Millicent looked at her granny, and then back to Khloe. "Now, I know we've not talked about cost yet, but my granny will be paying for everything, so when payments are ready to be made, just let me know and I'll have Granny send you the balance."

Khloe's ears buzzed from Millicent's constant chatter. She did everything she could to resist putting her hands over her ears and looked at the older woman who was about to reach into her black clutch, but Khloe stopped her by placing a hand on the woman's hand. "That won't be necessary, at the moment." She looked back at Millicent, and asked, "Um, what did you say your name was again?"

"My name is Millicent, Millicent Mosby," she said with a proud grin. The young woman gently fingered a chain of pearls around her neck, ever-so-slightly, flaunting her new bauble that adorned her stick-thin finger.

Millicent Mosby, Millicent Mosby. Where have I heard that name? After about five long seconds of chewing her lip, Khloe's eyes widened. Finally, she looked up at the young woman, only to see the newly elected Governor of Texas's daughter staring back at her, giving Khloe a slight nod. *Holy crap!*

"So, now that you know who I am...oh, and let me introduce you. This is my grandmother, Edith Mosby," she said, placing her hand on her grandmother's arm.

After Khloe and Edith shook hands, Millicent piped in, "Now, can we get back to talking about the big day?"

Khloe mulled her options. Being able to complete the order weighed heavily on her mind, but a possible shout-out from a powerful family could expand her business even more. *Goodbye, my quaint, intimate, and drama-free flower shop, and hello to big business in Texas*. After she quickly weighed her options, she knew she couldn't refuse, no matter how large the job would be, or how little sleep she would get.

"I'd be happy to help you, but..." she began, holding up her index finger, but before she knew what was happening, Millicent had leaned over the counter and pulled Khloe into a strangling hug.

"Oh, thank you, thank you, thank you!" she chirped in Khloe's ear.

Seconds later, Millicent seemed to remember her surroundings and that there were other customers were around, so quickly she composed herself, then once again said, "Thank you," this time in a whisper, as she straightened her navy shawl that lay gently over her cashmere, eggshell-colored dress.

Edith Mosby offered her hand to Khloe. "It's nice to meet you," she said. "I've read numerous online reviews and have heard so many great things about your store, so I told Millie we'd be in good hands by coming here."

"*Millicent*, remember, Granny?" the bride-to-be sternly but nicely demanded, giving Khloe an embarrassed grin.

"Yes, Millicent," Edith corrected. "I'm sorry, dear," she replied, patting her grand-daughter's arm.

As Khloe watched them interact, it was easy to see which one was in charge, and it certainly wasn't the mother of the newly-elected governor. It was also clear that whatever Millicent wanted, she would get—no matter if it was from her father, grandmother, or Khloe.

Blushing, Khloe said, "Well, thank you. I hope to prove you right." She looked around her store and saw a woman who had been waiting at the back of the line walk out, which led Khloe to realize that her time with Millicent was interfering with other customers' time. "Millicent, would it be okay if I call you later today? I'd love to talk in more detail about your wedding flowers." Khloe reached for a pen and notepad and pushed it toward Millicent, who wrote her home, office, and cell phone numbers down, along with her email address.

While waiting for Millicent to look up from writing what seemed to be a novel, Khloe surreptitiously rolled her eyes as the chimes on her door sounded again. When she looked at the customer who came in, she swallowed hard and her heart began to race. *Oh my gosh, you're handsome*, she thought, looking the stranger up and down. He wore a navy suit and sky-blue dress shirt. His thick, jet-black hair was combed to one side. When they made eye contact, he smiled. Khloe blinked and smiled back, but then refocused on Millicent.

"Well, I look forward to working with you, Millicent," she said, handing her a business card. "Again, I'll call you later today to discuss a time for us to meet. Should you ever have any questions, don't hesitate to call me. I'm available day and night, and my cell phone number is on there, too." She instantly regretted adding her cell number to her business card, imagining numerous late-night calls from Millicent.

"Oh, don't worry. I have complete faith in you, and I'll be looking forward to your call." She winked. Millicent took her grandmother by the arm and headed out of the store, leaving Khloe in a heat of panic. She didn't know if it was from the stress of working for the governor's daughter, the fact that all her waiting customers had lost their patience and left, or that the only client who was in her store was now coming toward her, and he was drop-dead gorgeous.

"Hello," Khloe said, watching him slowly glide his tall stature to the counter. When she tilted her head up, she added, "How can I help you?"

His almond-shaped, mysterious brown eyes stared back at her, and his full lips turned into a gentle grin. "I need a small arrangement, with lots of color—purples and pinks, perhaps. Do I need to order them, or can I take them with me now?"

"I believe I have just what you need," she said, hoping her response hadn't come out as suggestive as it sounded in her mind. "Follow me." She led him toward the walk-in cooler.

Feeling feverish, Khloe was thankful for the sudden blast of cool air. She made her way to a small shelf and reached for two mini vases, which she held up for him. The first one was made up of pink and purple tulips, along with baby's breath, which was placed in a rectangular silver vase. The other was filled with pink, red, and purple roses, placed in a clear, square vase. "Do either of these work for you?"

The man's smile widened, and he pointed to the roses. "Those are perfect," he told her, taking them from Khloe. When he did, his fingers brushed against hers, and she couldn't help but tremble. After holding a stare, Khloe put the unwanted vase back where it sat on the glass case, and then they walked out of the cooler and returned to the counter.

Focus, Khloe! She tried to pay attention to her work as she removed the price tag and rang up his order, but it was difficult, especially when her eyes wandered up to his, and to her surprise, she found him staring back at her.

"Having a good day so far?" he asked, making polite conversation.

Khloe couldn't help but let out a nervous laugh. "If you don't count the unwanted anticipation of working for who I'm assuming will be a very demanding bride-to-be, and losing customers who couldn't stay around to wait for me because my only employee is out making deliveries, then I guess my answer is yes." She knew she shouldn't have been talking about the wedding of the governor's daughter or other customers, but she couldn't help herself. "How about you?"

"My day's just beginning, so I'm pretty good."

"Ah, I see." She collected his change from the register and dropped it in his hands, managing to do everything she could not to melt from the warmth emanating from his skin.

Khloe printed the receipt and handed it to him, ever so slightly trying to glimpse if he had a band on his left ring finger, a little surprised when she saw it was naked. "Well, it was nice meeting you…" He looked down at the business card holder, taking one of her cards. "Are you Khloe?"

She nodded and said, "Yes, I am, and it was great meeting you, too."

When he turned around to leave, Khloe thought about asking him his name, but she stopped herself. *Just because he wasn't wearing a ring doesn't mean he's not married. He's probably buying flowers for his wife, so there's no need to wonder anymore about him.*

"Oh, I'm Derek Thomas, by the way," he said, to her surprise, when he stopped in his tracks and turned around.

She smiled, his sexy grin making her feel faint and wanting more. "Have a nice day, Derek," was all she could say as she balanced herself against the counter.

After Derek left, Khloe tried to focus on her customers and their orders, along with contacting Millicent to set up a meeting, and she was happy they'd even discussed a color pattern in a bit more detail, but she was too distracted by thoughts of Derek. From the way he looked when she saw him enter her store to watching him leave, she felt as if she had a fairy godmother hovering over her, telling her it was time to start dating again.

*****

That evening when Khloe got home, she quickly changed into her pajamas, pulled the cork from a bottle of red wine, and sat down at her computer. After opening her Facebook account, she typed DEREK THOMAS into the search field with curious enthusiasm. After scanning few images, her eyes finally landed on the handsome face popped up on her screen—the same one she'd seen earlier that day. With a smile, she clicked on it, hoping that his profile wasn't as secure as hers was. Unfortunately for her, his profile was protected, so she couldn't learn anything more about him, but just being able to see his picture was enough for Khloe. After a few minutes of staring at his perfect face, she decided to do a little more digging, so she closed the Facebook window and typed his name into the Google search engine. Seconds later, hundreds of results popped up. Taking a sip of wine, Khloe clicked on several links about his business, until she came upon one that read: Sister of Derek Thomas, Dead!, and she clicked on the link. She found it strange that it was an entertainment site that popped up, which led her to think it must be some coincidence that a deceased actress's brother had the same name. *Could it be the same Derek Thomas?* Deciding not to think too much about it, thinking it was some kind of hoax or the wrong Derek, Khloe decided to give up, after realizing it was almost half past eight o'clock.

"Handsome men like Derek are never single, anyway," she said, closing the browser window. She took a long sip, hoping the wine would stop any further thoughts of Derek coming back into her mind, then decided to order in sushi.

CHAPTER FIVE

Gabby

Dearest Gabriella,

I hope this message finds you well. Your profile says that you are new to Second Chances, *and so am I.*

To be honest, I really don't know how this online dating thing works, but my daughter-in-law has been trying for weeks to convince me that I should give it a try. Believe it or not, I gave in for a scoop of vanilla bean ice cream (I have a major sweet tooth).

Well, I guess it's time to cut to the chase and tell you the three things I'm looking for:

1) Someone to spend the rest of my life with. Yes, I know that everyone says that, but at our age, isn't that the truth?

Gabby laughed, then continued reading.

2) Being that I'm somewhat of an active man, I want someone who can keep up with me. I run each morning (okay, walking is more like it), support my community (I love living at a retirement center and attend monthly meetings), and on occasion, I attend cooking classes.

Ooh la la, I love a man who can cook, Gabby thought.

3) Most of all, I would love to meet someone who loves being around family. My wife (God bless her soul) and I only had one child, a son. His name is Jeff, and he's married to Jules. They have a five-year-old son named Andrew, and I'm very close to them and we get together quite frequently—mainly for Sunday brunch. It's important to me that the woman in my life loves—or at the very least—likes them.

Other than that, I'm not looking for anything specific as I love meeting new people and socializing.

Thank you for taking the time to read my message. Should you be interested in communicating further, don't hesitate to email me at harry.hoffman@gmail.

Have a wonderful rest of your day!

Harry Hoffman

Before Gabby re-read his message, she smiled at his picture, thinking how similar he looked to one of her favorite actors, William Devane, and how he seemed like a gentleman. She liked how he got to the point about what he wanted. She, too, wanted to find someone with whom she could spend her life. Over time, she'd begun to find cooking a hassle, and she'd love for someone to cook for her. But it was what he said about his family that tugged at her heartstrings the most. Gabby decided to email him back right away:

Dear Harry,

Thank you for your message. I must say that I was thrilled to receive it. As you probably read in my bio, this is the first time I'm trying online dating and am kind of relieved that you are, too (we newbies have to stick together, right?).

Anyway, here are a few things about me, and what I'm looking for.

1) I want someone I can laugh with. I spend my nights watching old episodes of I Love Lucy, The Carol Burnett Show, *and* The Dean Martin Variety Show. *(Speaking of Dean, I think I might need to replace my collection of that show because the DVDs are starting to skip…sorry for this random tangent.)*

2) Since I live alone, I often make casseroles or pots of soup and eat what's left over throughout the week. Cooking isn't my strong suit, so since you take an occasional culinary class, maybe you can show me a thing or two.

3) I was married to a wonderful man for forty-five years. He died of a sudden heart attack. We didn't have any children, but I've always loved the idea of having a large family. As for your family, it would be a pleasure meeting them.

I look forward to hearing from you, Harry, and hope you have a blessed day.

Gabriella Lewis

After reading over what she'd written three times, she clicked the send button, and her computer made a swooshing sound, signaling that there was no turning back, and that Gabby was officially in the dating world.

Later that day, Gabby received an email reply from Harry, which sparked back-and-forth exchanges that lasted for days. Each morning Gabby woke up to a sweet message from Harry, and she'd learned a lot about him—including the fact that his wife had died in a car accident over a year ago. Sharing similar tastes in gardening, torch songs, food and drink (especially a fondness for fine wines), and a passion for traveling, conversations between Gabby and Harry flowed naturally. She started to feel like a teenager, blushing at the way he always signed his emails, *Fondly yours, Harry*, along with the anticipation of what she'd learn about him next. After finally exchanging phone numbers, Harry called and asked her out for their first date at a neighborhood Italian restaurant. With his charming tone, feeling her heart beat with giddiness, Gabby couldn't refuse.

Dressed in a cream-colored pantsuit, Gabby took one last look at herself in the mirror. Her silver, mid-length hair was pulled into a loose ponytail, making her soft blue eyes stand out and her sharp jawline more defined. She stroked her oval diamond drop necklace, a gift from Charlie, and a sad smile crossed her face. A mist of acceptance—from Charlie and herself—enveloped her and she knew she was doing the right thing.

After making sure she had her favorite light pink lipstick, wallet, and glasses, she reached for her purse and left, feeling the least bit nervous to see Harry. Instead, butterflies of excitement fluttered in her stomach. She was ready to get the night started.

When she arrived at the restaurant, remembering what he looked like from seeing his picture, Gabby spotted Harry immediately. Struck by his even more charming looks in person, she was quite impressed at what she noticed first: his smile, wide and gentle, with a touch of compassion.

"Hi, Gabby," Harry said, standing to greet her and offering his hand.

"Hello, Harry," she said, allowing him to take hers, which trembled slightly.

Instead of shaking her hand like she expected, he gave it a delicate kiss. "It's lovely to meet you."

His white hair was slicked to the side and he wore gold-framed glasses. He was dressed in a white linen short-sleeved shirt, khaki pants, and brown dress shoes. Gabby giggled and sat down across from him. Almost instantly, they naturally engaged into conversation, not stopping until they were served one tiramisu, with two spoons, for dessert.

"So, Gabby, have you ever played bingo?" Harry asked, with a tilt of his head and a hopeful smile.

"You know, I haven't—I'm more of a words-game kind of person, but I'm always up for trying something new," she replied, taking the last sip of her Chianti as Harry signed the check.

"Well, I'm a member of a bingo group, and I was wondering if you'd be my date for Saturday night?"

As if it were second nature, Gabby clasped a hand over Harry's. "It would be my pleasure."

Gleefully smiling, he said, "Wonderful, I look forward to it." He pushed the bill away from him, then finished the last little bit that was left in his wine glass. "Well, Gabriella, I wish the night didn't have to end, but I have to get up early to go see my grandson's soccer game."

Oh, yes, his five-year-old grandson, Gabby remembered. "I'm sure Andrew will be happy to see you there," she said as they stood up from the table.

Both of them standing, Harry laughed. "I hope so because I love that kid to pieces." They stood, and Harry helped Gabby into her coat, then Harry placed his on after. Once they made their way out to the parking lot, they held a stare, for a moment, just before they embraced. Then, after a quick and gentle kiss on Gabby's cheek, Harry said, "Can I pick you up at four o'clock on Saturday?"

She blushed at the surprise of his kiss, brushing her hand over her cheek where his lips had been. She hadn't been kissed in so long, failing to remember all the tingling sensations that came with it. "I'll be waiting," she told him, finally able to speak. Seconds later, she watched him get into his blue Cadillac and drive away.

The whole way home Gabby thought about her dinner with Harry. He had been the same charismatic guy she'd been getting to know over email, and by the time she pulled into her driveway, she admitted to herself that she was smitten. From the way he laughed at her embarrassing stories about her culinary disasters, while she tried cooking for one—which they both agreed was hard to do—the way he let her babble on and on about Michael Bublé, and how his voice sounded as beautiful as Frank Sinatra and Dean Martin, to how she loved listening to how he shared stories about his family, it had been a perfect night with a lovely man. Gabby looked forward to getting to know him better.

When she got home, she sat at her desk and made an online order for a bonsai tree for Harry from Khloe's Flower Shop. She remembered how in one of his emails he had said those trees were his favorite.

After turning out the lights in her home and getting into bed, Gabby thought about how similar Harry was to her Charlie—yet they were so different.

Maybe it really is possible to have two loves, she thought as she drifted off to sleep.

CHAPTER SIX

Connie

When she pulled up at work, Connie glanced at her reflection in the rearview mirror. Feeling confident, she gave herself the sexiest wink she could manage, which didn't look that sexy at all. Then, she went into action, unbuttoning her shirt then re-buttoning but mismatching the buttons, so it looked like she and imaginary Walt had just finished up some quick, passionate lovemaking. She ran her fingers through her hair, slightly ruffling it up. Finally, it was go time.

As she made her way to her cubicle, nobody even noticed her, but that wasn't anything new. *Give it time*, she thought, already anticipating the reactions she'd get when the flowers, chocolate-covered strawberries, and champagne arrived. Until then, Connie focused on work.

At seventeen minutes until noon, Sharon still hadn't come by with Connie's order, so checking her inbox one more time, she clicked on Khloe's confirmation email she'd received earlier that morning.

Connie was beginning to panic because she knew her co-workers would be leaving at noon for lunch, and she didn't want them to miss what was coming—proof that someone loved her, even if it was all a ruse. When a few more minutes had passed, Connie couldn't take it anymore. She reached for the phone and dialed the number she knew by heart.

"Khloe's Flower Shop. This is Khloe," came a friendly voice on the other end of the line.

"Hey, Khloe. This is Connie Albright. I'm calling to check on my order that was supposed to be delivered about twenty minutes ago."

"Hey, Connie! Let me put you on hold and check on that."

"Great, thanks," Connie said, trying to remain calm and kind, but her blood boiled.

Seconds later, Khloe came back on the line. "Hey, Connie. I just called Sharon, and she's entering the building right now, so—"

"They're here," she said, quickly cutting Khloe off and hanging up the phone. She peered over her cubicle and smiled at Sharon, who was holding her delivery.

"Connie?" hollered Mia.

"Yes?" she said, trying to not to sound as flustered as she felt.

"It looks like Walt's done it again." Mia gave Connie a wide grin and pointed to Sharon.

Connie walked toward Sharon, giving her a quick wink. "Oh, they're beautiful," she said, doing her best to look and sound surprised as she managed to take the flowers, bottle of champagne and strawberries from Sharon.

Like bears to honey, her co-workers swarmed around Connie once again.

"Come on, Connie, tell us what the card says," piped Mia. "I just love Walt's cards. They even make me feel admired." She laughed, but when nobody else did, she tightly closed her lips and bowed her head.

"Yeah, and hurry up. I'm already late for lunch," said another.

Letting out a long sigh, Nicola crossed her arms and tapped her foot. "Con, that's a very sweet gesture, and it's nice to know you have such a kind...boyfriend."

Ignoring Nicola, Connie sat everything down on her desk, and then reached for the card and read it aloud. "You're the angel in my world! See you tonight so that we can enjoy these goodies! Walt." She held the card to her chest, casting a dreamy look on her face. "Oh, my gosh," she said, beginning to tremble, just for effect. "That has to be the sweetest thing ever," she said, knowing that the hefty extra expenses were well worth it, just by looking at her co-workers' faces.

"So, tell us, Con," Nicola began. "When can we see a picture of Walt? What does he look like?" she asked.

Crap. Connie hadn't thought someone would want to see a picture. She knew she had to say something, and fast. "Umm, Walt's...well, he's..."

Before she could think of something to say, Nicola waved her hand in the air and tilted her head back with a laugh. "It's okay, Con. You don't have to tell us a thing. We know you made him up." She smirked sarcastically at their co-workers, shaking her head. "Okay, ladies, let's go," she said, waving her hand, and in seconds, they followed her out.

Deflated, Connie sat back down at her desk, panic stabbing at her, and she began to sweat and shake. Her mind was spinning as she wondered what she should do. She knew it was time to take this imaginary man to the next level, eagerly anticipating for it to be the end of her workday.

When Connie's co-workers strolled back from lunch, they laughed as they passed her cubicle. But she was surprised when she spotted Sharon coming in behind them, this time holding a bouquet of two-dozen red roses. Thinking the flowers were probably for Nicola, Connie didn't give it a second thought until she heard Sharon behind her say, "Connie?"

"Oh, hey, Sharon. What's up?"

Sharon handed her the flowers and whispered, "These are from

Walt, too. Also, I hear the card is quite a sexy one." She winked, then quickly left.

Connie reached for the card, eager to see what it said.

This morning was amazing!

Yours, Walt.

"Oh, now what are these?" Nicola asked, standing with crossed arms and a curious, wicked grin.

"Just another arrangement from my love," Connie said, sounding defensive.

"What does this card say this time?" she challenged.

"Actually, I'd prefer to keep this one private," she said confidently, a successful effort to bait Nicola, who swiped it out of her hand.

After her eyes scanned the card, she looked up at Connie. "Okay, Con, I'll play your game and pretend he's real, but I still have my doubts." Nicola then looked Connie up and down and laughed. "Oh, honey, look at you." She pointed to Connie's shirt. "You can't even button your shirt right." She cackled a Cruella De Vil laugh and walked away.

"Bitch!" Connie murmured under her breath, taking a seat, swiveling herself toward her computer, feeling even more determined to strengthen her plan.

Tonight, she was going to make Walt come to life.

CHAPTER SEVEN

Khloe

The following week, Khloe looked up from the stack of cards she was writing and waved at Sharon. "Good morning."

"Uh, oh! What's wrong?" Sharon wrinkled her forehead.

"I'm fine," Khloe replied, with a fake smile and quick nod, hoping her best friend couldn't see right through her, because she wasn't in the mood to talk.

Sharon crossed her arms, lifting her brow. "You're not a good liar." She sat down beside Khloe and touched her arm. "Come on, you know you can tell me anything."

Where do I start? After a few seconds later, Khloe said, "Oh, I don't know, Sharon. I guess I'm really lonely, and I didn't realize it until last night when I was sitting home eating a huge portion of leftover chicken wings." She continued on, telling Sharon about her night of watching a sad movie and having a bit too much red wine to wash it all down with. "And then there's Derek, the guy I told you about, who I can't stop thinking about."

Sharon's lips twisted into a smile. "So, I guess you're ready to date—or at least think about it now," she commented, with wink.

Khloe laughed, and then nodded. "Yeah, I guess I am," she concurred.

"So, call the guy," urged Sharon.

After listening to Sharon give her several reasons and excuses why she could call him, Khloe rolled her eyes. While she loved her best friend, she didn't need Sharon to start sounding like her mother. "It's not that easy, plus, I don't have his number," she said, pulling her hair up into a ponytail with the white rubber band that had been around her wrist. She took a long sip of her coffee, deciding not to continue talking about a man who was probably married to a beautiful model-type woman, so she changed the subject. "So, how's the TARDIS sex going?"

Sharon giggled as she placed her purse on the shelf below the register. "Better than ever," she responded, beaming. "Well, I should get moving," she added then headed for the back room, taking notice of the large stack of messages that sat in front of Khloe.

"The orders are in the inbox, as usual!" Khloe called after her and continued to write the stack of cards. "Oh, and there's only one delivery, which needs to go out in the morning."

"I'm on it," Sharon responded back.

After writing the messages, she whispered, "Oh, wow," as she signed *Your secret admirer*, to go with a pink and red bouquet of flowers to Gabby, thinking how nice it was to see her moving on so well, because if Khloe was in her place, she didn't know if it would be so easy. Khloe thought back to the first time she'd met Gabby. She'd come in, wearing a black leisure suit, had on very little make-up, and wore black sunglasses. When she took them off to introduce herself, there were dark circles under her eyes. As she listened to Gabby tell her that her shop was recommended by a nurse at the hospital, she thought Khloe would be able to help with the flowers for Charlie's funeral, Khloe's heart ached for her, and instantly reached out to help Gabby with anything she needed. From that day on, there was something about Gabby that Khloe admired, and from the looks of it, Gabby was starting a new life.

Next up, it was time for Khloe to write Connie's message. Even though Khloe knew Walt was imaginary, she understood how lonely Connie felt, and a perk—no matter how small—could brighten up a day. Though things were a little different in Khloe's case, she admired Connie's tenacity to go after what she wanted—make-believe or not, which reminded Khloe how happy she was happy she was able to help Connie last week. When she found out that Sharon had car trouble and was late with Connie's delivery, she had Sharon deliver another arrangement right away.

An hour later, Khloe walked into the workroom to check on Sharon. "How's it coming?" she asked.

"Pretty well," Sharon replied, keeping her focus on the bow she was tying around the brown paper surrounding an arrangement. "Have you been able to concentrate on work and not think about Derek?" She did her best not to snicker, but a giggle escaped, and she burst out laughing.

Khloe rolled her eyes. "Actually, *Mom*, I focused just fine, though he's still right here in my heart," she said, with drama and sarcasm, placing her hand on her chest.

Sharon cracked up, which made Khloe laugh, too. "You think you're so funny, don't you?" After Khloe nodded, Sharon diverted the conversation back to work. "I'll be leaving shortly to make that one delivery."

Khloe tilted her head, looking over the arrangements, remembering it was to go to Mary Knight, someone they hadn't delivered to before. "You know what, Sharon, I'll take care of this one. I'd like to meet the recipient, and when I'm on my way back, how about I pick up lunch for us, too? A tuna sandwich from Tom's Deli?"

Sharon's eyes widened. "Oh, that sounds so good! I haven't had one of those in forever."

Khloe reached for Mary's arrangement, saying, "Great!" before walking out the door, but then she turned around, with her hand held up, and before she said anything else, Sharon took the words right out of her mouth.

"Don't worry. I'll handle things up front."

"Thanks so much," Khloe told her, and a minute later, Khloe was driving out of the shop's parking lot.

*****

As Khloe pulled up to a high-rise office building in downtown Dallas, she observed the perfectly manicured lawn, with an array of orange, red, and white pansies surrounding the building. Re-checking the suite number that was on the outside flap of the card, which was attached to the arrangement, Khloe carefully retrieved the arrangement from the floor of her backseat, walked up the narrow pathway, and headed to Mary's office.

"Hello, and welcome to Thomas and Associates. How can I help you?" asked a woman who sat behind a dark cherry wood desk. The woman, who looked to be in her early seventies, wore a light pink sweater. Her graying hair was pulled into a loose bun and her tortoiseshell glasses sat at the tip of her nose.

"I'm Khloe, from Khloe's Flower Shop, and I have a delivery for Mary Knight."

The woman blinked as she slowly stood. "I-I'm Mary Knight," she said, speaking quietly as she placed a hand on her chest, looking surprised.

Khloe held out the flowers. "Well, these are for you."

As Mary took the arrangement, Khloe watched her eyes light up, which was just one of the many reasons she loved her job.

"I can't remember the last time someone sent me flowers," Mary commented, placing the arrangement on her desk and reached for the envelope attached. Right at that moment, a door opened, catching them both off guard.

Before she saw his face, Khloe heard a man say, "Mary, could you please reschedule the meeting with Talisker, and I..."

Derek Thomas! Since meeting him, Khloe hadn't forgotten a single thing about him, including his deep, sexy voice, and now, here he was standing in front of her.

"Well, hello," Derek said as a smile crossed his face, halting in his place. "This is a pleasant surprise."

"Hi," Khloe said, her heart fluttering. "I was just making a delivery." She pointed to the flowers on Mary's desk.

Derek nodded. "Ah, I see," he said, not sounding the least bit surprised.

While Khloe and Derek stared at one another, Mary opened the card. "That is so sweet of you to send me flowers, Mr. Thomas, but why..." she began to say to her boss, but then she looked at Derek and Khloe's expressions as they stared at one another. "Ah ha! I get it now," Khloe thought she heard Mary mumble, but she couldn't be too sure because she was captured under Derek's spell. Seconds later Mary reached for her purse, put on her overcoat, and said, "Well, it was nice meeting you, Khloe. Mr. Thomas, I'm going to the bank and then to have lunch, but I'll be back later." Before Derek replied, Mary walked out the door, leaving Khloe alone with Derek.

"Well, I guess I should be going now, too," she said, shaking herself out of Derek's hold he had on her, when she heard the door shut. She took two steps back, about to leave, but Derek's smooth voice stopped her in her tracks.

"Khloe?"

She turned and looked at him, delightfully surprised to see him take a step toward her. "Have lunch with me today." It wasn't a question but rather a gentle request. *He's asking me to lunch?* He looked down at his watch, adding, "I have a meeting I need to get to right now, but maybe we could do a late lunch—"

"I'd love to," she interrupted him, sounding as if she were in a breezy trance, like she was lying on a secluded beach without a care in the world.

"How about we meet at The Thai Orchid?" Derek's grin widened as he put his hands on his hips, allowing Khloe to get a good look at him. She loved the open buttons on his purple and white striped golf shirt, exposing little black curls of his chest hair. His black leather belt had a shiny silver clasp that glistened in the light and brought attention to the waist of his black pants. Khloe couldn't pull her eyes away. "Khloe?"

Batting her eyes, she felt heat rise to her cheeks. He'd caught her staring at his pants. "Lunch…" was all she said, trying to do her best to get it together and stop acting like such a klutz in front of him.

"We could have Mexican, or even Italian, if you'd prefer."

She ran a nervous hand through her hair. "No, Thai is great with me, and I look forward to it," she answered, relieved her brain was working again, and that she was regaining consciousness from being invited to lunch with the most handsome man she'd ever met.

"Great! How about we meet there, let's say two thirty?"

"Perfect!" If Khloe didn't know better, she'd have thought she was having a heart attack, because her heart was racing way too fast, she'd begun to sweat on the back of her neck, and she was doing her best to balance herself in her shoes. "Well, I'll see you then," she said, and giving him a small smile and a wave goodbye, exiting as quickly as she could.

CHAPTER EIGHT

Gabby

Gabby clasped her hands together, eager to hear from Harry. She'd never sent a plant to a man before, but as Wilma and Clara kindly reminded her, this was her new life now and she should make the most of it.

While she waited to hear from him, Gabby caught up on laundry and tidied up her home. By the time she finished all her chores it was lunchtime, she still hadn't heard from Harry, and she was getting a little worried. What if he'd received his surprise and it scared him off?

Before she allowed herself to think more of it, she decided to call Fern. She needed to hear from someone that it was okay to wonder if she'd done the wrong thing.

"What have I done?" she asked after Fern picked up the phone. "After my date with Harry—"

"Oh, how was it?" she asked, interrupting.

Gabby smiled into the phone. "It was great. We had a wonderful evening. He's a very caring and sweet man."

"So, what's the problem?"

"I sent him a plant—a bonsai tree, which is his favorite," Gabby replied sheepishly, "and I have yet to hear from him."

Fern giggled. "Gabby, you didn't do anything wrong, and I'm

sure you'll hear from him soon. Besides, it's normal to think like this. It was your first experience back out there, and I'm proud of you—we all are. I think you should give it time." She paused, then smacked her lips and added, "Besides, it's not even noon. You don't know if his plant arrived yet."

She had a point. Gabby let out a deep breath, one she hadn't realized she'd been holding. "Thanks, Fern." Seconds later, Gabby confided in her friend, telling her more details about her date with Harry. After a few laughs, Gabby thanked Fern for helping calm her nerves.

"Darlin', you can always count on me. Now, if you don't mind, I'm off to report the news to Clara and Wilma, as I'm sure they want to hear all about your date."

Gabby laughed. "Okay, I'll talk to you soon," she said, and they hung up.

In the meantime, Gabby tried to busy herself by eating a grilled cheese sandwich and tomato bisque. *Why isn't he calling me?* She took an angry bite of her sandwich, pondering her next move. *Fine, if he doesn't call in the next five minutes, I'm done with him.* After five, and then ten minutes passed, she found herself too angry to eat and tossed her plate and bowl into the sink, almost breaking them, just as her phone rang.

"Harry?" she asked, panting into the phone.

"Gabby, darling," he began with a joyful tone. "I received my bonsai tree, and it's perfect. Thank you so much."

Gabby sighed with relief. "Oh, Harry, you're so welcome. I just wanted to let you know how much I enjoyed our dinner."

"I had a great time getting to know you, Gabby." He paused. "Are you okay? You don't sound like yourself."

"Well, if you must know, and I know this is silly, I was worried about not hearing from you. I started to think I'd been too forward in sending you the bonsai tree." She laughed nervously. "After all, we just met." Gabby closed her eyes and shook her head, knowing how childlike she was acting, but she couldn't help it. This was all new to her.

Harry roared with laughter. "Oh, Gabby, you had nothing to worry about. After going to Andrew's game this morning, Jeff and Juliet invited me to join them for brunch. I just got home and called you right away."

"I'm happy you did, and I'm glad you like your tree." Gabby let out a silent, relieved sigh. Not only was she grateful that Harry found his gift likable, she was relieved and happy that she hadn't scared him away.

"Yes, I do very much so, and I feel the same about you, too, Gabby," he said, his voice gentle. "I even told my family about you." He chuckled. "And my grandson, Andrew, is eager to meet you."

Not only does he like me, he told his family about me? Blushing, Gabby twirled the phone cord around her finger. "You can tell Andrew that I think his grandfather's a pretty cool guy."

They talked a few more minutes, but before hanging up, Harry said, "Gabby, thanks again for the tree. It really was sweet of you."

"You're very welcome, Harry."

"Well then, I'll see you on Saturday for bingo?"

"I'm looking forward to it," she said and hung up. Gazing out the window at the cool fall day, the sun shining brightly, she thought of Harry, and wished Saturday wasn't so far away.

CHAPTER NINE

Connie

When Connie got home that night, she climbed into bed with Buttercup and Tillman and opened her laptop. She typed "Walt Goldman" into a search engine and thousands of responses popped up. One by one, she clicked on images of men with the same name, but Connie was looking for a certain one—one who would match a certain criteria. He had to be single, live near her, wear glasses, have slicked-back jet-black hair, and could *not* be attractive whatsoever. After all, she had to pick someone who would look the part to be seen with her, thinking that a non-attractive nerdy-type would be perfect for the job. There was no way a handsome man was going to be convincing to her co-workers, knowing full well that sexy men like Henry Cavill and Channing Tatum weren't standing in line waiting to meet a girl like her.

By midnight, Connie still hadn't come across anyone who could play the role of Walt. Feeling overwhelmed and stressed, she decided to take one last chance on finding her man, which was to sign up for a free trial on an online dating site. She quickly created a profile, answered all the necessary information, and added a picture, which was her work ID—the best she could find on short notice. It wasn't the best picture of her, nor was it the worst—it was just Connie on a typical day—no frills or fuss, very little make-up, glasses, and a weak smile.

After clicking on "submit," she was granted access to pictures of hundreds of men. Finally, she came across a man with the name Walt Goldman. Her eyes widened, and her heart began to race. "That's him," Connie said in a whisper, readjusting herself as she sat up in bed, feeling recharged for her mission.

Staring back at him, Walt Goldman seemed to fit everything she'd required, including a few pimples on his chin and forehead. *He's perfect!* Connie cheerfully clapped her hands, feeling giddy, and began to compose a message to him:

Hi, Walt!

I came across your profile, and I love your picture. Seriously, you're so handsome! I could say that I'm a huge fan of French food, opera, British TV shows, and traveling, but that would be a lie, so let me tell you a little bit about myself. I'm addicted to chocolate, preferably Snickers bars. I love CCR and The Rolling Stones. I love The Bachelor *and* The Mindy Project *and am more of a homebody who would rather stay in for dinner instead of going out.*

I hope you find this honesty to be refreshing. I've heard horror stories about online crazies (a.k.a., liars).

Well, Walt, I hope to hear back from you, and maybe we can meet soon.

Have a good night!

Connie Albright

After reading over her message, she quickly clicked the send button, and did a mini-happy dance in her bed. There, it was done.

She'd contacted Walt Goldman, but what surprised her the most was that everything she told him was true. Now, all she had to do was wait for him to respond.

Shutting the laptop and putting it aside, Connie sank into her bed and closed her eyes. All her life, she'd dreamed of having a boyfriend, but sadly, her world hadn't turned out like the popular girls'. The one time she *thought* she had boyfriend was back in high school, but two weeks later word spread like wildfire through the school that Andy McMiller was only dating her to write his papers. Thanks to her, he had become eligible to play in the school's homecoming football game (after all, the team needed their star quarterback). Sadly, it had only been one big joke.

Though years had passed, not even food could comfort her, because it was parents and sister that she missed the most. They were the ones who had loved her just as she was, gave her as much confidence as possible...but that was before the accident.

CHAPTER TEN

Khloe

After stopping at Tom's Deli to pick up Sharon's sandwich, Khloe drove back to her store with the windows down. Derek was getting to her. She'd never had anyone affect her the way he did, and she didn't know how to handle it. She started to wonder why he wanted to have lunch with her. While Khloe thought she was pretty enough, she didn't think of herself as an overly attractive woman, who prided on the fact that she was to be a successful business owner. The only thing she could think of was that he wanted to talk business. *Yes, that has to be it!*

"Hey," Khloe said to Sharon when she walked back inside her shop. Khloe set her purse and the sack from Tom's Deli on the counter and took a seat to watch as Sharon arranged a cornucopia with an array of festive and holiday colors.

"Hey back," replied Sharon. "There, all done." She put her hands on her hips and stepped back to admire her work.

Knowing her mind was elsewhere, she tried to make her voice sound enthusiastic, saying, "It's gorgeous."

"You look stressed," Sharon commented, peeking her head into the brown paper bag.

"You couldn't be more right," Khloe said in a breezy tone, hoping to avoid all the thoughts rushing through her head as she picked on a cuticle, wishing she had time for a manicure. Between the holiday orders and Millicent's wedding, Khloe didn't have a moment to think outside the flower world—except, of course, her constant thoughts of Derek—and now their upcoming lunch. It was completely out of character for her to be thinking so much about a man she'd only been around twice. She'd sworn off thinking about men in a romantic way after the whole fiasco with Josh, so what was it about Derek that was so different?

"Uh, there's only one sandwich in here. I thought we were having lunch together."

"Yeah, so guess who works at Mary's office?" Khloe watched Sharon pull out her pickle, sandwich, and bag of chips, then watched as she popped a chip into her mouth.

Sharon wiped her hands on her apron, and then crossed her arms, waiting for Khloe to answer. "Who?"

Khloe grasped the table in front of her, finally saying, "Derek Thomas." *Handsome, sexy, and damn delightful Derek Thomas.* "Also, he asked me to lunch."

"Ooh la la!" Sharon said, clapping her hands after taking a small bite of her sandwich. "Yay! This is so exciting! Your mother is going to be so happy! Have you told her yet?"

Khloe laughed. "Are you crazy? No, I haven't told her anything because it *just* happened, and because there's no point, because it's only business."

Sharon whistled, then started chanting, "Khloe has a date! Khloe has a date!"

"Uh, no! This certainly is *not* a date," Khloe replied defensively, though a slight spark ran through her, wondering if it could in fact be a date. But she killed that thought, remembering that he was probably married. "Anyway, the arrangement I just delivered was for his assistant. I'm guessing he's looking to place orders for the holiday season for his clients, so it's just business."

"If you say so, but don't say I didn't warn you." Sharon looked Khloe up and down, then added, "You might want to freshen up before you go. Lip gloss and blush can do a lot for a *date*," she said, emphasizing the last word.

Khloe stood. "Sharon, stop," she said, this time more insistently. *I've got to be right about this, because I can't take the chance to get hurt again!* She went into her office and firmly shut the door behind her. She wasn't mad at Sharon, instead Khloe hoped her friend wasn't right—she didn't want to get her heart broken after she'd just pieced it back together.

She took two deep breaths, sat down in front of her large glass desk, and plopped her arms down, bowing her head onto the cool glass. After calming herself, she glanced up at the clock on her computer, realizing she had plenty of time to kill before meeting Derek.

To pass the time, she forced herself into work mode and did the best she could to concentrate—and not on Derek. Khloe did a search on Pinterest to find inspiration for Millicent because they were meeting the next day. Happy the bride had decided to go with extraordinary bunches of roses that would be displayed everywhere, Khloe wanted to be as prepared as she could for anything Millicent threw her way. After making a quick call to her wholesale distributor, Khloe was comforted by the fact that there shouldn't be a problem with the large order. She then sorted mail and shuffled through catalogs for gift ideas for her store and placed orders.

When her phone beeped, signaling that her lunch with Derek was in thirty minutes, she looked at the clock on her computer, noticing how quickly time had passed. Khloe took off her black-lace Tieks flats, reached into her bottom desk drawer, pulled out a pair of three-inch black heels, and slipped them on. While they weren't anything special, since she was meeting Derek for business, she figured she'd better dress the part. In preparation, she grabbed three purchase orders, along with several pamphlets and brochures, and stuffed them in her purse. Then Sharon's words popped into her head, so Khloe grabbed her compact mirror from her purse. She didn't think she looked that bad, but she could use more lip gloss after all, *only* because it was fall and her lips were a bit chapped. Reaching deeper into her purse for her a tube of Chanel's nuteral-colored gloss, she applied it to her lips. Finally, it was go time!

"Well, don't you look fancy," said Sharon when Khloe came into the front of the store. "I like the shoes, too." Nodding with approval, she added, "Very nice touch." A devilish smile crossed Sharon's face. "I usually don't wear my 'I'm horny' heels before seven, but hey—"

"Stop that," Khloe interrupted, trying unsuccessfully to hold in a laugh. "You're unbelievable!" She looked at her watch, noting that she needed to get going. "Well, I'm off, but I'll be back after lunch, so I'm trusting you to be on your best behavior and not tell customers I'm on a date," she joked.

"It'll be hard, but I think I can manage," Sharon joked back.

Khloe rolled her eyes. "Just call me if there are any problems." With that, Khloe was out the door to meet with Derek.

CHAPTER ELEVEN

Gabby

Gabby's life seemed to be blooming, and it was all thanks to the new man in her life.

When Harry had picked her up promptly at four o'clock on Saturday afternoon, he drove them to the small bingo hall. It was in a large dining room at the quaint retirement complex where he lived. Taking a seat beside her, he told Gabby about an easy way never to confuse the two bingo cards that were placed in front of her.

"Yeah, and what's the secret?" she asked, excited to play.

"It's called paying attention and being confident in your hearing." He pointed to his ear, where he wore a tiny hearing aid. "But the most important thing is to keep your eye on the prize."

"Oh," she said, her eyes widening. "What's the prize?"

Harry pointed to the stage. "See the boxes?"

Gabby saw two large boxes that were colored in bright, sparkly wrapping paper: one was white; the other, red. She nodded. "Yes."

"Well, in each one, there are several small boxes. When someone wins, they will be asked to pick a box. Now, there's one important thing." Harry leaned in closer to Gabby and whispered, "This isn't your typical bingo hall. There's all types of people here, so some gifts might be innocent, but some might not." A mischievous grin spread across his face.

Gabby widened her eyes again and tried to stifle a laugh. Dramatically, she put her hand over her mouth. "Oh my!"

Harry laughed, shaking his head. "Don't say I didn't forewarn you."

"I got it," she said, eager to begin. "Good luck, Harry."

"Sweetheart, I don't need luck. I've got you."

She batted her eyes just as the lights flickered, and a woman's voice announced it was time to begin.

On the fifth round of the first game, after double-checking she was right, Gabby stood and shouted, "Bingo!" After it was confirmed that she was a winner, the female announcer asked Gabby what colored box she wanted her gift to come from. She didn't give it a second thought, instantly picking red. Just as she did, fellow players began whistling and clapping. Feeling shy, she looked at Harry, who gave her a wink. His smile relaxed her, calming her enough to accept the overwhelming attention coming from the crowd.

After deciding to play another game, where neither of them won, Harry drove Gabby home, she invited him in and he joyfully accepted.

"You have a lovely home," he told her as she handed him a cup of coffee.

"Thanks, Harry. I'm quite fond of it." She sat across from him, and in a quick second, memories of her husband began to swarm. Charlie had given her a key to the house on their wedding day. While it had seen ups and downs and stood through dangerous thunderstorms and tornadoes, she'd thought about selling it after Charlie died, but she couldn't let go of his memory, nor did she want to—at least not yet.

Harry took a sip of his coffee and asked, "So, how did you like playing bingo?"

"Oh, Harry, I had the best time today," she replied with a bright grin. "It was so much fun, but most of all, I can't believe I won." She shook her head with a sigh. "I can't remember the last time I won anything." Standing, she continued, "Let me get the box, and we'll open it together." When she returned, she sat back down next to him. "I'm eager to see what's inside," she said, tugging on the white ribbon.

Harry placed his hand over hers to stop her. "Gabby, please, just remember my warning to you earlier."

Gabby shooed his hand away. "Oh, please, I'm sure I can handle whatever's in this box. It's not like I'm a prude or anything."

With widened eyes, a surprised smile crossed his face. "Well, then by all means, go ahead."

When Gabby removed the lid, at first she was in shock, but only for a moment, until she started laughing. Finally, after containing herself, she said, "Now I know why you warned me!"

Harry looked at the prize in the box and smiled sheepishly. "Hey, I did what I could."

Once again, Gabby burst into more laughter, and Harry followed along this time. Once they quieted down, they stared down at her prize, which was a red mini-vibrator. From the ones she'd seen in her younger years, Gabby was quite impressed how far they'd come. She hadn't used one in well over two decades. "I guess I'll have to give the old thing a try tonight," she joked, and then, once again, they chuckled until tears ran down their cheeks. Placing the box on the floor beside her feet and wiping the corners of her eyes, she told him, "Again, I had a great time today, and I thank you for inviting me. You're really fun to be around, Harry Hoffman."

"You're not too bad yourself, wild woman."

Gabby giggled like a teenager. "Very funny."

After chatting a bit longer, he reached for her hands and gently rubbed his thumb over her soft skin. "Would you like to come with me to my grandson's soccer game tomorrow? Jeff and Jules will be there, too. I know they would all love to meet you."

She was hesitant at first because she didn't expect to spend the whole weekend with him, or to meet his family so soon, but she realized it was just another step to possibly find love again, and she wasn't going to let it pass her by. "I'd love to."

CHAPTER TWELVE

Connie

The usually punctual Connie thought about sleeping in, but she couldn't. She'd been too excited to sleep. She found him—the man who she hoped would portray Walt. With a thousand thoughts running through her head, she had stayed up late writing notes, ensuring that there would be no pitfalls where Walt was concerned. Connie couldn't afford to mess this up.

After a quick shower, she threw on jeans, a white V-neck T-shirt, and an orange knitted sweater, then left for work, thankful it was casual day. "Thank goodness it's Friday," she murmured to herself, pulling in the parking lot and counting the hours until it was officially the weekend. With a bright smile she entered her office, ready to tackle whatever the day had to offer.

"Hey, Connie," Mia said, rising to greet her. "You just missed Sharon. I'm guessing she was dropping off another arrangement from Walt." Mia crossed her arms and leaned against her desk, observing Connie. "And with that grin you can't seem to wipe off your face, you certainly look like you had a good night. Walt?"

Connie quickly nodded. "Yep, I sure did," she said, and proceeded to her cubicle. She was surprised to find Nicola sitting at her desk, but what caught her attention even more was the swooshing sound of her personal email program closing. "Can I help you?" Connie asked the evil witch.

Connie watched Nicola's "caught" expression change to the brightest fake smile imaginable. "No," she said. "I found what I was looking for." Rising, she held out a thumb drive. "I just had to download a file for Mr. Boss Man," she said, pointing carelessly in the direction of their supervisor's office. Before Connie could reply, Nicola darted away, as though the building was on fire.

Connie slid her purse under her desk and noticed the already opened envelope that was attached to the flowers Sharon had delivered. *You've got to be kidding me*, thought Connie, reaching for the envelope. "Nosy witch," she mumbled, shaking her head at the thought of Nicola. Just in case others were looking, she took the card out of the envelope and read it, plastering an amorous smile on her face as she stared dreamily at the flowers. *In due time*, she mused silently about the stranger she'd sent a message to the night before. The ringing phone in the cubicle next to her prompted her to get to work.

At eleven fifteen, she was greeted by a swarm of co-workers who were passing by.

"Hey, Con, I forgot to tell you earlier, but nice flowers," Nicola said, stifling a laugh.

With that, the cluster of evilness behind her began laughing, too, making Connie furious as they filtered out of the office. Just as she was about to type "how to poison your co-workers" into a search engine, her email program signaled a ding. Quickly opening it, she smiled widely when she saw she'd received a message from Walt Goldman. *A real man named Walt is emailing me!* Before reading it, she took a breath to calm herself. Many seconds later, still feeling more anxious than ever, Connie leaned closer to her computer screen and began to read.

Connie,

Thanks for your message! When I opened your email this morning, the first thing I thought was, "Wow, Connie's a hottie!" Okay, that was a bad way to show you that I can rhyme, but it's the truth. Not only do you appear beautiful on the outside but on the inside, too.

Connie smiled warmly as her heartbeat sped up, and she continued on.

I must say that I was delightfully surprised and a little taken aback by your honesty. This is my third time trying online dating, so I've had my share of meeting dreadful and deceitful women. While it doesn't seem that we have many things in common, I'm sure there's something we can find to connect over.

I might be hanging out with the guys tonight, but if you're up for it, I'd love to get to know you and take you to dinner instead…that is if Cupid hasn't already hooked you up with an online stalker.

Connie had to laugh. "Okay, so he's charming and funny," she whispered to herself.

Thanks again for contacting me.

Call me anytime!

Walt

Connie stared at his phone number below his name and let out a breath. Not wasting any time, she reached for the phone and dialed his number.

"Hello?" said a man with a deep, sexy and confident voice.

Expecting to hear a less assured and squeaky voice, she was caught off guard by the sound of the manly voice on the other end of the line. "Um, yes, I'm calling for Walt Goldman, but I think I dialed the wrong number."

Connie was about to hang up, but before she did, she heard him say, "This is Walt," he said. "How can I help you?"

This to be some kind of mistake. From the picture on his profile, his voice was way too sexy to be the greasy-haired nerd. "Uh, this is Connie Albright—" Before Connie could continue speaking, she was interrupted.

"Hey, Connie! Wow, that was fast."

"Yeah. I just read your email and decided that there wasn't any time like the present."

He laughed. "Well, it's great to hear from you."

She smiled at his laugh. It sounded sincere and kind, and it was sweet to her ears. "Thank you," she said. "Anyway, I'm calling because I want to take you up on your offer for dinner tonight." *Was that too forward?* "But if you'd rather hang with your friends, I completely understand," she quickly added. Glancing over at the flowers she'd sent herself, hopeful that if she played her cards right, she'd have him doting over her, and soon enough, she'd be able to show the women she worked with that she was worthy of love—even if, at times, she really didn't believe it herself.

"Absolutely, but I know you're not into French food, so anything else with me is fine."

"Hey, as long as it's not French, then anything is fine with me," she replied. She sat back in her chair, hugging an arm against her waist, enjoying their conversation.

"Would you like to meet at Tequila Taco, say around seven?" he asked.

"That's actually my favorite Mexican restaurant!" she exclaimed.

"I'll have to remember that," Walt replied. He took a rushed breath, then said, "Well, Connie, I'm late for a meeting, but I'll see you tonight."

She sat forward and began to speak in a more businesslike tone when her bitchy co-workers returned from lunch. "I'm looking forward to it." She was about to hang up, but then she heard him say something.

"Oh, and Connie, I'll be the guy at the restaurant holding a white rose."

"Okay," was all she thought to say, and then the line clicked off.

As Connie put the phone down, giddiness surged within her. She couldn't wait to meet Walt. Though she found it strange that he mentioned that he'd be carrying a rose, considering they already knew what the other looked like, but she thought it to be a very nice gesture.

"Was that Walt?" asked Nicola, catching Connie off guard.

"That's none of your business."

"Oh, come on, you can tell me," she probed, sounding like a prosecutor in a court case.

"I don't want to bore you with the details about our hot and spicy relationship," Connie beamed, hoping to shut her up, and then turned back to her computer. Seconds later, she heard Nicola stomp away in a huff.

*****

Fixing Connie's makeup and brushing her hair were easy, but deciding what to wear was a different story. After struggling for thirty-seven minutes to come up with something appropriate, but sexy, too, she settled for the outfit she'd worn to work, sans the blazer. She added a purple scarf and a light, cream-colored cotton jacket, but when she looked in the mirror, she realized she needed one last accessory. With a sigh, Connie reached up to the top shelf of her closet for the only pair of high-heels she owned. She'd never worn them before, thanks to her clumsy, wobbly ankles and knees, but tonight was the night. After slipping on the three-inch gold heels, she held her hands out for balance and carefully walked to the mirror.

"Damn," she said out loud. She twirled around, amazed at how pretty—almost normal looking—she appeared, even for her. "I clean up good!"

When the alarm buzzed on her phone, signaling it was time to leave, she quickly fed Buttercup and Tillman, and then reached for her red clutch. She was ready to meet Walt.

Connie wasn't nervous as she made her way to the restaurant. Actually, she was more anxious about what her co-workers would say when she returned to work on Monday. She started taking notes in her head of what kind of arrangements she'd send herself the following weeks, and what their cards would entail.

When she pulled into the parking lot, she mumbled, "Ready or not, this is it," and got out of her car. Ever so gracefully, she walked to the restaurant.

When she opened the front door, the room was buzzing with patrons, and she began to scan for a man holding a white rose. From left to right, she saw nobody holding a rose, nor anyone that looked like him. At first, Connie began to feel deflated, thinking that Walt had skipped out on their date, but just as she was about to give in and go home, that's when her eyes stopped on an overwhelmingly attractive man who was walking toward her. Not even John Stamos, her favorite celebrity crush, compared to him. She looked him up and down, more than impressed with what she saw. He wore jeans, a blue and white plaid button-down shirt, and his hair was cut stylishly short. Connie was positive the alluring grin on his handsome, clean-shaven face had, could, would and had melted hearts. She began to wobble in her heels when she suddenly noticed the man was holding a white rose, and she froze instantly. *It's him!*

"Hi," he said, reaching out his free hand. "I'm Walt Goldman."

What have I done, what have I done, what have I done? With a knot in her throat, she found it hard to speak. Everything about this was wrong. He looked nothing like his online profile picture. Finally, she took his hand in hers, and when they touched, chills swept all over her body. At that moment, she was pretty sure she was playing the part of a heroine in one of her romance novels, because she'd never dreamed of a fantasy coming to life. *Send me to heaven now!*

"Hi, I'm Connie Albright," she finally managed to say.

CHAPTER THIRTEEN

Khloe

Seated in a booth at the semi-fancy restaurant, Khloe was comforted that The Thai Orchid was known as a hotspot for business lunches, instead of impromptu dates. She placed the black napkin over her lap and opened the menu just as a waitress approached.

"Hello, I'm Margot, and I'll be your server today," the woman said as she poured water into a glass on the table in front of Khloe. "Can I interest you in a Thai cocktail, or perhaps a glass of wine?"

Khloe would've loved a glass of wine to calm her nerves but decided against it. "Just water, please."

"Great. I'll be back once your companion arrives," she said, then disappeared behind two double doors that Khloe assumed led to the kitchen.

Khloe turned her attention back to the menu. After scanning through the decadent specials of the day, she decided to start with a bowl of Pad Thai soup, followed by the lunch portion of Panang Curry. Looking at her watch, she noticed Derek was five minutes late. If this were a date Khloe might be more anxious, but since it wasn't, she tried her best to act as casual and relaxed as she could— or at least she tried to, anyway. She reached for her water, and when she brought the glass to her lips, Khloe felt a hand on her shoulder.

That's when cool and calm Khloe disappeared, and in swept the Khloe who was suddenly hot, bothered, and aching with need.

"I'm sorry to have kept you waiting," Derek apologized. "I didn't think my meeting would run as long as it did. Have you been here long?"

When Derek took a seat across from Khloe, she got a whiff of his cologne, which smelled of a fresh combination of fresh oranges and pine. *Damn!* Khloe took another sip of her water—this time a much longer one—then she smiled at him and carefully placed her glass down. "Not long at all. Just enough time for me to figure out what I'm going to order. Have you been here before?"

"Yeah." He chuckled. "I come for business meetings at least three times a month or so." Derek reached for the wine menu that stood between them and flipped through the pages. "How about you?"

Ah ha! Just a business meeting. "Just once, but my friend and I sat at the bar. It was for a girls' night out," she said, thinking back to when she and Sharon had gone out together after work a few months before. That was the night they were hit on by two attractive men, and things were going fairly well. Though, when the bartender asked to see their IDs, the two boys quickly stammered an excuse to them and ran out of the restaurant. To this day, they still laughed at the memory.

"Well, I hear they make a killer cosmopolitan."

Khloe laughed. "You drink cosmos?" she asked, surprised that he indulged in what was normally thought of as a woman's drink.

Derek waved his hand, shaking his head. "Oh, no, not at all. I've just heard they're good here." His eyes were focused on his menu, quietly adding, "My sister used to love them."

Khloe noticed sadness in his eyes but didn't press. Instead, she opted to lighten the mood. "Well, I guess I'll have to try one sometime," she told him as their server approached.

Derek ordered an iced tea, interlaced his fingers, and turned his focus to Khloe. "Thank you for having lunch with me today. It certainly is a pleasure to have lunch with such a beautiful woman."

Flattered, Khloe took that as her cue to get down to business. "Of course," she said, reaching into her purse and pulling all the business materials she'd brought with her, along with a pen, while tyring to hide her blushing cheeks. "I look forward to helping you."

With a confused, squinting look on his face, Derek adjusted himself in his seat.

"I know what you're thinking," she said, trying to reassure him. "Flowers can be expensive, but I can work with you on a budget, so there's no need to worry." She flashed him a quick grin and wrote his name on the top of the form. "Now, let me tell you about our corporate holiday, seasonal, and executive packages—"

The side of his mouth curled into a grin that made Khloe weak in the knees, and glad she was sitting. "I think there's been some kind misunderstanding," he said, interrupting her.

"What…what do you mean?" Khloe asked, fumbling her words, and her heart beat faster.

Leaning forward, he crossed his arms. "I didn't ask you to have lunch with me today because I wanted to order flowers."

In a matter of seconds, she was pretty sure that if she were hooked up to a heart monitor, its alarm would be sounding, and a crash cart would be needed at any minute. Finally, it dawned on her that Sharon was right. *Is this really a date?* Then, she remembered what she thought she'd heard Mary say, "ah ha," and "I get it now." *What did Mary get and what does all this mean?* Had Derek sent flowers to Mary, hoping to see Khloe again?

"When I met you, I thought about asking you out, but I chickened out." He laughed, which made Khloe smile. "I guess what I'm trying to say is that I want to get to know you better."

"So, you sent Mary flowers, hoping that I'd be the one to deliver them?" When Derek bashfully nodded, Khloe asked, "So, tell me, what made you think I would accept your invitation?" Khloe bit her lip, taken aback by her own flirtatious banter, which seemed to be coming way too easily for her.

"You're here with me now, aren't you?" Derek surmised, raising his brow.

Khloe laughed again. "Good point." She thought for a moment, countering back with, "But what if I'm in a relationship, or even married?" she challenged, but once again, Derek had an answer.

"Maybe you're in a relationship, maybe not, but I doubt you're married," he said, pointing to her naked ring finger. "However, what I already know is that you're still here."

Khloe felt like she was a largemouth bass being reeled in by his charm. She knew it wouldn't be long until she became putty in his hands—and, just like that, she found herself thinking she would love to be in his arms. "What about you, Derek? Do you have a girlfriend or wife? A mistress?" *I mean, just look at you*, she thought, eyeing him up and down. He was like a walking sex god!

Derek shook his head. "No, I'm not seeing anyone," he said in a flirtatious tone. "I'm not married, nor do I have a mistress. I'm a one-woman kind of man," he said matter-of-factly. He raised his glass. "So, Khloe, what do you say, can we consider this our first date?"

He's single! Things seemed to be moving faster than Khloe's dates would normally play out, considering the enormous wall she'd put up since Josh, but somehow with Derek, it felt…different. She raised her glass as well. "How about I let you know when I'm headed home later?" she playfully suggested, clinking his glass with hers. As she took a sip, the water cooled her down, but her mind raced like a three-ring circus of emotions. *Is he really this freaking charming? Is this what it feels like to be physically attracted to someone who's so damn sexy?*

Can I trust him, and how the hell do I know for sure he's not taken? She was about to ask him that very question but decided against it, thinking it was too blunt.

Over lunch, they talked about everything—family, friends, travel, music, and food. Khloe told him about her parents, how she preferred '80s and '90s country music over contemporary, and her obsession with pasta. Their conversation flowed easily, and he seemed genuinely interested in what she had to say. She told him how much she had loved studying abroad in London, and how, as much as she enjoyed living out of the US, she was happy to be back home where she had her bearings. They shared a laugh when she tried her best English accent, failing miserably.

"Well, you get an A-plus for effort," he joked, sending Khloe into a fit of laughter.

"Hey, I try," she said, raising her shoulders.

When the conversation quieted between them, Khloe looked around at the nearly empty restaurant. She glanced down at her watch. *Eight minutes after five?* "Oh my gosh, I can't believe how late it is," she said, worried Sharon was going crazy without any help. She reached into her purse and pulled out her cell phone. "Do you mind if I make a quick call?" she asked, beginning to stand.

"Not at all." He reached for her hand and helped her out of her chair.

"Thanks," Khloe replied, not ready to let go of his hand, nor did she want to look away from his handsome face. "I-I'll be right back," she said, taking two steps backward. Finally, before she tripped over the carpet, ran into a table or chair, or did anything embarrassing, she twisted on her heel, hurrying out of the restaurant. Feeling the cool air cover her body, she dialed the store's number.

"Khloe's Flower Shop, this is Sharon. How may I help you?"

"Oh, Sharon, I'm sorry...Look, I'm still with Derek, but—"

"Wow, that must've been some lunch!" Sharon giggled, interrupting Khloe. "So, was I right, you know, about it being a date?"

Khloe smirked, only saying, "I'm not giving you any specific details, but if you must know, yes, you were right—"

Before Khloe could get another word in, she was interrupted by Sharon's boisterous laugh. "Ha! I told you so! Now, come on, spill it. How's it going?"

Khloe giggled into the phone, feeling like a schoolgirl. "We talked so much, I lost track of time. Look, I'll tell you everything another time, but I just stepped outside to call you and check in. How are things at the store? Was it busy?"

"Yes, but don't worry, it was nothing I couldn't handle. Right now I'm about to start closing up."

Khloe felt bad she had left Sharon at the store alone all afternoon, especially since it was the holiday season and she knew how chaotic it could get. "Okay, look, we're just about finished, so I'll be on my way back soon to help you."

"Khloe, you need to calm down, girl," Sharon said. "Please, stay and enjoy your time with Derek. I have everything under control, and I'll see you in the morning." Without another word, Sharon hung up.

Somewhat surprised her best friend had just hung up on her, Khloe knew Sharon was right. After all, it wasn't every day that Khloe had a lunch date with an attractive man like Derek —a very sexy businessman, who was dressed for power and seemed to have succeeded with his dreams—and was pretty sure her parents would give their seal of approval if they were to fall in love and get married. At that thought, a gust of wind brushed her face and she shivered, re-entering the restaurant and re-claiming her seat across from Derek.

"Everything okay?" he asked.

"Couldn't be better," Khloe said with confidence and gave him her most authentic smile. Knowing Sharon was taking care of everything at the store, she could focus solely on Derek and enjoy the rest of the time she had with him. "So, where were we?"

"Well, if I'm right, you're still deciding if this is a date or not." Khloe watched him quickly sign the check and then put his credit card back in his wallet. "So, is this it, or are you going to continue to let me schmooze you into saying this is a date?"

Taken aback by his sexy banter, which eerily reminded her of a very suave male character on her favorite soap opera, she stared into his eyes, batting hers, not knowing what to say.

"By your silence and the look in your eyes, I take that as a yes, and that our time together isn't over yet. Am I right?"

Khloe was surprised at how naturally she replied, "Yes."

CHAPTER FOURTEEN

Gabby

Gabriella was looking forward to going to Andrew's soccer game and meeting Harry's family. She peeked out the curtains and saw a light drizzle coming from the sky, but she wasn't too concerned about the game being canceled.

She'd never been to a child's soccer game before, but after taking a bit of time to decide what to wear, she settled on tennis shoes, jeans, and an old form-fitting blue and red nautical-themed sweater. She specifically picked the sweater because she wasn't worried about getting it dirty, yet still wanted to look nice. She pulled her hair back into a tight ponytail and lightly applied neutral-toned make-up. She looked in the mirror and saw a beyond-anxious but beautiful woman looking back at her. It was a side of herself she'd not seen since before Charlie died. Before letting the thought of him take over, she flipped off her bathroom lights and went downstairs to wait for Harry.

When he arrived at eight o'clock, she couldn't help but laugh at how adorable he looked.

"You like my attire?" Harry asked, raising his hands and spinning around in a circle. "It's my new tracksuit."

Gabby leaned against the door and put her hand over her mouth, laughing. "Harry, you look great, and I must say, I love the bright, canary yellow. It's so…you."

"Thank you." Harry hugged her, saying, "You look lovely."

After thanking him, Gabby picked up her purse from the entryway table and gave him a grin. "Well, I'm ready if you are."

"Great!" he said, reaching for her hand and leading her to his car.

When they pulled into the crowded parking lot, Harry pointed to the sky and said, "Looks like a nice day for a game."

"Cool, dreary, and rainy is good for soccer?" Gabby asked, raising an eyebrow.

"Yeah, it's just something Andrew says. Apparently, his team wins most when the weather's like this. I guess it's some kind of luck for them." Gabby followed Harry's lead out of the car and to the trunk, where he pulled out a red and green plaid quilt.

Wow, he's quite prepared, Gabby thought. Extending her hand, she said, "I'll take that," and then placed it under her arm.

Closing the trunk and locking his car, Harry asked in a chipper voice, "Well, are you ready to meet my family?"

"Absolutely," she replied. As they headed toward the soccer field, a wave of emotions—nervousness, anxiousness, and excitement—filled her body, hoping that his family liked her as much as she liked Harry.

The sidelines were filled with spectators of all ages. In the middle of the field, two teams of boys were dressed in uniforms, one wearing black and silver, and the other purple and green. Cheers and whistles sounded, signaling the start of the game.

"There he is," Harry said, pointing to a boy in a purple uniform with a bright green number on the back. "Number five."

Andrew had straight brown hair and his cheeks were red, as if he'd already been playing his heart out. He kicked the ball, then raced with the others to the white line between the goalposts. Then suddenly, he slowed to a jog. He gave a crooked smile and he waved eagerly at Harry. "Hi, Grandpa!" he yelled.

Harry waved back. "Hi, buddy! Keep it up!" He gave his grandson two thumbs up, and Andrew continued playing.

Gabby leaned into Harry. "He's adorable. I see where he gets his good looks."

Just as Harry opened his mouth to reply, a woman called out, "Harry, over here." Gabby spotted a young couple waving to them from the sidelines. The man wore jeans and a blue pullover, and the woman, an eager brunette, wore an adult version of Andrew's uniform top over a black long-sleeved shirt, along with skinny-jeans and knee-high designer black boots.

"That's Jeff and Juliet," Harry whispered.

"I never would've guessed," she said, playfully, and suddenly, she began to feel intimidated by Jules.

Harry gave her a comforting look. "I promise Jules doesn't bite," Harry said, referring to his overly enthusiastic daughter-in-law. "She's just excited to finally meet you because I've told her so much about you."

Moments later, Harry made the introductions. "Jeff, Juliet, this is the lovely woman I've been telling you about, the beautiful Gabriella." He circled his arm around her waist. "Gabby, this is Jeff and Juliet."

"Hello," said Jeff, extending his hand. "It's nice to meet finally meet you. You're all my father talks about."

Gabby took Jeff's hand and shook it. His eyes reminded her of Harry's—kind and gentle. "It's nice to meet you, too." Gabby then turned to Juliet and extended her hand, but before she knew it, Juliet had thrown her arms around Gabby.

"Oh, Gabriella," Juliet said, her arms wrapped tightly around Gabby's neck. Finally, she pulled away and held her at arm's length. "You're just as Harry described." She rested her chin on clasped hands, completely switching gears in a matter of seconds from devoted soccer mom to hopeless romantic.

During the game, Gabby and Juliet sat together on the quilt

Harry brought and got to know each other, while Harry and Jeff stood alongside them.

"Please call me Jules," Juliet told her. "So, Harry told me you two played bingo the other night. It was your first time, right? Did you have fun?"

Before she figured out how to respond, she felt her cheeks heat up to an alarming degree when she thought of the mini-vibrator, wondering if Harry had spilled the beans on the prize she'd won. "Yes, believe it or not, it was my first time playing. It was so much fun."

Then Jules leaned over and whispered, "Harry's very into you, Gabby. It's obvious by the way he talks about you."

"I hope it wasn't all bad," she said.

Jules placed her hand on Gabby's arm. "No, of course not. He cares very much about you," she said, leaving Gabby with warmth filling her heart. They turned their attention back to the soccer field, watching Andrew direct the ball down the field. When he scored, Jules bolted up and began cheering along with Jeff and Harry.

Gabby stood, too, and watched the precious but sweaty boy high-five his teammates. Minutes later, a referee blew a loud whistle, signaling the game was over. Andrew ran toward where they were standing and leaped into Jeff's arms.

"Hey, buddy!" he said with a hand raised to high-five his son. "You did great today."

"Thanks, Dad," Andrew said, trying to catch his breath, as Jules pulled a juice box from the mini-cooler and walked over to them.

"You did great, little man!" she told him, brushing away a few strands of hair from his flushed face and handing him the refreshment.

After he took a long gulp of his drink, Andrew reached for Jules, hugged her, then she put him down and he walked over to Harry. "Hi, Grandpa," he said, putting his arms around his grandfather's waist.

With two arms reached out, Harry picked Andrew up and placed him on his hip. "Congratulations on your win!" He also high-fived Andrew, then turned to Gabby. "This is the woman I was telling you and your parents about. Her name is Gabby."

Not wanting to scare him off, unsure if kids his age were still wary of strangers, she extended her hand. "It's nice to finally meet you. Your grandfather has told me so much about you."

He took another sip of his juice box, looking her up and down in the process, and then said, "Hi," to her in the sweetest boyish voice she'd ever heard, placing his small hand in hers.

"You were certainly the star of the game," she told him as she looked down at his hand in hers and smiled, not caring that his palms were dirty and clammy. His touch was so delicate that it warmed her heart, and she instantly knew she liked him.

As they all walked to the parking lot, Jeff and Jules invited Gabby and Harry out to lunch with them. Before Harry replied, he looked at Gabby, who answered for them.

"We'd love to," Gabby said, surprising herself. While she'd only spent a short time with Harry's family, she really enjoyed them, and from what she could tell by the way they treated her, they liked her as well.

Deciding on a restaurant close by, all five of them sat comfortably at the table, and that's when Gabby got to know Andrew. He liked spaghetti, which he gleefully pronounced as "pasgetti," enjoyed playing with his best friend, Conner, and his idol was David Beckham.

"I hear he's an awesome athlete," Gabby said to him before taking a sip of her iced tea.

"Yeah," he agreed, eagerly nodding his head. "Dad says I can be just like him when I grow up." He looked at Jeff and said, "Isn't that right, Dad?"

Jeff smiled proudly at his son. "That's right, buddy." He reached over and tousled his son's hair as the child shoved a forkful of spaghetti into his mouth. Jeff looked at Gabby, gave her a wink, and said, "Gotta love him."

"I can see why. He's set his goals high for himself, and there's nothing wrong with that." They all laughed, and Gabby felt Harry's hand on her leg. She turned to smile at him.

Jules, who was observing Gabby and her father-in-law, asked, "So, Gabby, tell us a little bit about yourself."

"Well, I love old movies, red wine, traveling, and I'm part of a Scrabble group, so I often study the dictionary." She turned to Harry, adding, "I also have a new love for playing bingo," and then she and Harry laughed. "Before my husband died, I also enjoyed cooking, but it's so hard to cook for just one." Gabriella felt a slight tug at her heart at the mention of Charlie and began to wonder how much about him she should share, or if she should say anything. *If I say too much, they might think I'm still not over him, but if I say too little, then I won't be honest with myself about my past and the husband I loved.*

"I'm sorry for your loss," Jeff said.

"Thank you," Gabby said with a wave of her hand and took the last bite of her salad. "It brings me peace to know he's in heaven and not in any pain."

"Nana's there, too, isn't that right, Grandpa?" Andrew's question silenced the table.

"Yep, she sure is," Harry replied with sadness in his eyes.

Just as Jeff opened his mouth to speak again, Andrew looked at Gabby and said, "Nana died in a car accident." Then, in the most serious tone manageable for a five-year-old, he asked Gabby, "Are you going to be my new nana?"

Nobody was prepared for his question as four sets of adult eyes widened.

Before Gabby had time to comprehend what Andrew had asked, Jules said, "Andrew, do you remember what we said about asking personal questions?" She then gave him a stern look. Noticing his empty plate, continued on with, "Why don't we go wash up?" Jules reached for Andrew's hand and headed for the restroom.

Me? Andrew's new nana? Now Gabby started to wonder what it would be like to have grandchildren. She and Charlie had tried to conceive for years, but it never happened. While it took her a while to make peace with not having any children, she did the only thing she could, and that was to accept she'd never be a mother. But, now that she was dating Harry, she was open to the idea of being a grandmother, though she didn't want to rush things.

"I'm sorry about Andrew," Jeff said to Gabby, interrupting her thoughts.

"It's okay." She smiled, with a wave of her hand, adding, "Though, I do have to say that it was quite a question. It's obvious he has a bright personality."

"Yeah, I've heard him ask some interesting questions before, but nothing like that." Harry blushed with embarrassment.

Minutes later, Andrew and Jules returned, and Andrew took his seat next to Gabby. He tapped her on the shoulder, and she turned toward him.

With a sullen face and sad eyes, he said, "Gabby, I'm sorry for what I asked you."

What an angel, she thought, his sweet face touching her heart. *How could I not love this little boy?* "That's very kind of you, Andrew. I accept your apology." She opened her arms and pulled Andrew into a hug.

After the check had been paid and they said their goodbyes, Gabby told Harry she wasn't ready to go home. Having had such a wonderful day, she was buzzing with energy.

"Well, where do you want to go?"

"I know just the place," she told him and proceeded to give him directions.

CHAPTER FIFTEEN

Connie

When Connie got home from having dinner with Walt, she felt like she was living her favorite childhood story, *Cinderella*. Her night went better than she could have imagined. He'd been attentive, charming, and funny, and she loved the way he looked at her—like she was the only woman in the world.

Connie plopped herself down on her bed and hugged her pillow. "Tonight was amazing, guys," she said to Buttercup and Tillman, who rubbed against her as she re-played the events of the date in her head.

"Your picture doesn't do justice to how beautiful you are," Walt had commented, handing her the white rose.

She'd blushed. "And, you're more handsome than the picture on your profile," she replied as they followed a hostess to a secluded booth in the corner of the Mexican restaurant.

He chuckled. "Yeah, my roommates got a hold of that photo after my mom dropped off a box of my stuff from my parent's attic." Walt paused when a waitress dropped off complimentary tortilla chips and salsa. After they each ordered a margarita, he continued, "Anyway, one night I was out drinking with the guys and I lost a bet, so they created a dating profile for me, using that picture. Thank goodness

I'm no longer that pimply-faced nerd I used to be." He flashed Connie a sexy smile.

She laughed. "No, you certainly are not. So, how old were you in that picture?"

"Believe it or not, that was me nine years ago."

"Wow," Connie said, wiping her mouth. "So, in nine years, the nerd turned into a prince. It sounds just like a fairy tale," she joked.

"Then I guess it suits me because I love a good fairy tale." Walt looked at Connie, who had a surprised look on her face, and then he added, with a raise of his shoulders, "Yes, just because I'm a guy, I can still admit that."

Connie was taken aback. She'd never known a guy who was so confident yet still attractive and nice at the same time. Finally, she said, "My favorite is *Cinderella*." Then, for reasons she didn't understand, she continued on. "I lost the book in a horrific car accident, and sadly, it was never recovered, and I never bought a new one." She looked up at Walt, who was staring at her with a peaceful and sorrowful expression, and she shook her head. "I'm sorry. I don't know why I keep talking…" She was thankful for the distraction of the waitress placing their drinks in front of them and taking their dinner order.

After they both took sips of their margaritas, Walt clasped her hand in his, and Connie felt herself turning to mush at his touch. "I don't mind at all, Connie. I like getting to know you."

Connie leaned back in her seat to take in what he'd just said. *He likes getting to know me!* "I like getting to know you, too, Walt."

"So, tell me about your family," he prompted. "Do you have any siblings?"

Instantly, Connie looked down at her lap, remembering she was alone in the world. *Not anymore*, she thought to herself, fighting off tears that threatened to spill out of her eyes. Finally, before answering him, she took a long sip of her margarita. "I had a family, but they all died in the car accident," she said, in almost a whisper as her heart began to ache. "It was a head-on collision, and miraculously, I was the only survivor." Then, Connie's voice turned monotone, her mind going back to the scene. "It was my and my sister's eighth birthday, and we were headed for Disney World. My dad was driving, Mom was in the front reading a book, and my twin sister—though, we looked nothing alike, she was the beautiful one, and I was the smart one—was listening to New Kids on the Block on her Walkman. As for me, I was reading *Cinderella* for what was probably the twentieth time that day…" She choked on her words as a knot got stuck in her throat, and as embarrassed as she felt to show any emotion on a first date—her very first one—she couldn't hide the tear that ran down her face.

Instantly, Walt jumped to her side of the booth and placed one arm around her. "Connie, I'm so sorry for the tragic loss of your family." After they held a steady glance, he reached for a napkin, dabbed at her eyes, and gave her a one-armed hug. "I can't imagine how rough your life has been."

"Thank you, Walt," was the only thing she could say, because she was taken aback by his tenderness. As if it were natural, she leaned against him and they sat there in silence. Finally, after a few deep breaths, Connie sat up and reached for her margarita. "I'm better now." She gave him a hopeful smile, to let him know she was grateful for his comfort.

"Anytime," he said, patting her shoulder just as the waiter placed their entrées in front of them.

While they bonded over tacos, Connie was still surprised that Walt hadn't gone back to his side of the booth as they shared stories about friends, work, travel, and she listened to him tell her about his family and past relationships. Connie surprised herself when she opened up to him, telling him about her true self, and how she grew up with a foster family who ragged on her. "I tried to be a happy kid, but I got out of that house the second I turned eighteen. They weren't violent or anything like that, but I could tell they saw me as…well, different. I had clothes, a roof over my head, and people who made sure I was alive, but in truth, I felt dead inside. Anyway, turning eighteen was a blessing, and I don't talk to them anymore, because in my mind, they really weren't my family." She paused before quietly adding, "It's not like they'd even care anyway."

"Well, you're so strong now." He tilted his head to take a look at Connie. "I just can't believe everything you've been through."

"It hasn't been easy, but, hey, what doesn't kill us makes us stronger." She tried to put on her best smile, and he laughed. While talking to Walt, Connie wasn't faking anything, nor did she feel insecure about telling him anything. After deciding to order another round of margaritas, Walt scooted closer to her, which pleasantly surprised her, making her heart race.

"I've never had a boyfriend, so I guess that explains why I'm unlucky with men. I mean, look at me," she said, waving her hand at her body. "In a way, I'm more like the ugly duckling," she said with a nervous laugh.

Walt reached for her arm, giving it a light squeeze. "You, Connie Albright, are not an ugly duckling and I can't imagine you ever being one," he said, brushing strands of her hair behind her ear.

Goosebumps instantly covered her body. That was probably the sweetest thing anyone had ever said to her, and Connie didn't know how to respond. All she could think about was kissing his perfect lips. *No matter what, do not get sidetracked from the plan.* However, each time she regained control of herself, minutes later, she lost it again.

After Walt paid the check, they headed outside, but Connie wasn't ready to say goodbye to him just yet—and the way he looked at her with his dazzling eyes, she sensed he wasn't ready either. "Well, thank you for dinner, Walt," she said, smiling sweetly. "I had a great time."

"I did, too," he said, as his eyes narrowed, looking as serious as could be. "Would you like to go out again? Maybe later this weekend?"

A second date? "Absolutely," she said, and then reached her hand out to shake his, loving how her skin felt in his delicate touch. Catching her by surprise, Walt pulled her into an embrace and wrapped his arms around her waist. She breathed in a faint combination of his cologne and tequila, and she couldn't imagine being anywhere else.

"It was nice meeting you, Connie," he whispered in her ear. When he pulled away, he placed his hands on her shoulders and pressed his soft lips to hers for what seemed like minutes, though was only a few seconds.

What an amazing kisser, Connie thought, as his lips and tongue teased hers, tasting like a combination of spice and salt. It was like she was born to kiss him. When Walt pulled away, he left Connie breathless, and they stared at each other for a moment before he broke the silence.

"I'll give you a call," he said, and with that he left Connie one drink shy of being tipsy, and very drunk on his kiss.

He kissed me, he kissed me, he kissed me! Her fingers brushing her lips, Connie watched Walt disappear into the crowded sidewalk.

CHAPTER SIXTEEN

Khloe

As Khloe followed Derek back to his home, she wondered what she was doing. In the past, when men invited her to their places she'd never accepted, because she didn't want to come off looking easy, especially on a first date. However, Derek seemed different, and not like a man who was after the one thing that most men had on their minds. Ironically, the more time she spent with Derek, that one thing was all Khloe thought about.

After turning the corner on White Creek Road, Khloe came to a slow stop and parked behind him in his driveway. She quickly reached into her console for a tube of lip gloss, ran it across her lips, then pinched her cheeks to give them a bit more color. After popping a mint in her mouth, she counted to three, got out of the car, and walked over to Derek.

"Welcome to my home," he said. Derek lived in a white-brick, two-story house. The trim was painted dark blue, which matched the window shades on each of the five facing windows, and the front door was painted red. "Come on, I'll in, I'll show you around."

When Derek reached for her hand, without hesitation, she placed hers in his and smiled, feeling the chemistry burn between them. "It all looks so charming, and I love the landscaping," she said, pointing to his burgundy Christmas roses and purple and white pansies that lay in a pot beside the door.

Derek chuckled. "Well, I really don't know a lot about gardening, or flowers for that matter. I told my landscaper I wanted to add color to my lawn during the fall and winter months, and it's nice to know that I have a flower expert's approval." Khloe giggled, and then they held a gaze while Derek managed to unlock the door with his free hand.

"Your home is beautiful," Khloe said when the tour came to an end in his living room. She took a seat on his white sofa, watching Derek slowly saunter across the room to his minibar. "How long have you lived here?"

"Not too long, maybe just over six months." He held up a bottle of red wine in one hand, and a bottle of beer in the other. "Beer or wine?" he asked.

"Wine, please." She was thankful she would soon be indulging in liquid courage, which would help her relax a bit more.

"Excellent choice." Within seconds, Derek had opened up a bottle of Cabernet, and they were clinking glasses. "To us, and seeing where the night takes us."

Khloe felt herself blush. She bowed her head and took a small sip, hoping that the redness on her cheeks would go unnoticed. "Oh, this is so delicious," she said, and swirled the wine in her glass. "I've always enjoyed a good Cab."

"Me, too, and I'm sure you've tried a fair amount, since your parents live in Napa, right?"

She placed her glass on the dark walnut coffee table in front of them. "You have no idea how true that is. I have boxes and boxes of wine at my store and at home—they're everywhere," Khloe joked, leaning back against the couch and laughing before she swiveled to face him. "So, you know a lot about me, but I hardly know anything about you. Tell me about yourself, Derek Thomas."

Derek shot her an enticing grin. "Well, as you know, I'm a sports and entertainment lawyer, and I own my firm. I love my job and take it very seriously. Sometimes too seriously," he said and chuckled to himself, "which I'm often told I work a bit too much."

Remembering she'd seen the title on his company's door when she made the delivery to Mary, Khloe's eyes widened with excitement. "So, I'm guessing you know a lot of celebrities, right?"

Derek nodded, giving her a wink. "I'd say so," he said, playing coy. "However, I can't reveal any of my clients, especially not the really naughty ones who pay me the big bucks to keep their stories out of the spotlight."

"Ah, okay, I get it now. You're like Olivia Pope on *Scandal*, always cleaning up people's messes."

"Yeah, let's go with that," he replied playfully, and nodded his head. "Anyway, I also like watching baseball and hockey, my favorite music is classical, and I love traveling—particularly to places I've never been." He paused for a second and took a long sip of wine before adding, "I'm also a family man. I talk to my parents—who live in New York—on a daily basis."

As Derek shared a few stories about his parents, it became obvious to Khloe he was a man who loved his family, and that was important to her. She didn't see her parents often but they had a close relationship, thanks to modern-day technology. "So, tell me about your sister. Are you two close, too?" When he didn't answer, that was when, for the second time that day, Khloe saw pain in his eyes.

Finally, after a few long seconds that left Khloe wondering if she should take the question back, Derek nodded. "Yeah, we are—I mean— we were really close, but she—" Just as he was about to finish his sentence, his cell phone rang. He took it out of his pocket and glanced at the number. "I'm sorry, but I have to take this. It shouldn't take long."

"Take all the time you need." Khloe watched Derek walk out of the room, and out of earshot. She reached for her wine, took a sip, and set it back on the table. Feeling a chill in the air, she tugged on a maroon throw that lay on the arm of the couch and placed it around her. Seconds later, Derek returned. "Everything okay?" she asked, sensing by the deadpan expression on his face that something was up.

"If you're cold, I can turn up the heat," he offered, ignoring her question.

She shook her head. "Thanks, but I'm good with this," she replied, holding up the blanket with one hand and reaching for her wine with the other. He sat back on the couch but this time he sat closer to her, and she could feel the heat between them rise, which she certainly didn't mind—and not because there was a chill in the air. When their eyes met, she smiled, not knowing what to do or say. Part of her wanted to wrap her hands around his neck, pull him on top of her, and start a heated make-out session, but she resisted the temptation. Instead, to distract herself, she found herself staring into her wine glass again, the bold and fruity aromas swirling in the air, floating just below her nose.

"More wine?" Derek asked, and when Khloe nodded, he poured more into her glass. "Are you hungry, too? We can order in, or we can make pizza," he offered.

Though they'd had a late lunch, they'd finished eating way before they left the restaurant, which was hours ago. "Now that you mention it, I am getting hungry, and pizza sounds perfect."

"Then pizza it is." Derek reached for her hand and led her into the kitchen to select toppings.

Settling on margherita pizza, Khloe, with the red throw still around her arms, watched Derek slice tomatoes, chop basil, and grate mozzarella. She was thoroughly impressed with his culinary skills, and was surprised her when he rummaged in his refrigerator to pull out a ball of pizza dough. "You have pizza dough just lying around? I mean, who does that?" she asked, laughing.

As Derek began kneading the dough on the granite counter's floury surface, he said, "Well, when you often work well beyond closing time for the pizza delivery, this is the next best thing." He shaped and tossed the dough in the air, just like Khloe had seen at pizzarias and in movies.

"Wow, Derek. I'm amazed at how well you do that. I wish I could, but my culinary talents stop at putting a frozen meal in the microwave."

"Oh, I'm sure they're not as bad as your British accent," he teased.

"Very funny," Khloe replied, giggling into her glass of wine.

He held the dough in one hand and reached for her with the other. "Come on, give it a try."

Khloe shook her head. "I think you've lost your marbles."

"You can do it," he said, giving her an encouraging smile. "I'll even help you."

"Fine." She flashed him a wide smile, hardly believing the words she just spoke. *Since when have I ever been this adventurous in the kitchen? Uh, never!* As many times as Khloe tried to bake or cook anything, her kitchen skills were simply rotten as an egg, and she hoped she wasn't about to embarrass herself in front of Derek. Gearing up for the challenge, she took the blanket off her shoulders and placed it on the back of an island chair. Then, with her stomach in knots, Khloe put out her hands, and Derek draped the dough over them.

"Now, stretch the dough gently by spreading your hands apart," he instructed.

Khloe tried to focus on the dough, but all she could think about was the fact that Derek was now standing behind her, and she felt his warm breath on her neck. Just like at lunch, his cologne still had an erotic effect on her, and her knees were weakening again. *Focus.* "Sorry, what did you say?" she asked, not having heard his next instruction.

He placed a hand on her shoulder, whispering, "Throw it when you're ready," in her ear, his warm breath sending chills over her body.

Khloe held her breath and flung the dough into the air, and she looked over her shoulder to see Derek's grin. As she stared at him watching the dough as it spun in the air, she noticed his eyes light up too. The next thing she knew, Derek's eyes weren't on the dough, but on her. Suddenly, she was lost in the dream of being with him—so much so that she, once again, couldn't hear what he was saying. Shaking herself back to reality, she looked to see the dough falling. Reaching her arms out, she was finally able to hear what Derek was calling out.

"Catch it." And, then, in one swift motion, he took her wrists from under the dough, pushing them toward the counter, saving the crust. "See, it's that easy." He gave her a smile and they gazed into each other's eyes.

When she looked away, she noticed that not only were they both covered in flour, but Derek was also still holding her wrists. "Yeah, real easy," she playfully replied, rolling her eyes and flashing him a frisky grin as his grip around her loosened. "Also, nice catch, by the way."

"Darlin', you haven't seen anything yet," he replied quietly, tapping her nose with a finger after letting go of her wrists.

Thirty minutes later, after they'd dressed the dough with the toppings, Khloe was sitting on Derek's deck on an outdoor sofa built for two, waiting for the pizza to cook on his grill. "Your view is lovely," she told him, taking in the large backyard and bright-colored flowers in artfully placed bushels.

"Thanks, I'm pretty happy with it." He looked around, observing his backyard's landscape, as he placed his hands on his hips. "So, I'm curious, what made you want to open your flower shop?"

Khloe always loved when she was asked this question, as it brought back happy memories. "Well, from when I was little, I've always loved flowers. My dad is a romantic, and he'd often send flowers to my mother saying how much he loves her, though, when I received my first arrangement on my tenth birthday, I was in shock when the deliveryman said they were for me, but it wasn't just about the arrangement. Overall, it's about what the message on the card says."

"What do you mean by that?" Derek asked as he tilted his head, his eyes squinting with interest.

"Words speak volumes. These days, with technology, you can send a flower emoji with a message saying, 'I love you,' or 'Just thinking about you,' which isn't personal at all, but when someone goes out of their way to send you an arrangement, making it a point to get a certain message across to the recipient, that makes me happy." She shook her head, knowing she was rambling. "Anyway, when I read the message and saw they were from my dad, it was an amazing feeling—like I was the most special person in the world, and I wanted others to feel that way, too."

He whistled. "That's very humbling of you, Khloe."

"Thank you."

For a moment, they sat next to each other in silence, enjoying the light breeze and watching the sunset, until Derek took stood to check the pizza off of the grill. "Ah, perfect," he said, then placed it on the pizza pan in front of them and started slicing it. "Dinner is served," he announced, reclaiming his spot beside her.

"This looks scrumptious!" Khloe said, truly impressed, taking her plate from him. "What's your secret to getting the crust so thin?" she asked before taking a bite.

"I hear if you have a newbie throw the dough into the air, and it almost lands on the floor, that does the trick—at least most of the time."

Khloe knew he was joking, even though his delivery was in a serious tone. She wiped her mouth with a napkin, noticing the adorable way he was trying to hide a grin. Trying her best to stifle a laugh, she replied, "You know what? I've heard that, too. Didn't they report something about it on *Dateline* or something?" in the soberest voice she could manage. Seconds passed, then Khloe broke, not able to keep in her laughter in, nor could Derek.

"In truth, it's all about the yeast, and the time you let it rest."

"Man, Derek, I bet you could teach me a thing or two in the kitchen."

"If you give me a chance, I just might," he told her, bringing his glass to his lips, his eyes never leaving hers.

She gave a tight-lipped grin and then she, too, took a sip. She wanted so bad not to act like a klutz, or say anything that would rub him the wrong way, though all she thought was, *I want to rub him the right way!*

"Everything okay?" Derek asked.

She nodded, placing her empty plate on the table, reached for her wine glass, took the last few sips of wine in her glass, then wrapped herself in the throw she'd brought outside with her. With a relaxed sigh, she leaned back on the sofa, watching the changing colors of the sunset. "It's beautiful out tonight, isn't it?"

"I think you're beautiful," he said, inching closer to her.

"Thank you," Khloe replied, feeling heat rush to her cheeks. Though she'd been called beautiful before, there was something special about the way Derek said it.

He brushed a loose strand of hair from Khloe's face and tucked it behind her ear. "What are you thinking?" he asked, placing his hand just above her knee and gently stroking her leg with his thumb.

She looked down at his hand, taking in the warmth she felt from under her pants, then slowly looked at him. "I…" Aware that Derek's lips were inches frim hers, Khloe found it hard to speak. The more he caressed her leg, the more aroused she became, and the more she wondered what it would be like to kiss him. *Is this all a dream?* When a gust of wind caused her to shiver, she knew it wasn't. Her heart raced and her mouth went dry, pretty sure it wasn't because of the red wine.

"You're thinking too much," he said, playfully tapping the top of her head with his index finger. "Come one, what's going on in that beautiful mind of yours?"

"Kiss me," Khloe blurted out. She looked up at him and his beautiful eyes stared down at her. Giving into Khloe's request, Derek cupped her face, pressed his lips to hers, and a wave of electricity shot through her from head to toe, goose bumps covering her body. Kissing him was so much better than she'd ever imagined it. With hints of wine, basil, and tomatoes, his lips were also sweet, like dark chocolate—Khloe's favorite—and it filled her with even more desire for him. She put her arms around his neck, pulling him closer and pressed herself against him, letting the blanket drop from her shoulders. She didn't want to stop, but he pulled away first. Breathless and dizzy, she tried to balance herself on the sofa, continuing to hold her arms around his neck.

Derek draped his arm around Khloe's waist. "I liked what was on your mind," he said, and Khloe quietly giggled. "Hey, it's getting a bit chilly out here. Would you like to go in?"

She nodded, then took his extended hand, and he directed them into the living room where, for the next few hours, between cuddling and kissing, Khloe and Derek got to know each other better, sharing more stories about their lives and their wishes for the future, over a second bottle of wine.

"To some, this is a silly question, but where do you see yourself in five years?" Derek asked her as they faced each other.

"Still loving my job, hopefully still living in my home or close to where I do now because it's near my shop, and maybe a pet or two. Honestly, I just want to be able to say that I'm happy."

"So, you see no man in your life?" he asked her, with a one-sided grin.

In the back of her mind, Khloe heard her mother chanting, "Say yes, Khloe, say yes." Instead, Khloe replied with, "Yeah, of course, I'd like to be in love, possibly even married with children, but right now, I'm taking it one day at a time." She took a large sip of wine, and then asked him the same question.

He scooted closer to her, then said, "I still want to be a successful lawyer, I'd like to be married, have at least two kids—maybe three—just living the dream as they say."

"That doesn't sound too shabby. I just wish the lucky lady lots of luck, because I'm sure you're going to be a handful of a husband—" she began to joke, but he silenced her with a kiss.

Several hours later, Khloe lifted her head from his shoulder and peered out the windows to see the sun rising. She looked back at Derek, watching his chest slowly rise and fall as he slept peacefully. His hair was in complete disarray, his dress shirt was wrinkled, but to Khloe, he was still as handsome as could be—possibly more so. *Damn, even at dawn, you're stunning.* She looked down at herself, pretty sure she looked like a hot mess, so she quickly ran her hands through her rumpled hair, hoping to at least look somewhat decent. Gently squeezing his arm, Khloe whispered, "Hey, Derek, I think it's time for me to leave. The sun's starting to come up."

Slowly, his eyes opened and he looked around the room, though before saying anything, he pulled Khloe in for a kiss. "Good morning."

She smiled, and then whispered, "Good morning," before kissing him again. "I think I should get goiong," she repeated, just as his phone beeped on the table in front of them. Derek reached for his phone, replied to a text, then put the phone in his pocket before letting out a long sigh, running his hands through his hair.

"Everything okay?" she asked, after seeing him tense his jaw. She sensed something was going on, and from the looks of it, it wasn't good.

He leaned back and took Khloe's hand. "I hope," he said, adjusting himself to face her. "What I know for sure is that I really like you, Khloe, and I want to spend more time with you."

Still accustomed to putting up a block with men, she saw two futures with him: the one where it most-likely ended badly; the other, where they they were serenaded by Peter Cetera through loudspeakers while they shared their first dance at their wedding reception. *Stop thinking like that*, she reprimanded herself, shaking away the silly images of wearing a mermaid, Chantilly lace wedding dress, with a champagne-colored ribbon wrapped around her waist. Though she knew Derek wasn't Josh, she fully intended to take it slow no matter what. "I'd love that, too."

"I think there's something I should've told you last night, but I didn't know how to—or even if it would happen. Anyway, I just found out I have to leave town this morning for, um, a case in…Chicago."

"Oh, okay. Well, they've got the best man for the job." She hoped she didn't sound as disappointed as she felt, and she ran a hand through her hair again. "Do you know how long you'll be gone?" she asked, standing to fold the throw they'd covered themselves with.

He stood next to her, taking the throw from her and carelessly tossing it on the couch. Hugging her waist, he pulled her close. "No, but we'll talk and text, and if you're a good girl, I might bring you back something."

"Oh, goodie," Khloe said, clapping her hands. "Will it be one of those Chicago-style pizzas?" she joked.

Derek laughed. "It might be, but Chicago has nothing on your pizza skills."

Playing with him, Khloe swatted his arm. Just as she began to say something, once again, Derek stopped her with a kiss. This time was more erotic than any had been before. The sweet yet sexy way Derek used his mouth felt like he was showing her how much he liked her, how much he was going to miss her, and she giggled to herself when she felt his hardness press against her thigh.

When the kiss was over, Khloe grabbed her purse, and then Derek walked Khloe out to her car. "I'll miss you," he whispered in her ear, after she opened the door and threw her purse into the passenger seat.

"I'll miss you, too," she said, noticing her guard had considerably dropped. "I'll also look forward to your calls and texts."

"I'll do the same, and I'm sure they'll keep me entertained during boring meetings I'll be in."

Behind Derek, Khloe noticed neighbors picking up their papers, as well as a few joggers out for a run. "Well, I should go."

"Yeah, but first, I have a question."

"And what would that be?" Khloe asked skeptically, crossing her arms.

With a mischievous grin and dreamy eyes, he asked, "Do you consider this the best—if not one of—the first dates you've ever had?"

"Ah, you still want an answer to that, do ya?" She wrapped her arms around his neck. "Oh, well, yeah, this was definitely the *best* first date I've had," she said, before kissing him.

"I'm glad I could make your first time special," he replied, grinning.

Khloe laughed. "I look forward to seeing you when you're back,"

Khloe told him as he pulled her closer.

After they shared one last, lingering kiss, she got in her car, waved goodbye, and began her drive home. "Here's to a new day," Khloe cheerfully piped to herself. While she knew she had a busy day ahead of her, one that would be long and tiring, it didn't matter, because she was pretty sure all she would be thinking of was Derek.

CHAPTER SEVENTEEN

Gabby

"So, the Crushed Grape, huh?" Harry asked Gabby as they took a seat on one of the couches in front of a decorative red granite fireplace roaring with warmth. Along the cork-inspired walls of the wine bar were giant oils and prints of grapes, glasses of wine, and lights that spelled out the bar's name. Large magnum bottles entwined with mini white lightbulbs that looked like tea candles acted as chandeliers.

"I thought this would be a perfect way to end what was such a wonderful day," Gabby replied, reaching for a menu that lay on the glass table in front of them.

"And I couldn't agree more," he said and took his glasses out of his shirt pocket. He put them on and proceeded to read over Gabby's shoulder. "What looks good to you?"

Gabby handed the menu to him. "I'm thinking about a house Cabernet. What about you?" she asked him, just as a tall, thin waiter greeted them.

"Hello, and welcome to the Crushed Grape." The waiter set down purple and green plaid napkins in front of them, and told Gabby and Harry about the all-day happy hour specials, which involved a flight of red and white wines and champagnes, along with a cheese tray. After agreeing on a flight of reds for Gabby and whites for Harry, and a cheese tray for them to share, they leaned back into the brown plush couch.

"I'm so happy you could meet my family," Harry told her, taking her hand in his. "They seemed to really like you."

She cupped his hand with hers. "And I really enjoyed meeting them. Jeff is so handsome—like his father, Jules is such a sweetheart, and Andrew, well, I adore him!" Just as Harry opened his mouth to speak, the waiter placed their wine flights in front of them and told them their cheese tray would be out shortly. Gabby lifted the first of five samples of red wine and turned toward Harry. "Thank you for allowing me the great joy of meeting your family. To today, with hopes of many more days like this one to come."

"You can count on that," he agreed with a wink, clinking together. Harry then placed his glass on the table and scooted closer to Gabby, tucking a strand of hair behind her ear. Gabby felt her cheeks turn pink, not minding how close he now sat to her, nor the way he gently touched her. "You wouldn't mind if I kissed you right now, would you?"

By now, Gabby's heart was thumping through her chest, and she was sure her face was beet-red from giddiness. Very slowly, she shook her head and closed her eyes, waiting to feel his lips on hers. When she did, seconds later, an erotic rush of delight raced through her—the kind she used to feel before she and Charlie made love. Not having had that feeling in so long and having it with Harry was just what she needed. *Do I want Harry?* she wondered, kissing him back, and like music being turned down, laughter around them, sparks from the fire, and sounds of champagne corks being popped faded away, because all she focused on was Harry.

"Um, excuse me, but I hate to interrupt," said their waiter with a little cough, and shyly Gabby and Harry pulled away from each other. "Here is your cheese plate," he told them, placing the tray on the table. Harry nodded at him, and the waiter started to walk away, then turned back on his heel, facing them. "It's nice to see that these days." Gabby and Harry looked at each other, confused.

"And what's that?" Gabby asked, scrunching her brows together.

"A couple so much in love," and before she could correct him—though she didn't know exactly what she'd say—the waiter hurried away looking more embarrassed than Gabby felt.

"Did you see how red his cheeks were?" she asked, covering her mouth. "I can only imagine what he must be thinking right now."

Harry laughed and handed Gabby one of the mini-forks. "I do agree with him, though."

"On what?" she asked, placing cubes of gourmet cheeses and a small amount of almonds and cashews with dried fruit and green olives on her plate.

"That we look madly in love." And then, after flashing Gabby a delicate grin, he gave a slight chuckle and popped a cube of cheese into his mouth.

"Funny, I thought the same thing," she joked back, but part of her wondered how the outside world saw them. Did they really look like a couple who were "madly in love"? *Do I love Harry? Is it too soon, though? What if…?*

Questions rushed through her mind as she talked with Harry and continued to enjoy her wines and cheeses. They watched as a band began to set up. When the familiar notes of "Unforgettable" rang out, Gabby and Harry looked at each other. Without a word, she knew what he was thinking. She placed her hand in his and they stood in unison, walked to the small dance floor and began swaying to the song, which was being sung by a man whose voice could easily pass for Tony Bennett's. Standing close together, with each slow move they made, Gabby and Harry stared back at one another. He held her close to him and brushed his cheeks with her hands. When the song was over, they stood still, not wanting to break the moment. Not even the clapping from other patrons at the wine bar interrupted the magical moment they shared.

"Thank you for the dance," Harry told her, just before kissing her gently on the lips.

"You're welcome," she replied, and let him lead them back to the couch. Taking a seat, Gabby now knew she was close to being in love again, but guilt of loving someone other than Charlie ate at her heart.

As they sipped the last sample of their wine, Gabby felt a little buzzed, though she didn't know if it was because of the alcohol or being around Harry. Deciding they were finished with wine and cheese, Harry paid the bill, but they stayed to finish what was left in their glasses, continuing to talk about Harry's family.

"They seem really great together," she commented after Harry told her the story about how Jeff and Jules met and married. "Speaking of marriage, would you ever want to get married again?" Gabby asked him, tilting her head.

Harry whistled. "Well, you're not holding anything back, are you?" he teased.

Gabby shook her head. "No, I'm sorry, I shouldn't have—"

He gave her arm a soft squeeze and nodded. "It's okay. I'm glad you asked." Harry took off his glasses and put them back into his shirt pocket, then swiveled to face her, giving her his full attention. "At first, no. My wife had always been my one and only, and I only had eyes for her. While I'm still heartbroken," he placed his hand on his chest, "I know that I have to go on without her." He smiled at Gabby, adding, "Since you've been in my life, my days are now filled with a renewed hope, and I know that having love in my life can still exist." His voice started to quiver, and he laid his hands on hers as he sighed. "That being said, yes, I'd love to get married again, not only because I know my late wife would want me to be happy, but because

I want to." After a hard swallow, he asked, "What about you, Gabby? Do you see yourself marrying again?"

Her heart melted because he wore a hopeful grin on his face and he'd spoken the same sentiments she felt. She no longer had to feel shy or guilty for talking about marriage with him—whether it would be with him or someone else. "Harry, you have no idea how happy I am to hear you say what you just did, because that's how I feel, too. You know, I loved Charlie, but at some point, I knew I needed to stop grieving over him, and I have to thank you for helping me do that. In the short time we've known each other, my heart is already open to love again, which is why I'm so grateful to you in my life— thanks for messaging me through the dating site, by the way." She let out a small chuckle and then in a quiet and serious voice, added, "I loved being a wife. Marriage and family mean everything to me, so, if I'm fortunate enough to be married again, then my answer is yes."

Without a word, Harry leaned over and kissed Gabby's lips.

*****

After Harry took Gabby home, she was still buzzing with energy. She wasn't ready to say goodbye to him yet.

"Can you stay for a while?" she asked him after she unlocked her door.

"I'd like that very much." After he crossed the threshold he closed the door, and she took him by the hand to lead him into her living room, and they sat down on the couch. She looked at his lips pressed tightly together and his dull eyes and sensed something was wrong. "Hey, are you okay?"

He nodded. "Oh, yeah, I'm fine. I was just thinking about life and how important it is to spend it with those with ones we care about." With a chuckle, Harry added, "Besides, it's not like we're getting any younger."

Gabby laughed. "I know what you mean. Family and friends are very important." She reached for his hand, gently placing it between hers, and then looked up at him. "You're important to me, Harry."

"And you are to me, too." With that, she allowed him to hug her, then he planted a gentle kiss on her forehead.

She looked up at him, noticing that he was asking approval to kiss her again, so, with her eyes, she said yes. When she felt the delicate sensation of his soft lips, she began to wonder what it really would be like to be part of Harry's family. She'd be a wife to Harry, stepmother to Jeff, a stepmother-in-law to Jules, a step-grandmother to Andrew. Even though she'd just met them, she had a feeling she belonged in Harry's family.

Moments later, she pulled away from him, breathless.

"What is it, my darling?" he asked.

"Harry, I've never been with anyone but Charlie, but something about the thought of being with you makes it all seem right. It's like…" She shook her head, trying to think of what she wanted to say, but all that came out was, "I want to be with you." Once the words were out, she knew in her heart she truly meant them. Sure enough, she was falling in love again, and it felt good. Managing to finally look at Harry, she saw nothing but love, and, of course, eagerness on his face. Instantly, as if it were natural, Gabby reached for his hand and led them up the stairs to her bedroom.

CHAPTER EIGHTEEN

Connie

Connie woke up, thankful it was the weekend and excited to hear from Walt. To burn nervous energy while waiting for him to call, she decided to go to the gym in her apartment complex. She hadn't been in a few months, and knew that it would do her some good. Slinging her gym bag over her shoulder, she headed out the door.

Though she typically felt insecure about her figure, today she wasn't bothered by it because all she could think about was her magical date with Walt. She hopped on the treadmill, plugged her ears with headphones, and began jogging. After getting her heart rate up a bit, she increased the speed and kept going until the fifty minutes on the timer buzzed. "Wow," she said as she hopped off. As she headed back home, Connie was amazed at how great she felt. While she'd only had one date with Walt, she sensed that maybe his presence in her life was more than just to play the part of her "boyfriend," but to help her get her life in order. In the back of her mind, though, Connie knew she didn't deserve to feel so blissful, considering the devious way she was going about it, but she couldn't help herself.

After returning from the gym, Connie still hadn't heard from Walt. So, to be sure she didn't miss his call, she brought the phone into the bathroom with her, placing it on the outside ledge of the shower. Hours later, when he still didn't call, she decided to watch one of her favorite movies, *Love Potion #9,* to try and take her mind off things. Just as she hit "play," her phone buzzed. She smiled when she saw Walt's name on the screen.

"Hello?"

"Hey, you," Walt said, sounding out of breath.

"Hi." She giggled into the phone. "What's up? You sound like you've been running a marathon."

He chuckled, then explained he'd been busy helping a friend move, but he'd love to see her later.

"I'd love to see you, too," she said, feeling warmth rush to her cheeks. Warmth rushed to her cheeks.

After they decided on something fun to do he said, and Connie gave him her address, Walt said, "Great, I'll see you soon," and then hung up.

Right away, Connie quickly got to work tidying up her apartment. She didn't want him to see the messy woman she really was—at least not yet.

After things were picked up, she hurried to her bedroom to get ready. Since they'd decided to go to an outdoor flower garden, which Connie heard was a great place for photos, she wanted to look her best—just in case she or Walt brought out their phones and started clicking away. She settled on a new pair of dark green corduroy pants, a black V-neck cashmere sweater (the one she only wore on special occasions, though she couldn't remember when she wore it last), and her favorite pair of black flats. Connie took one last look at herself in the mirror just as her doorbell chimed. *Just breathe,* she thought as she quickly went to answer the door.

When she opened it, Walt's eyes bugged out. "Wow, you look stunning."

Connie eyed him up and down, once again liking what she saw. Under a black leather jacket, his gray T-shirt showed off his chiseled torso, his jeans hugged him in all the right places, his hair was slicked back, and his woodsy cologne tickled her nose. Turning her lips up in a grin, she replied with, "Thanks. You look handsome yourself."

"Are you ready to go?" he asked.

"Yes." She reached for her purse and closed the door behind her. She smiled when Walt grasped her hand as they walked down the hallway, out of her apartment complex, and to his white BMW convertible.

On the way to their destination they had a relaxed conversation about the weather and their day. When they arrived, Connie was stunned by the beauty of the garden. She spun in a slow circle and took in the tall bushes that were etched into quarter-moons, which led into four separate paths. Between each of them lay white square stones leading to trails in different parts of the park. She took in the bright colors of flowers and plants, along with all of the visitors who swarmed the place with smiling faces as they posed in front of cameras. Connie felt like she'd been whisked away into a fairy tale, because never in her life had she seen something so magical—except for Walt, of course. "Wow, this place is beautiful," she whispered to him.

"I know, isn't it?" Walt said, taking her hand in his and leading her toward a fountain. "Here," he said, handing her a penny he'd pulled out of his pocket. "Let's make a wish together."

Connie took the penny, held it to her lips and closed her eyes, thinking of a wish she'd want to come true. *I wish that someone would love me the way my imaginary Walt does.* Seconds later, she flipped the coin into the fountain.

Walt followed suit and turned to her. "What did you wish for?"

Grinning, Connie waved a finger at him. "I'm not telling you because if I do, it won't come true."

"Fair enough," he said, taking a step toward her, then brushed the back of his hand alongside her face, his eyes staring deep into hers. "I could look into your eyes forever."

"Thank you," she said with another giggle, knowing he'd probably used that line with all his previous women before, but she had to remind herself to not get too wrapped up in this real life fantasy she'd created. "Hey, how about we grab a bite over there?" she suggested, trying to distract from her shyness, along with the erotic thoughts racing through her head as she pointed to a man dressed in a hot dog costume.

"I'll follow you," Walt replied with a wink, holding out his hand.

She took his hand in hers. "With pleasure."

Minutes later, Connie and Walt sat beside each other at one of the many picnic tables scattered around the garden and bit into their hot dogs.

"This is nice," he said after taking a sip of his water.

"The weather is perfect," Connie said, and she looked up at blue sky, only noticing a few clouds. "You picked a great day to come here, considering it's not too cold out." Connie hadn't brought a jacket, but she was warm enough in her sweater. However, if she did get cold, she was sure Walt would help keep her warm. Just the thought of that made her blush, and she gave Walt a quick smile, taking the last bite of the chocolate chip cookie they bought to share.

"I'm glad you're having fun, but there's something I want to show you," he said, sounding direct, yet secretive at the same time.

"Oh, really?" she replied flirtatiously. "And what is that?"

"Well—" he began, but at that moment, a gust of wind came and swept up their napkins, sending them flying. With a little help from other patrons, Connie and Walt picked up the napkins along with their paper plates and threw them away.

"Well, I guess we're done with lunch," Walt joked.

"Yeah, I guess so. Now, what were you saying about something you wanted to show me?" she asked.

"Come on." He motioned to her with his finger, giving her a sly grin as he held out his hand.

"Your wish is my command," she joked with a salute and placed her hand in his, allowing him to lead them down a pathway to a secluded part of the garden.

"Oh, my goodness," she whispered, standing frozen, taking in the view. "It's gorgeous." She scanned the crescent-shaped area where they stopped, with all different kinds of roses exuding a delicate, sweet scent. She walked over to a bush and bent down to smell a circus rose. "This is simply heavenly!"

Without any hesitation, Walt took out his Swiss Army pocket knife and began cutting the stem.

"Walt, what are you doing?" she said, worried that he'd get in trouble for picking the flower. She pointed to the security guard who stood in the center of the garden, keeping watch for any flower thieves.

"Don't worry about it," he said casually, which made Connie uneasy. While it was a sweet gesture, Connie was a rule-follower, and she never liked getting in trouble. "In honor of my grandmother, my parents donated this part of the garden, so I think security will let this one go," he said, pointing to the guard who now had his back to them. "Connie, will you accept this rose?" he asked, holding out the flower to her.

"Yes," she said with a laugh at the cheesy question, remembering how she'd told him she loved watching *The Bachelor,* and before she could say anything else, she felt his lips on hers. As the hot sun beat down on them, Connie's heart melted. Kissing Walt made her feel like she was in her own fairy tale, and she felt that when their lips were together, he was transforming her from the frumpy girl she had always been to a beautiful princess she always wanted to be. His sweet lips sent a wave of sensual chills over her body, and she tasted chocolate on his tongue. He wasn't forceful, but he wasn't gentle either. Walt was just right. *Holy crap, you're a kissing god!* she thought. Slowly, not wanting to break contact, she reached her arms around his neck, bringing him closer to her, not bothered by the roar of an airplane flying above, the water trickling from the fountain, or the joyful laughter of boisterous children from across the way. Connie was too busy kissing him, and began wondering what it would be like to be intimate with Walt.

When their lips parted, Connie looked up at him, seeing everything she'd ever wanted in a man staring back at her. "Again, thank you," she finally managed to say, though she wasn't sure if she was thanking him for the rose again, or this time, the kiss. The more she looked at him, she had an overwhelming urge to suddenly tell him the truth—that though she found him for all the wrong reasons, but was falling for him for all the right ones. Maybe one day, she'd tell him the truth, but not now, because at that moment, everything was too perfect.

"Hey, do you want to go back to my place?" She let her heart and mind do the talking. She looked up at him, never feeling so confident in her life, and if she had to bet on it, she was pretty sure Walt was thinking the same thing.

He pressed his lips to hers again. "Yes, but before we do that, how about we capture a picture of this moment, so we'll always have it?"

"I'd love that," she said, and in seconds, they were posing together in front of the rose bushes. To any onlooker, it would seem they were a normal, happy couple in love, not just some ruse invented by Connie.

CHAPTER NINTEEN

Khloe

When Khloe got home, she took a quick shower and dressed in jeans, brown knee-high boots, and a lavender cashmere sweater. After blow-drying and curling her hair, then carefully applying make-up, she zoomed out the door and headed to work.

On her way there, she thought about her perfect date with Derek, wondering how she got so lucky to meet him. Though he'd be in Chicago, she was already looking forward to receiving phone calls and texts from him. However, until he was back, she planned to focus on work, including her meeting with Millicent, which she was trying to stay positive about, hoping the bride-to-be wouldn't be hell to work with.

"Hey, you," Sharon said as Khloe entered her shop. Coming from the workroom, carrying a large arrangement that she placed on the center of the shop's cherry wood table in the middle of the store. "Do you like it?" Sharon asked, pointing to the tall, clear glass vase, which was decorated in an orange and brown Thanksgiving-colored theme. "I know it's a couple of weeks away, but I thought why not start getting in the spirit of it, which might incresease the chances of people placing their holiday early orders. Also, just to be sure, I made sure it was manageable to keep up with until after the end of the month," she added, pointing to the foam packs inside the vase.

"I love it!" Khloe gushed. "And I love the flowers you chose." Khloe admired the roses, Gerbera daisies, and lilies, along with baby pumpkins, brown crystal ornaments, and pine cones that layered the bottom of the clear vase. It was a stunning arrangement, and from the looks of it, she knew she could easily sell it for a hundred and fifty dollars. She patted Sharon on the back. "You did a beautiful job."

After taking a bow, Sharon smirked, then changed the topic. "So, I think you have some explaining to do," she said, waving a finger. "How was your date with Derek?"

Just hearing the name *Derek* made Khloe blush. "It was great," she replied with a bright smile, and tilting her head up at the ceiling. "No, in fact, it was more than that. It was perfect. We had such an amazing time, and he's so charming." Though her night with Derek was more than she could've ever imagined, she was trying not to jinx anything with him, but she wanted to share her happiness with her best friend, too. "From lunch yesterday, to this morning, we talked non-stop, well, except for the time we were sleeping, of course."

Sharon widened her eyes and stretched her neck out, clearly surprised by Khloe's behavior. "You *slept* with him?" Sharon asked, sounding shocked.

Just as Khloe was about to tell Sharon about dinner and spending the night with him, the chimes on the door rang. "Look, there's so much more I want to tell you, so why don't you come over tonight? That is, unless you have plans with Leonard?"

She shook her head. "Nothing is more important than hearing how your night went with Derek, so I'll be there." She then added, "By the twinkle in your eyes, I can tell you're already smitten."

Khloe couldn't deny it. "You know, I really think I am, and I have a good feeling about him, too. I know it's way early in this relationship—or whatever it is—but I love spending time with him."

A wide grin crossed her face. "Oh, Sharon, I just can't wait for you to meet him." Khloe was beaming as she bounced on the tips of her toes.

"Oh, Khloe, I'm so happy for you!" She gave her a quick hug.

"Thanks, doll," she said to Sharon, before she watched her cross the store to help a customer who was wandering through the shop. Khloe still had an hour before Millicent was to arrive, so she went into her office and started preparing for their meeting. She laid out a spread of photo albums that contained a wide range of Khloe's Flower Shop's portfolio, two notepads—one for Khloe, the other for Millicent—a few purchase orders, along with a split of Mumm champagne for the bride-to-be, chilling in a bucket of ice in the middle of the table. Looking over the set once more, Khloe was ready for Millicent. She looked at her watch, noticing she was supposed to arrive any minute, so Khloe sat down at her desk, where she returned a few emails. Five minutes later, Millicent still hadn't arrived, so Khloe peeked into the front of the shop to find Sharon. "Hey, when Millicent Mosby arrives, would you please send her back?"

"Yep, no problem," she replied to Khloe, handing a receipt to a customer who stood in front of her.

"Thanks," she said, then walked back into her office. Khloe had always been a planner and followed her calendar religiously, so she considered her time important, though knew that sometimes unforeseen things happened. She halted from tapping her nails on the edge of her desk and jotted down more ideas for Millicent. Twenty minutes later, and with several pieces of paper written and drawn on, Millicent still hadn't arrived so she decided to call her. On the third ring, Millicent answered.

"This is Millicent Mosby," she grumbled into the phone, sounding out of breath.

"Hi, Millicent, this is Khloe—"

"Oh, Khloe," she said, interrupting her, and her voice now in a sweet-as-sugar tone. "I'm so sorry, but my meeting with the event planner ran way late because my previous meeting with the bakery went overtime—I guess I spent too much time explaining the shape of the cake. I mean, how hard it is to explain that I want it to look like a crystal chandelier? Maybe I should hire a bakery from L.A.," she thought outloud. Without missing a beat, she added, "I'm sorry for the random tangent, but I guess it's just not my day. Anyway, I'm on my way right now and should be there soon. Does that still work for you?"

"Absolutely!" Khloe replied.

"You're the best," Millicent cooed, before hanging up.

Khloe swiveled in her chair, headed for the coffee machine and made a new pot, because she had a feeling she was going to need a strong cup to help power her through the meeting with Millicent. Just as Khloe put the cup to her lips and took the first sip, she heard Millicent's high-pitched voice. "Hi, I'm late for a meeting with Khloe Harper."

"Please follow me," she heard Sharon say.

"Oh, Khloe," Millicent said, almost leaping in her arms. "I'm so sorry I'm late."

Surprised by Millicent's embrace, Khloe patted Millicent's shoulder and gave Sharon a wink that it was okay for her to go back to work. When Khloe and Millicent parted, Khloe pointed to the table and chairs in a small corner of her office. "Please take a seat, and we'll get started." Khloe walked to the table and then asked, "Can I offer you a cup of coffee, water, a soda, or even a glass of champagne?" She held up the small bottle of Mumm Napa, one of the many bottles her parents had sent her.

Millicent pointed to the champagne. "Definitely the champagne! I just love anything with bubbles!" She had a youthful grin on her face—one that could be easily mistaken for a kid being offered an ice cream cone with three scoops of double-fudge chocolate ice cream, covered with rainbow sprinkles.

Khloe carefully poured the champagne, watching Millicent eagerly clap her hands and walk toward the table.

Millicent's eyes stayed focused on the champagne being poured, casually dropping her designer purse on the floor beside her, and took a seat. "Thank you," she said to Khloe, taking the champagne flute in her hands. Before she put the delicate glass to her lips, she added, "I so needed this." And with that, she emptied half its contents.

Khloe had to laugh. "Rough day so far?"

In reply to Khloe, Millicent rolled her eyes with a nod of her head. "Very, but everything is good now," she said, tracing the rim of her flute with her fingertip.

"Great!" Reaching for her notes and portfolio picture book, Khloe took a seat next to Millicent, saying, "Okay, to get started, I have a few questions for you." After asking the basic questions about the specific date and time of the wedding, address of the ceremony and reception, along with a few other minute details Khloe needed to know, she slid her floral portfolio toward Millicent. "Before we discuss any specifics of what I had in mind, here are some photographs of what we've done for past weddings, birthdays, and other events."

Millicent pulled the book toward her and started flipping through the pages, with a blank expression.

To Khloe, that meant Millicent was re-thinking her choice. As Khloe watched her client, she quickly hoped to wash away the detachment that crossed her face, not wanting to disappoint the governor's daughter. If Khloe were a betting woman, she'd wager pouring more Mumm into Millicent's flute could make the bride-to-be happy and content. "Would you like more champagne, Millicent?" she asked, holding up the bottle and hoping it would possibly get Millicent to verbalize any feelings she had about anything she saw in the portfolio.

Millicent extended her arm to Khloe and allowed her glass to be re-filled without replying.

"I do like this," she told Khloe, pointing to a rose bouquet where two rows of white roses circled around two red roses, to which Khloe nodded and told her it was a popular choice.

"Oh, well, then I can't have that one, can I?" Millicent rhetorically commented, and turned the page. Finally, on the last page, Millicent's jaw dropped. "This is it." She beamed up at Khloe, pointing to a large white rose bouquet, scattered with real crystals around it, with the stems covered in white satin, along with more crystals. "Wait, this is *not* a popular item, right?"

Khloe leaned over and nodded, eyeing which one Millicent was pointing to. "No, that one is new, so nobody has ordered it." She wanted to tell her that she'd created it herself and that it was the exact bouquet she wanted if she ever got married, but she decided to keep that to herself. "I think it's a lovely choice." Khloe continued to point out that it was a pretty penny since the crystals weren't fake, and even suggested adding color crystals, which led Millicent to leap head over heels about that idea, telling her she'd think about the color and would get back to her.

Once her bouquet was picked, Millicent leaned back in her chair, excitement wearing off, and then she began biting her lip.

Catching Millicent's sudden relaxed composure, she said, "If you change your mind, we can work on something else. I'm sure I can create something you'd love—something original—and just for *your* wedding!" However, Khloe was hoping it wouldn't come to that, but on the other hand, like Millicent told her, she had a tendency to change her mind.

Millicent shook her head. "No, I'm pretty sure that I'm sticking with the all white bouquet, with the crystals. Though, I'm the governor's daughter, not just any ordinary person. Oh, and I just found out that the wedding will be featured in three Texas wedding magazines," she commented, her eyes beaming, though from her monotone voice, Khloe sensed there was something up, but she didn't dig. "I need this to be the most spectacular event that anyone's ever seen," Millicent said with a yawn, and then ran her hands through her hair.

That's when Khloe knew she needed help, and she needed it from her biggest competitor, Madam Pluma. Being a larger shop, with double the clientele, they scored big when they signed a contract with a secret wholesaler. The word in the flower shop business was that Mrs. Pluma, the owner, wanted to keep her wholesaler to herself, and she'd never tell anyone who they were. Just thinking about having to make the call to Mrs. Pluma, and ask her—okay, beg, if she was being honest—to give her the name of her wholesaler and to see if her store could in any way help with the Mosby wedding, made Khloe's stomach twist with nerves. "Absolutely, that's definitely something we can do! Millicent, I will do everything possible to meet your highest expectations with your wedding flowers. Now, besides flowers, tell me what your vision is—from the ceremony, cocktail hour, if there is one, of course, along with the reception—so I get a feel of the ambiance and what flowers would work well." Khloe turned the page in her notepad, flipped it toward Millicent, and took copious notes and drawings, which were not that different from the images she'd shown to Khloe on her phone, on the day they'd met.

An hour later, having taken only a few short breaths while giving Khloe a perfect description of what she wanted, Millicent said, "Well, Khloe, I cannot thank you enough for helping me today." She pointed to Khloe's stack of notes (which covered the flowers for the rehearsal dinner), the bridesmaids (all fourteen of them), her bouquet, her father and her fiancé's boutonnières, along with the ones for the fourteen groomsmen, and several hundred flowers for the reception. "I can't wait to see how it's all going to look," Millicent said, beaming again. "I just know it's going to be beautiful." With a sigh, she sat back in her chair and looked down at the engagement ring on her finger. "You know, my granny was right when she said that everything will come together, and I feel that way now," Millicent said in a quiet voice, straightening herself in her chair. "Also, I wanted to apologize how I acted the first time we met. You were really nice to me and Granny, and I can only imagine you must have thought I was spoiled brat, or probably something worse. I guess I should relax a bit with all the wedding stuff, huh?" It didn't seem like a question to Khloe, but rather a realization, as Millicent clasped her hands and placed them on the table. "It's just hard being the governor's daughter, and the pressure of the wedding being the main event…" Millicent shook her head, and gave a faint smile in Khloe's direction. "Anyway, I'm sorry, and I promise not to be a bridezilla, so if I ever get out of line, please let me know. I guess my main focus is that the wedding will be featured in magazines, which adds even extra added stress—which is why I feel *everything* has to be perfect."

A little surprised by Millicent's apology and by her venting, Khloe replied with, "Thank you for your apology, but there's no need." In sales, Khloe had learned quickly that not everyone is nice, and customers thought they could spit demands whenever they wanted.

The two held an understanding glance, until Millicent asked, "Are you married?"

Millicent's question surprised Khloe, and she caught a glimpse of the large rock Millicent wore on her left hand. "No, I'm not married."

In surprise, Millicent's eyes bugged out. "I'm sorry to ask you this, but why not? You're a very pretty woman, and I know that any man would be lucky to have you."

Khloe blushed. "That's very kind of you to say, but for right now,

I'm taking it one day at a time," she said with raised shoulders, thinking of Derek.

"Well, are you at least dating? Come on, there has to be someone you're interested in," Millicent said, tapping her hands on the table.

Before Khloe was about to responded to Millicent—with what, she didn't quite know—her phone rattled the table. Eagerly, she reached for it and saw it was a text from Derek that read: On the plane! I'll call later. Miss you! Beaming, Khloe replied with: Miss you, too! Safe travels! Talk to you later. She put her phone back on the table. "Sorry about that."

"Ah, ha!" Millicent exclaimed with a loopy grin. "So, you *are* dating someone."

Khloe couldn't hide her smile. "Well, I wouldn't really call it dating—we're only starting to get to know each other, but yeah, I guess I could say there's someone I'm interested in."

"Aww, yay," Millicent cooed, adding, "Being in love is the most wonderful thing in the world."

Without giving any reply about being in love, Khloe stood up, capped off the half-drunk bottle of Mumm and put it back in her refrigerator. Talking about her personal life with a client wasn't something she usually did, nor did she want many people knowing her business, so she changed the topic. "Well, I think we made a lot of progress today—"

"Wait! I'm not letting you off that easy," Millicent playfully snapped, pointing her index finger at Khloe. "You do agree, right?" She stood up, inches away from Khloe. "Tell me, isn't being in love the most wonderful thing in the world?" Waiting for her answer, Millicent stared dreamy-eyed into Khloe's eyes, almost like she was trying to be convince Khloe to join some kind of lovers' cult.

Could Khloe see herself dating Derek? Yes. Could she see a possible future with him? Well, that answer would have to wait. So, to satisfy Millicent, she nodded and said, "I'm sure it is."

"You're funny." Millicent let out a sigh and rolled her eyes. "Well, when the time comes for you, don't let the one get away. Believe me, I know firsthand." Then, in one swift swoop, she drained the rest of her flute's contents. After licking her lips, she picked up her purse, draped it over her shoulder and said, "Thank you for everything, Khloe. I have complete faith and trust that you will help make my wedding the most beautiful anyone's ever seen."

"You're so welcome," Khloe said with enthusiasm. After scheduling another appointment, this time at the governor's ranch where the wedding and reception would take place, Khloe led Millicent to the front of her shop. "Again, please don't hesitate to call me should you change your mind about anything, or need anything, because it's completely okay to do so." Khloe smiled at Millicent, trying her best to cover up her growing stress level, imagining what the upcoming months of creating Millicent's abundance of flowers for her wedding would be like, especially considering this was her biggest job. Just knowing it would be for the governor's daughter, where she imagined numerous high-class guests who were in the public eye would be in attendance, was nerve-wracking enough, *but* what ate at her stomach, making her nauseous, was the fact the wedding would be in magazines across the state, which meant her flower shop would be mentioned. *I have to pull this off!*

"Oh, believe me, I will," she said, opening Khloe's office door. "Bye." She waved and then wobbled out the door.

Khloe hurried to catch up to her. "Millicent, are you okay to drive? Would you like to take some water or coffee with you?"

She waved Khloe away. "I'm fine. Besides, my driver is here. Champagne doesn't usually affect me like this, so don't think that I'm a weakling," she said with a laugh. "I forgot to eat this morning, but you really don't eat veggie and protein shakes, do you?" She gave off a small chuckle, adding, "I guess my bride boot camp diet is working, which is good for my fiancé's upcoming campaign." Taking a couple of slow steps to a black town car, where a man stood holding a passenger door open, Millicent said, "All political wives are forced to look great, so no excuses, right?" and then gave one last wave to Khloe, before she not so gracefully slid into the car. Seconds later, Khloe stood watching until the car drove away.

When Khloe walked back into her store, she saw Sharon hand a large arrangement of pink and yellow roses to a male customer, along with his receipt, and then he walked out the door. "Hey, how's it going?"

Sharon closed the drawer on the cash register with one swift move of her hip. "Just fine, but let's skip the small talk. Now that nobody's here, tell me more about Derek and your date."

Khloe snickered. "I'd love to, but I have some work I need to get done. How about I tell you tonight? Come at around eight. We'll order sushi and have a girls' night in…that is, unless you have a TARDIS sex date with Leonard."

Sharon laughed. "Ha, ha, very funny! Like I told you earlier, nothing means more than hearing about about you and Derek."

Khloe laughed. "Okay, okay, you'll get them," she promised before walking back to her office, knowing it was time to take care of some serious business by calling Mrs. Pluma. She held her breath ring by ring, waiting for someone to pick up.

"Madam Pluma, this is Rory."

"Hi, Rory, this is Khloe from Khloe's Flower Shop. Is Mrs. Pluma available?"

"Umm, just a minute, let me check," the chipper woman said.

After almost five minutes passed, Khloe was about to hang up and walk the few blocks to Madam Pluma's herself, but Rory came back on the line. "Um, who did you say you were again?" After Khloe repeated herself, Rory said, "Oh, sure, no problem, please hold."

Seconds later, Mrs. Pluma came on the line. "Khloe Harper, how nice to hear from you. How's business, darling?"

"It's going great," she said, speaking with confidence, not fazed by Mrs. Pluma's forward question. Khloe was aware Mrs. Pluma was known to keep a watchful eye out for struggling flower shops so she could swoop in and take them over, just as she'd done with the previous three stores she now owned. Khloe wasn't worried about Mrs. Pluma—or anyone—taking her store away from her, because she wasn't struggling and she worked hard to make it what it was, which was one of many reasons why this call was so important. "Anyway, I was calling you because I need a favor, and I thought maybe you could help me out with something."

"Oh, and what would that be?" she asked, in what Khloe took to be a less than surprised tone.

After Khloe explained her situation about needing help with Millicent's wedding, she took a slight pause before asking, "Mrs. Pluma, I know you don't give your wholesaler's contact number to just anyone, but I thought that maybe this once, you'd make an exception…I promise I won't share the name or number with anyone else." Nervously, Khloe bit her lip as she waited for Mrs. Pluma to respond, and while she didn't want to, she spit out her last card as a way of begging. "I'd be willing to give you a percentage of the final balance of the wedding."

Mrs. Pluma echoed a slight laugh. "You know, Khloe, only one other person knows who I use as a wholesaler, and I'd like to keep it that way, *but* since I'm a family friend of Governor Mosby—he told me he didn't want me working the wedding because I'd be receiving an invitation. That being said, I'm going to help you."

Khloe couldn't believe her ears, and in a matter of seconds, she found herself writing down the number of By the Dozen, relief washing over her. "Thank you, thank you, thank you, Mrs. Pluma. I promise I will keep this just between us."

"Now, when you call them, be sure to ask for Falcon, and he will help you out with whatever you need." She paused, smacked her lips, and then added, "Now, I wish you luck with this elaborate challenge, Khloe, but if there's anything you need, don't hesitate to call me back."

Khloe thanked Mrs. Pluma again and hung up the phone, feeling droplets of sweat on her forehead, hardly believing what a simple and peaceful conversation she'd had with one of the most reputable women in the Texas flower business. She sank into her office chair, silently thanking her lucky stars. *One step done, and millions more to go!*

*****

Later that night, Khloe poured more red wine into her glass, saying, "Though, in the end, the conversation wasn't as bad as I thought it would be. I got what I wanted and needed, and I'm really hoping the wholesaler will come through for me."

"Oh, I'm sure everything will be just fine. After all, if By the Dozen helps Mrs. Pluma, I'm sure you have the right people to help with Millicent's wedding, and don't forget, I'll be by your side, every step of the way," Sharon said with a wave of her hand. "Cheers, my friend. I know everything will come together beautifully." They clinked their glasses together, both took a sip of wine, and then she said, "So, enough of this work talk. Spill it, girl, and hold nothing back."

Khloe giggled, feeling her cheeks turn pink. "Well, after lunch with Derek, I followed him back to his place, where he gave me a tour of his lovely home, then he opened a bottle of wine and we talked for a bit." She paused to take a sip of her wine. "Then, a few hours later, and after a lot of getting to know each other, we made homemade pizza for dinner."

"We?" she asked, tilting her head. "I don't mean this in a bad way, but, honey, you're horrible in the kitchen," Sharon said, popping a piece of a California roll into her mouth.

Before reaching for a salmon nigiri and curling her legs under her, she gave a playful tap on Sharon's knee. "Oh, hush, I'm not *that bad*, but he encouraged me to try something new, so I did. Anyway, after dinner, he kissed me." Khloe was going to continue but was interrupted by the shrill tone of Sharon's voice, and watched her raise her hands in the air as she performed some kind of happy dance, while sitting on the floor. Once Sharon resumed being quiet to let Khloe speak, she added, "Sharon, everything about the night was perfect. After dinner, we went back inside, sat on his couch, and got to know each other a little bit better—"

"I bet you did," Sharon said quietly, with a giggle.

"Derek's soft-spoken, sweet and caring, and he really listens," Khloe said, and she began to daydream once more about the time they'd shared together. "He's really a wonderful man, and I'm looking forward to getting to know him, but those lips of his…mmm, they're simply irresistible." Shaking her head back to the present, she casually added, "It was so hard to leave him this morning, and, like I told you, no, I didn't sleep with him. I simply slept *next* to him, on his couch."

"When are you seeing him again?" She adjusted herself next to Khloe, leaning against the couch, holding her wine.

"That's the thing. I don't know."

"What do you mean, you don't know?" Sharon asked, sounding alarmed for her friend. "Wait, he isn't married, is he?" After Khloe reassured her that since the moment she met him she didn't see a ring on his left hand, nor any female garments around his home, Sharon continued, "So, what's with the uncertainty about seeing him again?"

"Well, he's an entertainment and sports lawyer, so traveling is part of his job, of course. This morning, he got a text and told me he suddenly had to leave for Chicago, and he doesn't know when he'll be back." Khloe reached for her wine glass, holding it close to her, and sighed.

"But you think there's more to the story?" she asked, reading Khloe's mind.

She really didn't want to read too much into Derek's sudden trip, but how could she not when she still felt the burn from finding those emails and texts in Josh's phone? Khloe knew Derek was different, so she wanted to give him the benefit of the doubt and didn't want Josh to scar her for other men, because it wouldn't be fair to her or them. Khloe shook her head, not really knowing who it was she was trying to convince—herself or Sharon. "I trust Derek, but—"

"It's the Josh thing still, isn't it?" she asked, interrupting Khloe's thoughts.

Without a word, Khloe nodded. "Part of it, yeah, I think so. Also, I think it's the urgency of him having to leave town so suddenly, which sends me a red flag, like I did something wrong..." she said, and then just stopped, because she knew she was crazy and that his leaving wasn't because of her. Sighing again, she sipped on her wine. "With everything I went through with Josh, I'm trying to remember Derek isn't like that cheating bastard and believe that he won't hurt me." Seconds later, her phone beeped, and a smile crossed her face when she saw it was a text from Derek.

Long day of meetings, going to dinner now with partners, for yet another meeting. I will call you when I get in bed. Hope your day went well. Miss you!

Eagerly, Khloe replied with: Busy day here, too! Can't

wait to hear your voice...Miss you, too!

Bringing the glass back to her lips, she felt Sharon's eyes on her. "What?" Khloe asked.

"I've never seen you act like such a teenager, jumping the moment your phone beeps, and acting like a yappy poodle who knows no boundaries." Sharon eyed Khloe over the rim of her glass. "It wouldn't hurt to play hard to get."

Khloe giggled. "I know, and you're right. I'm just happy. I really like him, Sharon, and I don't want to mess things up."

"I'm happy for you, Khloe, I really am, but just be careful," she said, patting Khloe's arm in a motherlike way.

"Thank you. That means a lot to me." They held a quick glance before Khloe said, "Now how about we open another bottle of wine, and I'll put on a sappy, old movie?"

"Sounds wonderful, darling, just wonderful," Sharon said with a dramatic accent as she put the back of her hand on her forehead.

"Excellent," replied Khloe. She jumped up and walked into her kitchen where she looked at the clock, seeing that it was just after eight thirty. Knowing it would be hours until she heard from Derek, Khloe planned to keep having fun during her girls' night with Sharon.

*****

Shortly before one in the morning, Khloe woke to the jarring sound of her phone ringing, and Derek's name flashed across her screen. She sat up in her bed and ran a hand through her tousled hair. "Hey, you," she said in a whisper.

"I know I probably woke you, but I didn't want to go to bed without calling."

"I'm glad you did." She leaned back into the pillows, still groggy from sleep. "How was your dinner meeting?"

"It was fine but very repetitive, covering a lot of the same things that were discussed earlier on in the day." There was a small pause, then Derek said, "Well, it's late, so I'll let you get back to sleep. I'll text and call you later."

"No, I want to talk to you," Khloe mumbled, with her eyes shut.

Derek laughed. "Khloe, go back to bed, and we'll talk tonight."

"Okay," she replied, giving in to him as her heavy eyes began to close.

"I miss you, Khloe," he said, and with that he hung up, leaving Khloe wishing he weren't so far away and that she was snuggling against him as she slept.

CHAPTER TWENTY

Gabby

The next morning, Gabby woke up to a naked Harry, who was sleeping soundly beside her. She stared up at the ceiling and whispered, "What have I done?" While being intimate with Harry had been everything she imagined—he'd been gentle and it revitalized her—it had also been very…different. She'd never been with anyone other than Charlie, but that didn't bother her as much as the guilt she felt, because she still considered herself a married woman. Though, after a few deep breaths, Gabby reminded herself she wasn't having an affair; she was simply getting on with her life.

Craning her neck, she saw the clock on her nightstand read just past eight, not remembering how long it'd been since she slept so late. She quietly slipped out of bed and within half an hour was showered and dressed. When she came out of the bathroom, Harry was no longer in her bed. "Harry!" she hollered, quickly making her way downstairs. *Would he leave without saying goodbye?*

"Gabby, darling, there you are," he said, handing Gabby a mug after she'd found him in the kitchen. "I hope you don't mind that I made us coffee." He pointed to her machine on the counter. "It's no wonder you have the instructions out. That's quite an advanced machine."

The coffee pot was the first thing she'd bought after Charlie died. Keeping the old one would only have added salt to her open wound. While trying to use the high-tech machine was difficult, but it brought her joy to know that she learned how to use it on her own.

"Ah, yes, that machine...while I think I've mastered it, there are some mornings that I wish I'd bought a less fancy one." She took the cup from him gratefully and sipped. "Thank you." She paused, weighing her next words. "Listen, Harry, about last night—"

He raised his hands in the air to stop her. "It was wonderful being with you. It's the first time in a long time I've felt this happy."

Part of her felt the same way, but she decided she didn't want to hurt him by telling him that guilt was eating at her. Instead, she simply smiled and nodded. "Yes, it was nice," she mustered, as even more guilt chewed a hole in her heart.

"Well, I have to go," Harry said, placing his coffee cup in the sink. "But, I'll call you tonight."

"I look forward to it." Gabby followed him to the door ask asked, "Oh, could I have Jules's address? I was going to send her some flowers. She was so nice to me yesterday."

After giving Gabby the address and a gentle kiss goodbye, Harry left her with puzzling, mixed emotions. She shut the door, leaned against it, and closed her eyes as her mind raced. *What in the world am I doing?* Shuffling into the living room to think, she reached for a picture of Charlie, sat down on the sofa, and stared into his eyes.

"I love you, Charlie, but I'm lonely. I need you to tell me that what I did last night didn't hurt you—that it didn't hurt us." While she knew it was silly that she was talking to a picture of her dead husband, she wanted his blessing that it was okay to move on with her life, so she started telling him about meeting Harry, and that she might be falling in love.

Minutes later, when she closed her eyes, she heard Charlie's voice say, "I don't want you to be lonely, my angel. Until we're together again, live your life, my love."

Tears rushed down her cheeks. Looking up to the heavens, she smiled. "Until we meet again, Charlie." She pressed her fingers against her lips, and then lifted them into the air.

*****

After talking to Charlie, Gabby felt better and was ready to play Scrabble, hoping that by attending the church service that had ended prior to meeting with her Scrabble group, she would be able to focus on the game and come out a winner.

"Well, Gabby, we've been playing for an hour now, and you still have yet to tell us about what's going on with Harry," said Wilma. "Come on, spill the beans."

Gabby laughed. She reached into the bag and picked out three tiles: an E, an X, and an S. *Just my luck!* She looked over at Fern. "I thought you told them everything already."

They all laughed, then Clara replied, "She did, but we want more details."

"Well, yesterday I met his family, and they're so kind, and I'm absolutely crazy about his grandson."

"And...?" asked an encouraging Wilma.

Where do I begin? Deciding to share details through her tiles, she placed three letters on the board. "That will be twenty-four points, please," she said to Clara. When Clara didn't make a move to write down the score, she looked around the table and saw her friends' jaws drop. "What?" Gabby asked, raising her shoulders.

Fern reached over and touched her arm. "Are you trying to tell us something?" With wide eyes, she looked to Wilma and Clara, and then back at Gabby.

Clara nodded at Gabby. "Well, are you?"

Gabby grinned. They all looked back down at the word, *sex*, and gaped at Gabby. "Yes, I slept with him," she said and nonchalantly sipped her coffee as her friends gasped.

Wilma exclaimed, "Oh my God!"

"So…how was it?" Fern asked as her cheeks turned rosy.

Next, Gabby looked at Clara, the most sensitive in the group—the one who she knew she could relate to the best. "But what about Charlie?" Clara asked. "Have you forgotten about him?"

Her friends' questions were valid, and she wanted to answer them, hoping it would help her unscramble all the emotions she had. Turing to Wilma, she said, "It's not something I planned on happening, it just did. Besides, it *wasn't* our first date. It was our *second*," she said with emphasis. "Anyway, like I was saying, it wasn't a thought-out decision, but there's something about him that makes me feel so comfortable. It's like he's my…" she said, trying to think of how to describe their relationship, and then finally she said, "He's my second chance."

After they all cooed and awed, Gabby turned to Fern. "As for how it was, while being intimate with Harry was different, it felt nice to have someone hold me that way." She gave a faint smile. "I had second thoughts, but the more I think about it, the more I realize I needed it to happen—you know, as a way for me to move forward." She paused, twisted in her chair, and took Clara's hands. "No, I haven't forgotten about Charlie, nor will I ever. We had a wonderful life together, and we loved each other very much. But now that he's gone, I've realized I can't live the rest of my life alone. I don't want to. Now, I know it might sound silly, but I've talked to Charlie and he's given me a sign that he's okay with me moving on with my life, and for that, I'm grateful."

"Thank you for telling us," Fern said, and the others smiled in agreement.

She looked around the table at her friends. "Now, can we get back to the game?" They nodded, but Gabby felt their eyes on her as she reached for the bag that held the tiles.

CHAPTER TWENTY-ONE

Connie

"Are you sure you want this?" asked Walt after they arrived back at Connie's apartment. They'd fallen onto the couch, unable to keep their hands off of each other, until they both decided they'd be more comfortable if they headed to her bedroom. While Connie had tidied up the place, her bedroom was the only room she hadn't cleaned because she'd never expected they'd end up in here. Since she never had a guy in her bedroom before, she figured there was no point in making the bed, or even throwing everything in her closet, so her clothes weren't scattered everywhere.

"Yes," she said, panting and desperately wanting him. This was what she'd been waiting for her whole life—sex with a man like Walt. Seconds later, when his tongue flicked her nipples, and she'd entwined her fingers through his hair, feeling too eager to be shy about her body, Connie let out the breath she didn't know she was holding before closing her eyes. Finally, Walt rested his body on top of hers, and she reached down and felt his hardness, which was an only inch away from her warmth, a shy grin crossed her face, not believing she was touching a penis. Seconds later, when Walt entered her slowly, with pleasure in her heart, she opened her eyes to look at him, trying to convince herself that this was real and not a dream.

"You're beautiful, Connie," Walt whispered. He caressed her cheek then kissed her lips as he gently thrust in and out of her.

She cried out with joy as tears welled in her eyes. Nobody had ever told Connie that she was beautiful, much less while making love to her. She blinked her tears away and refocused on what Walt was doing to her. *I'm having sex with a man who thinks I'm beautiful, so chew on that, Nicola!* She found it sad she was thinking about Nicola when she and Walt were becoming one, but she couldn't help it. Walt had been her mission, but now, he was more than that. He was a man who thought she was beautiful and she didn't want to let him go.

After their lovemaking, Walt rolled off Connie and they lay on her bed, each trying to catch their breaths.

"That….was…incredible," Connie said, finding it hard to speak, blown away at the high she was experiencing. She turned on her side to face Walt. She scooted closer to him, and he draped his arm across her naked hip. "Can I tell you something? I have a couple of confessions." Connie gnawed on her lip, worried he'd run off, and that her plan would go down the drain, but after what they'd just shared, she felt a genuine connection to him. He wasn't just a game anymore.

"You can tell me anything, Connie."

"Nobody has ever called me beautiful before." Right after her confession, tears stung her eyes, but she wiped them away.

Walt brushed her cheek with the back of his hand. "That's hard to believe, because I think you're attractive, funny, charming, and you're a devil in bed." He raised his eyebrows, and she couldn't help but laugh. "But, you're more than that, Connie." He rested his hand on her chest, just above her left breast. "You have a very loving heart, and you're a beautiful person on the inside, too."

Connie stared at Walt for what seemed like minutes. She didn't know what to say. "Thank you, Walt. I think you're amazing, too." She flung her arm over him and squeezed for dear life, wanting to stop time. It had been the best day of her life. "Thank you for accepting me just as I am," she said. Never in her lifetime did she think she'd ever have a *Bridget Jones* moment of her own. She kissed Walt again, and as she did, she felt a type of warmth in her heart that she'd never felt before.

"What's the other confession?"

She looked down at her naked body sprawled out on her bed and quickly reached for her comforter to cover herself. Even though he'd just seen all of her, now that they weren't all over each other, she was still insecure about her body, especially with what she was about to tell him. "Well, you were incredible—the whole experience was so unlike what I thought it would be. I mean, I've heard horror stories about losing your virginity, but this was more than I could ever have asked for."

Walt stared down at Connie and started to laugh.

"Um, what's so funny?" she asked defensively, as she brought the covers closer to her body.

His eyebrows raised and he tilted his head, looking surprised. "Connie, are you telling me you're a virgin?"

"Well, not anymore, thanks to you." She laid her head back on her pillow, but before she could say anything else, Walt had stripped the covers off her, and, once again, was on top of her.

"What—what are you doing?"

He gave her a wicked smile. "Well, now that I know you were a virgin, I have a few moves I'd like to show you. Tell me, Connie, do you like to learn?"

"I love to learn," she replied, without any hesitation or any of her insecurities holding her back.

CHAPTER TWENTY-TWO

Khloe

"What are you wearing?" Derek asked Khloe, catching her by surprise on a lonely Sunday night. It had been six days since Derek left, and Khloe missed him more each day. Though they texted frequently throughout the week, their nightly conversations were what she loved the most, and for the past two nights, their phone calls became more and more in-depth, and—at times—even a bit racy, which by the time Khloe hung up with Derek, left her panting for more.

She paused, thinking how silly the whole thing was, and asked, "What? Are we in high school again?"

"Just help a guy out," he replied encouragingly, making Khloe laugh.

"Oh, I get it," she said, as seductively as she could manage. "You're desperate for a little action?" Knowing Derek wanted her sent color to her cheeks and set her body on fire. She'd never had any kind of conversation like that on the phone before, because she was too shy, but Derek made her want to give it a try. *Damn him and his suave, sweet-talking ways. I can't believe I'm considering doing this.*

"Come on," Derek urged. "I don't know when I'll be home to kiss those beautiful lips of yours."

"Well, since I'm a nice girl, I'll tell you," she bashfully whispered into the phone. "I'm wearing a red silk camisole and very short black lace boxers," she said, in what she hoped was her most seductive voice. Khloe lifted her hand and fiddled with the red straps, waiting for him to reply.

"That sounds so hot," he murmured. "Now, tell me what you'd want me to do to you if I were there with you." Khloe sunk deeper into her pillows, closed her eyes, and imagined him on top of her, kissing her neck as waves of erotic sensations surged through her, and she moaned. "Come on, Khloe, tell me. I don't bite."

Oh, but I wish you did! The thought of him nibbling into her flesh made her short of breath, and she realized the conversation was getting a little too worked up, especially since they'd only spent one night together. "I think it'd be better if you'd just come home so I can show you myself—" she began, just as she heard a knock at the door, stopping her in her tracks and wondering who would be stopping by so late—and without calling. "Um, hey, Derek, I gotta go. Someone's at my door." She got out of bed and threw on her oversized white cashmere robe.

"At this hour? It's past midnight. Look, just to be safe, let me stay on the line. I wouldn't want someone to hurt you."

Walking to her front door, she wished she had a peep-hole, so she reached for the heavy, glass trophy she won last year for Best New Flower Shop in the metroplex, thinking that if she were in some kind of trouble it would protect her—or that it could at least injure her intruder—while she'd run next door to get help. "Who's there?" The only thing she got was silence. "Nobody's replying," she whispered to Derek, holding the phone tight and waiting a few seconds. She turned to go back to her room, thinking it was maybe just a gust of wind or something, making the autumn wreath thump against her door, but when she did, she heard knocking again. She repeated the question, but, still, nobody answered. "Look, I'm just going to answer it," she told Derek.

"Okay, but be careful, Khloe," Derek warned.

With her heart racing, she placed her hand on the doorknob, slowly opening the door, and peered out into the darkness. After a few seconds of noticing nothing out of the ordinary, she widened the door's gap. Though she didn't see anyone, she thought nothing of it when she saw a car parked across the street, and then saw its lights flash, along with a beeping sound. She told herself it was just the neighbors who'd already gone inside and locked the car from inside their home. "It was nobody," she said to Derek, walking back into her home, but a strong breeze of a familiar scent wafted under her nose and she stopped in her tracks, pausing for a second. Moments later, something made her turn around, and when she did, Derek was standing in front of her, catching her completely taking her off-guard as she raised her hands in defense. "Derek!"

"Hey, beautiful," he said, grinning down at her. Derek tapped a button on his phone, slipped it in his dress pants pocket, took two large steps toward Khloe. Wrapping his arms around her, he kissed her on the lips.

Mmm, I've missed this! After she pulled away from him, Khloe shook her head, hardly believing Derek was standing in front of her. Finally, she realized she was still holding her phone and trophy. "What—what are you doing here?" she asked, looking up at him. "Wait, how do you know where I live?"

"I'm an attorney, so I have my ways," he replied. He cupped her face in his hands and kissed her again, softly this time. "Come on, let's go inside and I'll tell you everything." He draped his arm around her shoulders as they went inside.

After offering him a glass of water, which he declined, Khloe led them to her couch in her living room, deciding she'd give him a tour of her place at a later time, because she wanted to catch up with him first. "This is such a great surprise!" she told him, facing him with her knees tucked under her, holding his hand. "Though, for a second, I was a little creeped out."

"Well, I'm glad my head caught a break from that weapon," he replied, pointing to the trophy on the table that sat in front of them.

Khloe laughed. "Yeah, sorry about that." She raised her shoulders. "But these days, you can never be too careful." She leaned over to kiss him, and when she did, he pulled her onto his lap. When their lips parted, Derek, with a devilish yet sexy grin, said, "So, about these pajamas you were telling me about..." With the tip of his finger he caressed Khloe's ear and trailed it down to her collarbone, opening her robe as he caught a glimpse of her red camisole. "Ah, looks sexy," he told her.

She sighed and shook her head. "You, sir, aren't going to get off that easy."

"Oh, really, and why is that?" he asked, running his hands through his hair.

"How was your trip? I mean, I know you were way busy in meetings and all, but did you get everything accomplished?"

"Do you really want to talk about work right now?" he questioned her with a smirk.

"Okay, we won't talk about it. I'm just glad to have you back. Now, come on, tell me how you found out where I live?"

"That, my darlin', is a secret, but if you really want to know, I had Mary search for your address right before I got on the plane, and when I landed, I came directly here."

She put her arms around his neck, leaned her chest against his, and then whispered, "Well, I'm glad you did."

"Oh yeah?" he asked.

She looked at him, hoping her smile and body language answered for her, as they held a steady gaze for what seemed like minutes, until they couldn't fight it anymore. Seconds later, like magnets, their lips connected again, and before Khloe knew it, her robe was being tossed across the living room. She felt Derek's lips on her neck as the pads of his thumbs caressed her nipples through her silk top, and not even the vibration of her phone that lay on the table in front of them could distract her. Tilting her head back, Khloe wondered if she was living in a dream, because she never wanted to wake up, allowing Derek devour her with his mouth.

*****

Khloe woke up with her arm stretched over Derek's naked torso. Somewhere in the middle of the night and between fooling around, they'd eventually made it to Khloe's bedroom. While they didn't have sex, Khloe could have been easily swayed, because she was definitely more than tempted.

Leaving Derek still sleeping, Khloe got out of bed and went into her kitchen to make a pot of coffee, while she dreamily reminisced about her night. From the moment she turned around to see him at her doorstep to waking up next to him, everything about it felt natural. It was like they belonged together.

"Good morning," Derek said, entering her kitchen and taking Khloe out of her thoughts about her mother's recommendation on what kind of china pattern she and Derek should register for their wedding, when she slightly mentioned Derek to her mother in an email the previous week.

"Hey, you," she said, turning to see Derek standing in her doorway, dressed only in purple and white-striped boxers. *Damn!* After eyeing him up and down, she handed him a cup of coffee and planted a kiss on his lips. "Sleep well?" she asked, leading him to the living room, where they took a seat on the couch.

"I did. That is, once we finally went to sleep." He blew on the steaming cup of coffee and then winked at her.

She blushed. "Yeah, I'm sorry about that, but I just couldn't help myself. Having you home is quite a treat."

Derek took a hard swallow, put his coffee cup on the table, and then said, "Yeah, about that…Khloe, I need to tell you about something."

She didn't like where this conversation was going, nor did she like his stern and serious tone or the sober expression plastered on his face. "What is it?" she asked, mimicking him by putting her cup next to his, getting ready for whatever it was he had to tell her. As calm as she tried to stay, her stomach was in knots, as she impatiently waited for him to speak.

Derek ran his hands through his hair, as he searched for words. "I don't know where to begin…"

She reached for his hands, placing them into hers, hoping with all her might that whatever he had to tell her wasn't going to be unwelcome news. "At the beginning would be a good place," she commented, trying to lighten the mood, which didn't help, because Derek's expression and body language didn't budge. "Derek, whatever it is, you can tell me," she said.

"I didn't go to Chicago." With a solemn expression, Derek bowed his head, but only for a second, and then looked back at Khloe. "I've been in L.A."

What?! Khloe's heart turned cold, and she hoped she'd heard him wrong, but by looking in Derek's eyes, she knew what he was now telling her was the truth, and that he'd lied to her. With a thousand questions running through her head, she didn't know where to begin. When she opened her mouth to speak—shout at him, really—her voice was steady and quiet. "Oh," was all she finally managed to say as she let go of his hands.

"I'm sorry I lied to you. You have to know that it was never my intention to hurt you, but what's going on is a private, family matter, and I really couldn't—I can't talk about it. At least, not right now. I hope to be able to tell you everything very soon." He sighed and reached for her, caressing her cheek with his thumb and wiping away a tear that was falling. "You have to believe me when I say that. I want to tell you—I really do."

She turned her head, escaping his touch on her skin, avoiding making eye contact, blinking away her tears as she scooted away from him. *Be strong, Khloe, be strong!* "Are you married, Derek?" she asked in a whisper, sinking herself into one side of the couch, holding her arms tight against her, waiting for his answer. She turned back to face him, now glaring at him.

"Gosh, no," he said, defensively, "Khloe, I told you I wasn't married on our first date."

"Well, Derek, excuse me, but you told me you were going to Chicago and you went to L.A., so how am I supposed to believe anything you say?" she snapped back, her voice in a high tone.

He put his hands up and shook his head. "Okay, okay, you're right." He inched himself toward her, as if testing the waters, and when she didn't stop him, he continued on, until their knees were touching. "Khloe, we're in the early stages of getting to know each other, and I don't want that to stop, but right now, there's some legal drama going on in my family, and nobody knows about it. We're very private people, and we need to stay that way—at least for now."

"Look, Derek, just save us both some time and tell me the real truth." She put on a brave smile—one she hoped he didn't think she was faking—and, choosing not to believe him but rather what she thought to be true, said, "So, you're married but are going through a divorce. Fine!"

Derek clenched his fist and held it to his lips, taking in a deep breath, looking directly at her. "Khloe Harper, I swear to you, I have never been married, I'm *not* married, nor am I going through a divorce. Please, if you believe anything I say to you, believe that."

She bowed her head and put her index fingers on her temples, hoping to fight off a headache she imagined would be coming any minute. "I just don't know what to think about any of this," she told him honestly. Khloe's heart ached, not only for herself, but for him, too, because what if he really was telling the truth, and she was just guarding her heart? She lifted her head and looked into his eyes, wanting more than anything to be the trusting woman she was trying to become, but hearing that Derek had lied to her, she didn't know if she'd ever be able to trust him—or any man—again. When she saw no sign of where to begin to forgive him, she stood up and began to pace as she bit her nails, suddenly feeling naked in front of him. If she was going to give him the benefit of the doubt and they were going to get through this, she wanted to let him see her in the raw. Feeling Derek's eyes on her, she stopped in her tracks and faced him, asking, "So, if it's a legal family matter, why couldn't you just tell me that, and that you were going to L.A.?" She placed her hands on her hips. "Don't sugarcoat it for me. Come on, Derek, give it to me straight."

Derek scooted himself to the edge of the couch and clasped his hands together. "What's going on is a very serious matter, and in the legal system, as of right now, there are certain things that I can't share, nor do I trust people with the knowledge of the seriousness of this case."

His words cut her like a knife, even more so than his lying to her. "Oh, I get it now," she said, before letting out a sarcastic laugh. "Not only did you not even try to trust me, you didn't think you could." She looked down at him, and their eyes met. In a whisper, Khloe said, "You didn't even give me a chance." While their time together had been short, she wished he'd seen that she wasn't one to gossip, and that she could be trusted.

Derek shook his head as he stood to meet her. "That's not what I meant, and you know it."

"Then what the hell do you mean?" By now tears filled Khloe's eyes, and they began to streak down her face. With the back of her hand she wiped them away, hopeless and wondering what to do, feel, or think.

He stood up, took two big steps toward her, and gripped her arms. "Khloe, what can I do to make you believe me, and to understand?"

"I don't know," she said through sobs. "I just wish you hadn't lied and knew you could trust me. It might seem like a little thing to you, but that's not how I work in relationoships. I want to trust you, but how can I, especially *if* you want things to still work between us?"

Derek was silent, looking serious—with squinted eyes and a tense jaw—as she watched him contemplate his response. "I promise you, the second I know I can tell you everything, I will." He wiped a tear away from her cheek and gave her a gentle smile. "Please?" he begged. "I don't want to lose you or what we can have." His eyes held steady on her lips for a moment, and then Derek bent down and kissed her lips, and when she didn't pull away, he drew her closer to him, placing his arms around her, letting her fall into him.

Khloe needed closure to his lie before she could move on. "Is there anything else you need to tell me—anything at all? Because this is your chance," she mumbled, against his naked, warm chest.

Derek reached for Khloe's hand and kissed the back of it. "Yeah, actually, there is something," he said, sounding drained.

Oh, what could it be now? she thought, but didn't say anything and tried her best to keep her emotions in check.

"I have to go back to L.A. in just a few short hours." He waited to see how Khloe would react, and when she nodded for him to continue, he did. "We're in the last few stages of this whole thing being over, and I'm hopeful that after this, I don't expect to have to go back." He sighed, and Khloe sensed his relief that he'd told her everything—or at least she hoped she was right. "There, that's everything I can tell you up to this point. I really hope I haven't messed anything up for us, and that you can trust me."

Knowing she was going against everything she believed, telling herself never to trust a lying man again, she wanted to at least see if they could jump this hurdle, so Khloe decided to take the high road, and at least give him a second chance. Placing her hands on his broad naked shoulders, she felt comfort in the warmth of his skin. "Okay, Derek, but please, don't lie to me again." After he promised her he wouldn't, she kissed his lips, and she tried to quiet her mind from all the negativity, to prove to herself that Josh hadn't broken her for every man who came after him. Khloe held onto Derek, kissing him hard and passionately, hoping to ease her heart, as she tasted his sweet, hazelnut-flavored coffee-flavored lips, loving how they teased and tested her body's boundaries. When they separated, she asked, "What time do you have to leave?"

"In a few hours, so I still have some time."

"Okay," she said, reaching for her cell phone to let Sharon know she'd be late, but when she did, her eyes widened to see so many missed calls and texts from Millicent. With a sigh, Khloe began typing to Sharon, adding to see if she could please call Millicent and let her know she'd be getting back to her later that day. In an instant, Sharon replied, telling she would take care of everything, which Khloe was thankful for. Yes, maybe professionally, it looked bad on the outside that Khloe was choosing love rather than to help a customer, but there were no second guesses about it—she'd choose Derek each time. "Then let's make the most of it," she said, tossing her phone aside, and they fell together onto the couch.

CHAPTER TWENTY-THREE

Gabby

Gabby's last stop on her list of errands was to Khloe's Flower Shop.

"Hey, Gabby," Sharon said when she entered. "I haven't seen you in ages. How have you been?"

"I'm good," she said dreamily as a quick image of Harry flashed in her mind. "It looks like y'all are in the fall spirit. Everything looks so beautiful," she commented, looking around the shop.

"Thanks," Sharon replied. "It's not hard to do, especially since we've been experiencing below-average temperatures this season."

"Tell me about it," Gabby said with a wave of her hand and pulling her cream-colored coat around her. "Anyway, I was wondering if Khloe was in today?"

"Actually, she hasn't come in yet, but is there something I can help you with?"

"I hope she's okay," Gabby said.

"Oh, she's fine. I just think she needed the morning off."

"Well, in that case, I'm needing to place an order." While Gabby was closer to Khloe, only because she saw her more, she'd known them equally and had a friendship with Sharon, too. "I want something beautiful—something multi-colored and very feminine."

After taking down Gabby's order, she looked her up and down, noticing she had more of a glow than she normally did. "You look happy this morning," she commented.

Gabby couldn't contain her happiness anymore. "I think I might be in love again," she confessed.

"Gabby, that's wonderful news," she said. "I'm so happy for you!"

"Thank you, dear," Gabby said. "His name is Harry, and I got to meet his family, and I adore his precious grandson, Andrew." She laughed, remembering the boy asking if she'd be his new nana. "Anyway, the arrangement goes to Harry's daughter-in-law, Jules Hoffman."

"Great, and I'm assuming you want this delivered. Do you have an address for her?"

Gabby nodded and handed Sharon a sticky note. "Here it is," she replied, sliding the piece of paper toward Sharon.

"Do you need anything else today," Sharon asked, before processing the order.

"You know what, actually, yes I do, though, I need to take this one with me."

"Okay, and for this, what are you thinking?"

Having placed the second order, a single red rose which Gabby held in her hand, Sharon held out a small bouquet of white daisies.

"What's this?" Gabby asked.

"Just a little something from me and Khloe. We want you to know how much we admire you. It seems as if your life is coming up roses," Sharon told her.

"Thank you, Sharon. You're too kind. Have a good rest of the day, and be sure to give Khloe my best."

After Gabby left Khloe's Flower Shop, she realized it was the first time she'd wholeheartedly admitted to herself that she was falling in love, and it felt darn good. Now it was time to head to a place she hadn't been in quite a while, not that she'd forgotten, but she'd been too afraid it would hold her back from the healing process. When she pulled up to Highland Memorial Cemetery, she reached for the rose on the passenger seat, got out of the car, and pulled her coat closer to her. Though the sun was out, it was a brisk day in Texas, which had been Charlie's favorite type of day. Gabby walked over to a tree and took a seat on the bench next to it. Beside it was a white gravestone etched with the words: "Charlie Lewis: Forever devoted husband and friend."

"Hi, my love," she whispered, not knowing how to begin to say what she needed to get off her chest. While he'd given her a message that it was okay to fall in love again, she needed to have closure with their past in order for her to move on with Harry. "I'm sorry about not visiting lately. I've been trying to get on with my life, but it's damn hard without you." She pulled a tissue from her coat pocket and dabbed her eyes.

"Charlie, I miss you so much, and for months I wished that losing you was a nightmare, and that I'd wake up to find you next to me." She paused for a moment, then, with hesitation, continued. "I—I've been seeing someone. His name is Harry, and I know you'd like him. In a way, he's similar to you," she said, and began to tell him a little bit more about Harry, along with letting Charlie know that Harry would take care of her.

"I think I love him, and I'm pretty sure he loves me, too. Charlie, I want to be happy again." She gently lowered herself down to his gravestone and put her arms around it. "Please, tell me you still love me, and that I can love again."

As she pressed her lips to the stone, a gust of wind blew her hair. A wide grin crossed her face, knowing it was a message from him. "Charlie, oh my first love," she said as happy tears ran down her face. She stayed there for a few minutes as acceptance began to sink in. Finally she stood, placed the single red rose beside Charlie's grave, then said, "I'll always love you."

*****

While Gabby was making herself dinner, consisting of a bowl of rice and beans she'd bought at the store earlier that day, her phone rang. "Hello?"

"Hello, lovely," he said. "How has your day been?"

"Pretty good, yet busy. I ran a few errands and then came home before the rain started." She peered behind the curtains, seeing that the weatherman had correctly predicted the torrential downpour late in the afternoon.

"Yeah, it's pretty bad out. Jeff said they lost power for a few minutes, and that when he was out earlier he saw several accidents on the highway."

"Yikes," she replied as her microwave beeped. Placing her phone between her ear and shoulder, she reached for the hot bowl then grabbed a fork, and placed her steaming entrée on the kitchen table. "Well, I'm glad to know you're home safe and sound?"

"Yes, my dear, I am, and you, too, as well. That was actually one reason I called. I wanted to make sure you're okay."

She smiled at the sincerity in his voice. "That's awfully kind of you, Harry." She couldn't remember the last time someone had called to check on her, excluding the many phone calls she'd received after Charlie died. "What was the other reason you called?" she asked before taking a bite.

There was a short pause before Harry answered. "Well, I wanted to make sure we're okay...I mean about us, about what happened."

Swallowing, Gabby put down her fork and closed her eyes. "Harry, before we get into that, there's something I need to tell you."

"Oh?" he asked carefully, as though sensing the tension in her voice.

Hesitant, only because she didn't know how he'd react, Gabby said, "I went to Charlie's gravesite today." When he said nothing, she continued with, "I told him about you—about us. I hope you're okay with that."

"Gabby, Charlie was your husband, and it wouldn't be fair of me to be upset or hurt that you talked to him, or that you told him about us. He was your past, and I'd like to think that I will be part of your future."

"Oh, Harry," Gabby said, swooning into the phone. "Thank you for saying that, and yes, I'd love for you to be in my future." She smiled. "Now as far as what we shared, it was absolutely wonderful, and I have no regrets."

Happy she'd been honest with both men, Gabby took her cordless phone into her living room, where they continued talking for hours, leaving her meal left uneaten as she allowed herself to enjoy the feeling of falling in love again.

CHAPTER TWENTY-FOUR

Connie

Connie spent most of her Saturday and Sunday in bed with Walt. He reluctantly left before dawn on Monday morning but told Connie to go back to sleep. So that's what she did, after giving him one more goodbye kiss. When her alarm buzzed later that morning she stretched in bed, thinking about the amazing weekend she had with the man of her dreams. For the first time in forever, Connie looked forward to starting her day.

Deciding to change up her attire a bit, Connie pulled a never-worn emerald-colored pantsuit out of her closet, then reached for the heels she'd worn the night she met Walt. Surprisingly, she'd managed to walk somewhat well in them, so she wanted to wear them again. *This is going to surprise the hell out of Nicola!* Along with a change in wardrobe, she wore a noticeable amount of make-up, and even curled her hair. Giving herself a once-over in the mirror before she left, she saw something she'd never seen before. "I am beautiful," she said to the image staring back at her. After giving herself a confident smile, she fed her cats and then headed to work.

During her drive, she decided to do something she'd never done—she rolled down the windows, allowing the wind to blow in her hair, and turned up the music. It was as if a new Connie had taken over. Just as she was about to put the car in park, the song "It's Your Love" came on. She rolled up the windows, listening intently and thinking about Walt. When the song was over, she reached for her purse, then made her way to the front steps of the building with a wide grin on her face.

She opened the doors and chirped, "Good morning, Mia," watching her co-worker frantically type.

"Good morning," said Mia cheerfully, not bothering to look up.

It was out of character for Mia not to look her in the eye each morning, but Connie figured she was focused on her work, so she didn't think too much about it. She walked to her cubicle, passing not only Nicola, but the pack of bitchy women, too. When she saw their eyes pop open and their jaws drop, Connie just kept on smiling, imagining what they were thinking.

Connie sat at her desk and reached into her purse for the picture Walt had taken of them at the flower garden. She stared down at it, smiling at the memory of their perfect day. Before she placed it on her desk, she kissed her finger and put it over Walt's face. With a relaxed sigh, she stashed her purse under her desk and turned on her computer. While she waited for it to boot up, she went to the kitchen and poured herself a cup of coffee. On her way back she walked past Nicola, chirped a "Good morning," and kept walking. Connie could tell by the way Nicola glared back at her that she was taking note of Connie's dramatic change in appearance, and she didn't like it.

When it was almost noon, Connie headed to the office freezer to retrieve a Lean Cuisine and was shocked to find a red rose bouquet waiting for her at her desk when she returned. She squinted, confused, because she'd been so busy with Walt that she'd forgotten to send herself flowers that week. She quickly opened the card and read it.

"Hey, Con," Nicola said, sneaking up behind her, nearly scaring her to death. She pointed to the roses. "Those are pretty, but—" and that's when she stopped mid-sentence. That's when Connie watched Nicola's eyes go directly to the picture of her and Walt. In one quick move, Nicola reached for it and raised an eyebrow. "This," she spit out, "is Walt?"

"Yes, that's him," Connie replied, proud to call him hers.

"Hmm," was all she said, then placed the picture back on the desk. "So, what does the card say today?" she asked. Before Connie had a chance to pick it from the bouquet, Nicola grabbed it and began reading. "I had a great time on our second date. I love getting to know you, Connie, and I look forward to spending another weekend with you in bed! Walt."

Oh, shit! This can't be happening!

"Second date?" Nicola inquired with a deceptive grin, sounding like a detective who'd just cracked a case. An evil grin spread across her face.

Connie looked at Nicola, swallowed hard, and blinked. Connie was about to reply that there must have been some misunderstanding at Khloe's Flower Shop, until Connie stopped in her tracks, seeing something she'd never seen on before—a genuine, sweet smile form on Nicola's face. Curious to see what had caused it, she saw Walt coming toward them.

"Uh, I'll be right back," Connie said, then scampered out the glass double-doors toward him. Ignoring his hello, she grabbed his arm and pulled him back into the lobby.

"Honey, are you okay?" Walt asked.

"Yeah," she said quickly, nodding her head to assure him. "I just didn't expect to see you. Wh-what are you doing here?"

He held up a bag from Einstein's and smiled. "I thought I'd surprise you with a bagel sandwich for lunch."

"You're so sweet," Connie said, kissing him on the cheek and wishing that the prying eyes she felt watching them through the spotless glass doors weren't Nicola's. "Thank you for dropping this by. I'm sure I'll enjoy it." She turned to look through the doors, and suddenly she felt like she'd been kicked in the gut when she saw Nicola was rushing toward them. "Well, I need to get back to work now, but I'll see you soon—maybe even tonight." Connie gave Walt another quick kiss, this time on his lips, pressed the elevator button, and began walking back to her cubicle when she heard him speak.

"You know, I really like you, Connie. You're an amazing woman," Walt said, which made Connie halt in her tracks.

She turned around and rushed into his arms. "I like you, too, Walt." As he held her, she looked up at him, not remembering of being this happy—ever.

She hated to ruin the moment, but she had to get Walt out of her office and into the elevator before Nicola came to spill her secret and ruin her life.

"I have to get back to work, but I'll call you later." After another kiss, one that lingered a bit too long, the elevator doors opened, and Walt walked in and waved goodbye.

But just as the doors were almost shut and Connie was off the hook—for now, Nicola walked out of the office and into the lobby, and placed her hand in, stopping them from closing. "Walt?"

"Nicola, please don't!" yelped Connie, but it was too late.

Connie watched as the elevator doors opened and Walt walked back out, as if in slow motion. "Yes?" he asked, flashing Nicola a dashing grin and placing his hands in his pant pockets.

Nicola reached out her hand to him, which he took. "Hi, I'm Nicola Grayson. I'm a friend and co-worker of Connie's." She flashed Connie her signature fake grin, and then looked back at Walt. "I must say, Walt, I've been loving the arrangements you've been sending her. They've been absolutely beautiful, and the messages on the cards," she began, as she started to fan herself in an overly dramatic way. "Well, they just leave me wanting more." She giggled.

With a confused look, Walt turned to Connie, who was in such shock that she was unable to speak. Her world was crashing down on her, and she didn't know how to react. However, what she did know was that if Walt was going to find out the truth, it had to come from her. Finally, with sad eyes along with a guilty conscience, she looked at him and firmly said, "Walt, I need to tell you something. It's important that we talk right now." She reached for his hand, but he didn't budge.

"What's going on here?" he asked in a somber tone, one Connie didn't like one bit, walking out of the elevator, with a confused look on his face looking back and forth at Connie and Nicola. While he waited for an answer, he took his hands out of his pockets and crossed his arms.

After a few seconds of earth-shattering silence, Nicola spoke first. Putting her hand on Walt's arm, she said, "You see, Walt, your Connie isn't as innocent or sweet as you think she is."

"Please don't do this, Nicola!" Connie roared, glaring at her. Tears began streaming down her face, ruining the make-up she'd worked so hard to make perfect.

"Oh, honey, it's not like you could keep the secret forever," Nicola said with an evil laugh and wave of her hand. She took a step toward Walt. "You see, Connie's been sending herself flowers, courtesy of a Walt Goldman. When I questioned her about her boyfriend—the imaginary one I *knew* she had—I did a little snooping of my own. It turns out that she'd set up an online dating profile to find a guy who had your name. There are several files of notes she'd written on what the qualifications were, what your story would be, what she'd tell people. Oh, honey, the list goes on and on, and I hate to be the one to tell you this, but you were nothing to

Connie but a fake, and a game to her—one that she will never win."
She looked over at Connie, scoffing as she looked her up and down.
"Connie is nothing but a loser, and that's all she'll ever be."

Walt remained silent as his eyes darted between Connie and
Nicola, but his jaw tensed more by the second.

Finally it was Connie's turn to speak. "What are you trying to do to
me? Why are you telling him this? It's none of your damn business!"

"Sweet, innocent Connie, the one who stole what was going to be
my sole account right from under my nose. You knew I was after that
multi-million dollar hospital's business, and how dare you take it
away from me," Nicola challenged. "Also, as a professional, one
should know never to leave their computer unlocked when they're
away from their desk."

With her mouth agape, it all made sense to Connie now. Not that
Nicola had ever been nice to her, but after her boss handed over a
large account to Connie, there was a definite change in Nicola's
behavior and words toward her. "You bitch!" Connie, said, more
than ready to fight her right on her fake, perfectly-shaped nose. She
took one step forward and was about to tackle her, but Walt put his
arm around her waist, stopping her. "Leave! Now!" Connie screamed
at Nicola, pointing at the doors that led to their office.

Nicola put her hand to her lips, and with sarcasm, said, "Well, I
hope I haven't said too much, Walt. You look like a nice guy, and I
couldn't stand the thought of you being hurt." She gave him a wink,
pulled out her card from her red silk bra, exposing it under her black
blazer, and handed it to him. "Call me some time." Then, like the
snake she was, Nicola slithered back to her cubicle.

"Walt…please, you have to give me a chance to explain," Connie
said, taking a step toward him, the moment Nicola was out of the
lobby.

Without looking at her, Walt pressed the button to the elevator and raised his hand to stop her. "Just tell me one thing. Is everything she said true?" he asked.

With a knot in her throat, very quietly she said, "Mostly yes, and I'm so sorry. Can we just talk about this, so that I can tell you everything?" While she begged, she watched his body deflate. "I didn't mean to hurt you. I only wanted someone in my life who treats me like you do. Please, Walt, say you forgive me." She looked up and saw nothing but animosity in his eyes. "Walt, I'm…I'm so sorry."

"Why didn't you just tell me?" he asked with a sarcastic scoff. "I thought you were different—at least it seemed that way, but as it turns out, I didn't know you the way I thought I did. I truly liked you, Connie, but I do not like being lied to." The elevator doors opened and Walt stepped in.

"Walt, please don't go," she pleaded, but there was nothing she could do. She watched the only man who had called her beautiful disappear into the elevator and seconds later, the doors shut. Alone and completely heartbroken, Connie fell to her knees. For the first time in her life, she knew how it felt to watch the love of her life walk out on her.

What seemed like hours later, Connie picked herself up and went back to her cubicle, ignoring the callous looks from the women she worked with. She was sure that Nicola had spilled her secret to everyone else—and that mascara was streaked all over her face. However, none of that mattered to her because she was numb.

Connie sat down at her desk and tried to work, but she just stared blankly at the blinking cursor.

Though her time with Walt had been short, he'd taught her that she deserved better. Being with him had given her a taste of what her life *could* be like. He'd made her believe in herself. *Connie Albright, you're better than this!*

"I can't do this anymore," she said, standing.

She was tired of working at a job she hated, she was tired of being a laughing stock, and she was tired of feeling alone in the world. *It's time for a change!* She quickly tossed the small amount of belongings she kept at work into her purse. She didn't care if she was causing a scene. After one last look around, she headed to Nicola's cubicle a few feet away.

"Oh, hey, Con," Nicola said with a bright smile, as if nothing had happened. "What can I do for you?"

"Nicola, since the day I met you, I wanted to be just like you. On the outside, you appear to be everything that any man would want." Connie paused when Nicola seemed to be holding in a laugh, but she would not allow herself to feel defeated. "I was wrong, because I want to be nothing like you. You're evil. I could stand here and say that you ruined my life, but the truth is, you didn't." Connie smiled down at her nemesis, who sat motionless with a blank look on her face. "Thank you for showing me who I really am, which is someone way better than you'll ever be."

With that, she marched out of her office without saying anything to her boss and not bothering to look back.

CHAPTER TWENTY-FIVE

Khloe

After giving Derek a kiss goodbye, Khloe watched him drive away, and then she closed the door behind her and leaned against it, blissfully thinking about the last few hours they'd spent together. She was proud of herself for being honest with him about why she was so angry. He told her he understood and that he'd give her all the time she needed to gain his trust and he also promised to make it up to her by apologizing with his lips and hands.

While they hadn't had sex, she was still giddy about seeing him and could only imagine what it would be like to be intimate with him—the way his lips would brush aginst her skin, the way his—then her thoughts halted when she heard her phone ring, and looked at her caller-ID.

"Hello to you, too, darling," her mother said, after Khloe picked up. "Are you busy?" Without missing a beat to give Khloe time to reply, she continued with, "If not, you should be planning your trip to Napa for Thanksgiving. You know how good a bottle of Cab goes with my famous stuffing."

Khloe gave a slight laugh. "No, I'm not busy, and believe me, I wish I could be with y'all, but with everything going on at work, I just can't leave Sharon." She took a seat on her couch, pulling up a blanket and draping it over her legs, hardly believing that Thanksgiving was the following week.

"Khloe, is it just me, or do I sense something else is up with you?"

"You know me too well, Mom." Tossing her head back, she giggled like a schoolgirl into the phone, and proceeded to tell her mother about Derek, him surprising her, excluding his lie, because once her mother knew he'd hurt her little girl, her mother would be put off by him. Besides, Khloe looked at it as if they were starting over, so there was no point in talking about the past.

"Well, we can't wait to meet him," she replied, and then she went into a tangent of questions, comments, and what their children would look like.

"Mom, you have to slow down," she told her, shaking her head. "We just began dating, and I'm trying to take things slow."

Sighing into the phone, "All that matters to me is that my baby's happy."

Khloe smiled. "I am, Mom." She looked at her watch and realized it was coming up on lunchtime; she needed to get to work and return Millicent's calls. She jumped up, and while she pulled out what to wear and started her curling iron, they talked a bit longer. "Well, I have to go, but I promise that once Derek gets back from L.A., so that you two can meet, we can FaceTime," she told her, after turning on her shower.

"Perfect! Your father and I can't wait." Then, just as her father crossed her mind, her mother added, "Oh, and just so you won't worry, your father is doing just fine—actually, he's out golfing again." She sighed, adding, "I swear, it's like he's a new man. Anyway, have a good day, and I love you."

"I love you, too, Mom, and know that I really hope to see you two soon." She hung up and quickly got a move on with her day. An hour later, Khloe looked herself over in the mirror, texted Sharon she was on her way, and then out the door she went, with a wide smile on her face that couldn't be contained.

When Khloe came through the door to her shop, Sharon said, "Well, well, there you are," giving her a one-sided grin.

"Hey," she replied, placing her purse on the counter. "Thank you so much for taking care of everything this morning. I really appreciate it."

"No worries at all," Sharon said, craning her neck to eye Khloe up and down. "After all, I know it must've been important for you not to come in. So, why don't you tell me all about that deliriously bright expression on your face." She sat down on a stool behind the register and patted the one next to her. "Come on, girl, spill it."

Khloe sat down next to Sharon and began talking a mile a minute. "I'm just glad I didn't injure him by throwing the trophy at him," she giggled. "I just can't believe he surprised me!"

"I bet he is, too. After all, you do have a mean fast ball," she commented, reminding Khloe of their short-lived softball team, squeezing Khloe's arm. "How exciting!"

She shook her head. "The whole night was amazing, and I can't tell you how great it felt waking up next to him."

Khloe's face lit up, and then it must've turned sour, because Sharon asked, "So, what's up with the sudden grim look on your face?"

Instantly she felt her shoulders deflate. "He lied about where he'd been."

"What? Then where the heck has he been?" Sharon asked, sounding in pit-bull mode, ready to guard her friend.

Khloe raised her hands, hoping to calm Sharon down, because after what she'd been through in the past twelve hours, she didn't want the emotions to get the best of her again, and by Sharon's actions and tone, she could tell Sharon was already on the attack. "I appreciate your wanting to jump to my rescue, but before you hunt him down, let me explain." As she sighed, Sharon straightened herself on the stool and crossed her arms, transforming herself into listening mode.

"What the hell, Khloe! He didn't have to give you specifics, but he could've told you he was in L.A. What I'm curious about is what kind of family matter is this? I mean, are we talking murder?" After Khloe rehashed everything for Sharon, she was less than pleased with Derek's betrayal to her best friend.

Khloe shook her head. "No, of course not!" *At least I don't think so!* "Look, as mad as I was at him, he explained everything, and he swore he's not married and there is no other woman. It's simply a family matter."

"And you really believe that?" she asked, scoffing.

"Well, at first, no, but I do now," Khloe admitted. "Sharon, with all the pain Josh caused, I didn't think it was possible to fall for someone again. I put up a wall, but I'm ready to start dating. I know lies are lies, and not every relationship is perfect, but until Derek gets back from L.A. and when he can tell me everything, I've decided not to worry or stress about this."

"I think you're wise to want to move on, which is what I've been encouraging you to do, but do you really think Derek's the right one to move on with? He lied to you. And to me, it seems like quite a big thing not to tell you about."

Khloe nodded. "I hear you loud and clear, my friend, but I truly believe he wouldn't lie to me if he didn't have to, and whatever the reason is, I'm sure it has to be good."

"Oh, Khloe, you know I love you, right?" she asked, rhetorically. "I wish you the best, but please, just watch your heart, okay?"

"I'm doing the best I can, and we're taking it a day at a time."

"Fine, but if he hurts you again, I *will* hunt him down and kick his ass," she said, punching her arms out like a boxer.

Khloe laughed. "Ha ha! I'll be right there with you." She hopped off the stool as the chimes on the door signaled a customer coming in, letting Sharon take care of the customer because it was time to get to work and contact Millicent.

*****

As Khloe sat on her couch, she thought back to the day's events, including her multiple conversations with Millicent, who she'd to apologize profusely to for not returning her calls and texts as soon as she'd received them. So, once she'd gained her customer's trust back, Millicent pulled a one-eighty on her and changed her mind on her bouquet numerous times that day. By closing time, it was a little after seven, and she was ready for some comfort food and wine, but before she left, she made sure everything was cleaned up and ready for the following day as far as orders were concerned. Later that night, after scarfing down a hearty portion of vegetable lasagna she'd picked up from the Italian restaurant next to her shop, Khloe was on her third glass of wine and it was a little before eleven, Texas time. Aside from Derek's texts saying he was taking off, and then again when he had landed, they hadn't been in contact all day.

Deciding to get in bed, Khloe casually slid under her new white satin sheets, turned off the TV, and read a bit of her romance novel to put her in the frame of mind to sleep, but that didn't distract her from the fact that Derek hadn't called. Neither did turning back on the TV to watch an episode and a half of of *Friends*.

Where was he? she wondered, trying not to allow her insecurities to get the best of her. *Just relax, Khloe, he'll call.* After a few minutes of trying to calm herself, she turned off the lights, along with the TV again, and laid her head on the pillow. She reached for her phone, thinking there was nothing wrong with calling him. She dialed his number, and then waited for him to pick up.

On the third ring, someone picked up. However, instead of it being Derek, she heard a very young, childish female voice. "Hello?"

Khloe's eyes widened and her heart pounded with panic. "Um, sorry, I must have the wrong number," she said, and quickly hung up. *There must've been some mistake.* Khloe glared at the phone as she carefully dialed his number again, confident she'd hear his voice on the other end of the line this time.

"Hello?" said the same female voice, this time sounding annoyed.

Tears welled in Khloe's eyes, and her heart turned cold. *How could I be so stupid! Of course, he has daughter, so he must be married.* Though, as much as she didn't want to admit it, in the back of her mind she knew it was too good to be true to give Derek another chance. Stiffening her bottom lip, not wanting to belive what she now thought to be the truth, she said, "This is Khloe Harper. I was calling for Derek Thomas. Please tell that lying, low-life scumbag what a jerk he is, and that we're over!" It was times like this that she wished she had a home phone so she could have the satisfaction of slamming the handset back in its cradle. All she could do was forcefully press the "end" button. Starting to sob heavily, she fell back into her pillows.

She felt so foolish. "Damn you, Derek. Damn, you!" she shouted, punching her mattress with her fists as hard as she could. Once she felt she'd won the boxing match, she reached for a tissue on her nightstand and wiped her eyes free of tears. She reached for her phone and was about to call Sharon, just as her phone rang. When she saw Derek's name flashed across her screen, she hit the ignore button, but he kept calling. After repeating that cycle five times, Khloe finally answered and yelled, "What the hell do you want?" into the phone.

"Khloe, please, don't be mad," he said quickly, and Khloe heard him panting. "It's not what you think. The girl who picked up is my—"

Part of her wanted an explanation, for him to tell her it had all been a big misunderstanding, but she was finished with his excuses. Interrupting him, she hissed, "I know, Derek. She's your daughter, so I really don't care what you have to say, or listen to anymore of your excuses." Derek had obviously lied to her again, and there was nothing he could say or do this time that would fix it.

"Khloe, just give me a chance to explain."

She reached for a tissue on her nightstand and furiously wiped away the tears that welled in her eyes. "Derek, *your daughter* answered your phone, so don't try to tell me that you don't have a family, because now I know the truth!" she snapped. Feeling weak again, she sniffed into the phone. "You know, I really liked you. I thought you were different. I thought giving you a second chance was the right thing, but I was wrong."

"Fine, I'll tell you everything now. The truth is, I'm in L.A. because—"

"I don't care," she barked.

"Khloe, just tell me what you want me to do. I'll fix this any way I can."

Lie to me, shake me awake, and tell me this is all a dream, and that giving my trust to you wasn't a mistake. "Lose my number. Oh, and Derek, go to hell!"

After Khloe hung up, she was beyond furious. She felt like an idiot for letting her guard down—a first for her in years, and all she got for it was a broken heart. Curling into a fetal position, Khloe cried until the sun came up.

*****

When Khloe's alarm sounded at six thirty the next morning, the last thing she wanted was to get out of bed and start the day, but she figured she couldn't lie in bed forever, pining over Derek, especially during the busy holiday season. She needed something to focus on and that would be her work, no matter how tempting it was to hibernate under the covers. Slowly she made her way to the bathroom, hopped in the shower, and submerged her head under warm water, hoping to ease the sting of her shattered heart.

An hour later, just as she was about to leave for work, her phone rang, and she saw Derek's name on the screen. After the third ring she picked up—only because if she didn't, she imagined he'd be calling all day long, and she didn't have time for distractions.

"We need to talk," he said after she picked up. Sighing, she sat down on her couch with her head hung down. "Please, Khloe," he pleaded, in a gentle, coaxing tone.

Going on only a few hours of restless sleep, Khloe thought it was better to rip off the Band-Aid. "Fine, Derek, I'll listen." *Be strong*, Khloe told herself, preparing for what Derek had to tell her. She heard Derek take a relieved sigh, and then he began.

"Have you heard of the actress, Brooke Ireland?"

"Of course, hasn't everyone?" she replied with sarcasm, not knowing where this conversation was going. "She was an amazing actress who died in a horrific plane crash three years ago, but what does she have to do with anything?"

"What the public doesn't know is that she had a daughter who, at the time, was three."

Khloe scrunched her face. "Um, okay…"

"Khloe, Brooke was my sister—when acting, she used a different last name—and I have a niece. Her name is Savannah."

"Derek, I don't have time for games—" she began, shaking her head, not believing he'd stoop to something so low as to think that the death of a beloved actress would somehow change things for them, and when she told him just that, he cut her off.

"Please listen to the rest of what I have to say."

"Fine." Khloe closed her lips, thinking that the sooner he told her, the sooner she could leave for work and all this drama would be over and she could start tending to her broken heart.

"I had to keep it a secret because the press would have a field day with what's going on. Khloe, I'm adopting Savannah." With piqued interest, Khloe's eyes widened but she kept her lips shut, wanting to hear what he'd say next. "Since Brooke's death, Savannah's been living with my parents, where they make sure she stays out of the spotlight. In my sister's will, it was her wish that I adopt her. I'm in California because Brooke's lawyers are here, and it's easier to handle things in person. My parents are taking care of her during the day, but I get to spend some time with her at night. Before you called last night, I told her she could play a game on my phone before she went to bed, then, when I was putting her to bed, she said some 'lady' called for me, and she sounded really mad. That's when I knew it had to be you, so I called you back right away."

Khloe put her hand over her heart and closed her eyes, now realizing why the voice that'd picked up sounded so young. *It was his niece who answered the phone?* "Oh, Derek." She wanted to believe everything he'd told her, but as much as it pained her not to believe him, she didn't know how many more lies she could take. Though, as mad as she still was at him, now that she knew what he'd been keeping from her—and what she hoped was the whole truth—that all he wanted to do was protect Savannah, made her heart melt. "I— I don't know that to say. I'm so sorry for...everything—the loss of your sister, having to deal with everything your family's been though, and of course, for Savannah."

Khloe had watched all of Brooke's movies, and she felt like she knew the actress personally, but she never knew she'd had a daughter. From playing the evil vixen in *Stay Away, He's All Mine* to the sweet, yet sassy heroine in *The Invitation*, she'd been an amazing actress, an

A-list star, and the paparazzi couldn't get enough of her. Years ago, when Khloe would be shopping at the grocery store and would see Brooke's face plastered across the tabloids, she felt sorry for her, because of the horrible ways the tabloids ate at her like vultures, always judging her weight (even if it were for a role, or even going in and out of the gym make-up free), publishing unattractive shots they always seemed to manage to get of her on days she was shopping for groceries, and for constantly reporting that she was an alcoholic and a drug abuser. "She was a brilliant actress."

"She definitely was."

"So, Savannah's six, huh?" Khloe commented.

Derek laughed. "Yeah, and she loves watching her mother's movies and sometimes tries to imitate having an adult voice. She loves to act, but for now, I'm going to try to keep her guarded." He paused and let out a breath. "Khloe, I'm sorry I didn't tell you—I know now that I should've been honest with you about everything."

She opened her mouth to say that everything was okay and that all was forgiven, but instead, she said, "Derek, I just don't know what to think about this." She ran her hands through her hair, then added, "I think I just need some time to process all of this."

"Look, I don't know how the outcome will be with Savannah, but I want you in my life, and in Savannah's, too, if I'm fortunate to be granted custody. Now that you know everything, please tell me you want the same thing."

With all her heart she wanted to say she'd forgive him, and they could try to make it work, but something stopped her. "I—I…it's a wonderful thing what you're doing, raising your niece, but you lied to me. I just wish you would've told me the truth from the beginning, or at least have given me a chance to be trusted."

"I had to keep Savannah safe. The press would be all over this," he said, repeating himself.

Tears ran down her cheeks, ones she didn't know she were on the edge of falling out, but she didn't care anymore. "What did you think I was going to do, call the tabloids and say, 'Hey, Brooke Ireland's brother is adopting her daughter, and I can give you all the exclusive details'?" She knew that was a cruel remark, but she had to make a point. "I'm not like that, Derek, and I'd like to think that you knew that before you decided to lie to me!"

"I get that, and I know it's all my fault. I'll do anything to help us move forward."

"Derek," she said, her heart palpitating, "I need to think." In a whisper, she added, "Please—"

"I'll give you all the time you need."

"Thank you." After a long moment of silence, Khloe looked at her watch. "Look, I need to get going."

"Yeah, sure. I need to run, too. The ruling could happen at any moment—it might even have happened. Would it be okay if I called you later tonight?"

"I don't think that's a good idea right now," Khloe said.

"I'll respect your wishes, but you have to believe me when I say I didn't mean to hurt you."

You have no idea how I wish that were true, you...handsome jerk!

"Khloe, I won't stop trying to earn your trust and make this up to you, and I won't give up on us."

"Bye, Derek," she said, and then after waiting a long five seconds without another word between them, Khloe heard her line go dead. When her phone went back to its home screen, she sat on her couch to grieve for a few seconds. Now that she knew the truth, she'd give anything to tell Derek she was sorry and that she understood his reason for lying, but on the other hand, she couldn't help but feel betrayed. The only thing she knew was that it was time to go to work, and that she'd deal with the situation later. With one last blow of her nose, a quick wiping away of the tears, she took a deep breath, grabbed her keys, and headed for work.

*****

The second Khloe walked in the door, she began to cry uncontrollably, thankful there were no customers around.

"Khloe!" Sharon hopped off the stool in the front of the shop and walking up to her friend.

Khloe threw her arms around Sharon as if she were clinging to a life preserver. "He told me everything, and now I don't know what to do," she said through her tears, allowing herself to fall apart in front of her best friend.

"Come on, let's go back to your office," Sharon said, leading them down the hall. Once they were seated—Khloe in her desk chair and Sharon across from her—Sharon coaxed in a whisper. "What happened, sweetie?"

Khloe reached for a tissue. "I wish I'd never met Derek, or let myself open up to him." She cried harder, burying her head in her hands. Minutes later, she looked up to find Sharon pushing a cup of steaming hot coffee in front of her.

"Here, drink this," Sharon said.

Khloe took a sip right away, not worrying about getting burned because she'd already checked that off her list for the day, thanks to Derek.

"He's married, isn't he?" Sharon asked, taking a guess.

She shook her head, and then began to speak. After Khloe gave a quick summary of her conversation with Derek, she added, "I'm just trying to pull my thoughts and feelings together." She leaned back in her chair. "What would you do if you were me?" She sighed. "Could you forgive him, Sharon?"

"Everyone's different, Khloe…" Sharon began.

"So, now you're defending him?" she asked in a huff, narrowing her eyes.

Sharon leaned her arm across Khloe's desk and shook her head. "No, I'm not defending him. I'm just telling you what I think. Yes, it's shitty that he lied to you, but I now see why he did."

"I do, too," she admitted, "but you know I'm a trustworthy person. I would never betray anyone."

Sharon cocked her head and smirked. "Khloe, honey, you've only been on one date with him and spent a morning together. While I'm sure he thought he could trust you—and now he knows he *can*—he was just protecting his niece. Savannah is his main priority, and if you're going to be in his life, you need to understand that."

After thinking about it for a moment, she knew Sharon was right. "Okay, I see your point, but you get mine, too, right? After Josh, it's really hard for me to trust a man, so when a good one lies to me— no matter how little or how big—it's like adding salt to previous wounds." When Sharon nodded in agreement, Khloe continued, "I know his intentions were good, and it absolutely warms my heart to know he has such a gentle soul toward children, but—" Khloe's phone buzzed, interrupting her. She took her phone out from her pocket and looked at the screen. "It's from Derek."

"Well, what does he say?"

"He says, 'Thank you for hearing me out. Know that you're on my mind all the time.'" Khloe thought about responding, but decided it was best to keep her mind on work. "Look, customers will be coming in shortly, and I need to go over the orders and write the cards for today's arrangements."

"I've already taken care of everything," Sharon replied. "All I have to do is make a few last arrangements, and then they'll all be ready for pick-up and delivery."

Khloe stood, walked over to her friend and hugged her. "I

couldn't do this without you. You know that, right?" she asked. She looked around her office, noticing the Christmas catalogs were piling up, bills needed to be paid, and Millicent was like a ticking time bomb, who she expected to change her mind yet again. This all led Khloe to think that at any second she was closer to popping a bottle of Mumm and drinking it herself, not caring if she were at work or not, because her stress-level was at an all-time high.

Sharon nodded. "I do, but I think it's best that you go home. Take a well-deserved day off."

Khloe scoffed at the idea. "Oh, I'm fine. I'll splash some water on my face then be back to normal, and nobody will know that my heart is broken."

"Well, as someone who knows you very well, I'm making a judgment call for your sake." She reached for Khloe's arm and tugged her to the front of the store, where a couple had just entered. "I'll call you later," she said, nudging Khloe out.

With a sigh, knowing Sharon was right and that she wouldn't give up, she said, "Okay, fine. I'll call you later," before she bowed her head and quickly walked out of her shop.

CHAPTER TWENTY-SIX

Gabby

Now that things with Harry were smoothly sailing along, Gabby sensed that something about her had changed for the better. Even while doing simple and mundane tasks, like laundry and the dishes, she whistled and even on a few occasions, caught herself smiling for no reason. Despite dealing with seasonal allergies that had been bothering her, she was deliriously happy, and it was all thanks to having Harry in her life.

She was about to head to the grocery store when her house phone rang.

"Hey, Gabby, it's Jules."

"Oh, hello, Jules," Gabby said. "How are you?" She sniffed into the phone.

"I'm great. I'm just calling to say hello, and to thank you for the beautiful flowers. You didn't have to do that."

"I'm so happy you like them. You were so kind to me, so I just wanted to send you a little something as a thank you."

"Well, I assure you that I love them. Harry tells me things with you two are still going good," Jules said in a giddy tone and the joy in Jules's voice warmed Gabby's heart.

Gabby giggled. "Yes, Harry and I are good…well, everything

except for a case of bad allergies, but it's nothing I can't handle."

"Well, if there's anything you need, just know you can always…" she began but then stopped speaking, and then Gabby heard Jules say in a muffled voice, "Yes, but only if she's up for it." Seconds later, Jules was back on the line. "Gabby, would you mind if Andrew talks to you? If you're not feeling well enough for it, I completely understand."

Gabby smiled to herself. "Of course, put him on."

"Hi, Gabby," Andrew said cheerfully.

"Hello, sweet boy. How are you?"

"Great! Since it's teachers' serve day, I'm home from school, and I'm making pancakes with Mommy."

Gabby laughed. "I think you mean Teachers In-Service Day."

"Yeah, that's it," he said, giggling.

"Well, are you having fun?"

"Yes, lots and lots! Mommy's been spilling flour all over the floor." He took a deep breath and continued talking faster. "And when she flipped a pancake, one of them landed on our dog's back, but Smokey didn't mind," he said, speaking in an overly exaggerated voice.

Gabby shook her head, imagining the mess in the kitchen and how much fun they were having. "It seems like you two are having an awesome day."

Changing the subject, Andrew asked, in the sweetest voice she'd ever heard, "Gabby, will you come to my birthday party tomorrow?"

"I wouldn't miss it for the world," she said without any hesitation.

"Yay!" he shrieked, and then she heard him tell his mother the news. "Well, Mommy wants to talk to you. See you tomorrow," he said.

"I take it by Andrew's excitement that you'll be able to make it to his party, but please know that you if you have other plans, I

185

completely understand," Jules said when she came back on the line. "With all his friends, the bounce house, and the soccer entertainment at the park, I'm sure Andrew will get over it."

"There's no other place I'd rather be, and it sounds like a great time. Can I bring anything?"

"Just yourself. Oh, and maybe a flask, too. There will be a lot of rowdy kids around, so you might need it," she said, and they shared an understanding laugh.

After they said their goodbyes, Gabby pulled out of her driveway and was on her way, not only going to the store, but to get a birthday present for Andrew, too.

*****

Gabby had managed to persuade the manager at the sporting goods store to sell her their life-sized cardboard cutout of David Beckham. Though she knew he was probably just short of half her age, she briefly considered keeping the handsome poster for herself to look at, but decided it was probably best to give it to Andrew. Then, after making a quick stop for groceries, she cheerfully walked through the door of her home.

Still reeling from her allergies, she needed to eat even though she probably wouldn't be able to taste anything. She prepared a mini shepherd's pie, and just as she placed it in the oven, her doorbell rang. When she opened it, a wide grin spread on her face, staring at the best medicine, who was holding a bouquet of pink and white roses. "Harry, what are you doing here?"

"I came to see how you're feeling," Harry told her, sounding concerned. "Those allergies still got you down?"

Gabby nodded, reaching to pull him inside. "You're very kind to come by," she said, and he handed her the flowers that were wrapped in caramel-colored butcher paper. "Thank you for the lovely bouquet."

"You're welcome, my dear," he said, hugging her and planting a kiss on her cheek. "Khloe's Flower Shop is the best in the town."

"I couldn't agree more," she told him, adding, "I just put a shepherd's pie in the oven." Reaching for his hand, she led him into her kitchen, where he sat down at the dinner table and she proceeded to put the flowers in a glass vase.

"That sounds fantastic!" he said with excitement as his eyes lit up. "I'm starving," he added, patting his stomach. As he watched her, he said, "So, I heard Andrew invited you to his party tomorrow. I'm really happy that you'll be there."

"Of course. I wouldn't miss it for the world." Gabby set the vase of flowers in the center of the table and placed her hands on her hips, admiring the bright colors. "You know how much I love your family."

"I do, and they love you, too." He reached for her hand. "Do you mind if we go in the other room and talk?"

"That would be perfect," she told him with a sniffle. She grabbed a tissue and they took a seat on her couch. "I'm sorry. I must look like a wreck," she said. For two days she'd stayed at home, under the influence of allergy medicine that still hadn't helped her feel better. Though she'd showered and changed clothes earlier that day, she was sure her hair was puffed out in a ball of frizz and her eyes were bloodshot from all the sneezing she'd done.

"You look beautiful," he told her as he put his arms around her.

"Oh, Harry," she replied, shaking her head, with a laugh. "So, what did you want to talk about?" she asked. At that, she noticed his heartbeat increase. When he didn't say anything, she pulled away from him and placed her hand on his shoulder. "Harry, are you okay?"

Very slowly, he nodded. "Yeah, in fact, ever since I met you, I have been better than I have in a long time."

Gabby smiled. "So have I."

"Well, I've been wanting to tell you something, but that night—when we made love—it changed me, Gabby."

"What are you trying to say, Harry?" she asked him, not quite sure where the conversation was going. She felt her own heart start to beat faster.

"Gabriella Lewis, I'm in love with you," he said in one swift breath.

Gabby's eyes filled with tears, and she placed her arms around Harry's neck. "Oh, Harry..." She reached up and touched his smooth, delicate face, as images of how their love story started, to where it was at that moment, played in her mind. "I love you, too." She felt surprised when her own words melted her heart. After she leaned over to kiss him on his lips, she asked, "Do you want to go upstairs?"

With enthusiasm, Harry nodded, but then he hesitated. "But what about the shepherd's pie?" he asked, pointing toward the kitchen.

Gabby waved her hand. "Let it be. If it burns, it burns. After all, I told you I'm not a good cook."

CHAPTER TWENTY-SEVEN

Connie

What a disaster of a day, Connie thought, swerving in and out of traffic with both hands clutched tightly to the wheel. Thanks to Nicola, Connie was sure her life was over. She pleaded with Walt, to get him to understand her point of view, and that while the part about why she wanted to find him in the first place was true, she was truly falling in love with him, but his anger didn't waver. Though, with her luck, she knew it was too good to be true to have something so precious—a man like him—in her life, before he was either taken away by a beautiful woman or leaving on his own will.

Now that the damage was done, there was nothing she could do to salvage the situation. She had another plan: Connie was going to reinvent herself. Wiping away the smeared makeup on her face, she put on lip gloss, hoping at least it would make her look more presentable. She got out of her car and walked through the doors of her local bookstore, making her way to the self-help section. Thirty minutes and over a hundred dollars later, she got in her car and drove home.

Watch out, world! Connie Albright is starting a new life! she told herself, unlocking her front door.

Earlier in the day, the sun was shining and Connie was in love, now heavy storm clouds floated above her, and now her relationship with Walt was over. She made it home just as it began to thunderstorm. She put down her purse and sack of books, then zombie-like, walked slowly to her bed. With Buttercup and Tillman by her side, she snuggled under the covers, allowing herself to mourn the loss of Walt in her life. Thinking back to the night she created her dating profile, the first time she met Walt, their first kiss, and remembering the way he'd made love to her...it was too much for her to handle, and she started to cry heavy tears, finally letting go of everything she'd been keeping in for so long. She tried to mend her broken heart by releasing the embarrassment and hurt of being ridiculed by her co-workers and the sadness of feeling so alone that she'd needed to create an imaginary boyfriend, along with finding a real one and losing him.

Finally, after she couldn't cry anymore, she closed her eyes, mentally and physically exhausted.

*****

Things didn't get better for Connie, they only got worse.

It had only been a full seven days since her world fell apart. Taking an angry bite out of her fifth large Snickers bar that day, she clicked the order button on her laptop, comforted in the fact that her second pizza that week would be arriving shortly. Her apartment looked like it'd been hit by a tornado. She'd eaten most of everything in her pantry (excluding the few things she had that were healthy because who wanted to eat well while nursing a broken heart?). Greasy takeout containers hadn't been thrown away, and candy wrappers were strewn everywhere. She hadn't showered in days and knew she was beginning to smell, but she didn't care. *Nobody wants to see me anyway*, she thought.

Connie reached into her wallet for money to pay for the pizza when she accidentally pulled out the picture Walt had taken. With her fingertip she traced their faces, remembering that special day as tears stung her eyes. She stared at the photo for a while, wondering where he was, and what he was doing. Did he miss her or even think about her? "Probably not," she mumbled to Buttercup and Tillman, who looked at her curiously. She reached for them, holding them close to her as she leaned on them for comfort. "I love you two," she said and turned on the TV. Because her life couldn't get any more miserable, she settled on *The Way We Were*, which was almost over. She reached for the box of tissues and prepared for another heavy cry—not only for Katie and Hubbell, but for her and Walt, too.

As the credits rolled, Connie was a ball of tears. When her doorbell rang and she dabbed her eyes, tightening the belt on her coral robe before answering it.

"Whoa," said the teenage pizza delivery boy, taking a few steps back. "Are you okay, miss?"

"I'm fine," she replied with a fake smile, holding out his money.

"Well, you don't look okay. Do I need to call someone for you?"

"Just give me the damn pizza," she said, snatching the box from him. Without caring about her change, she threw him the twenty-dollar bill and slammed the door in his face. "Asshole!" she hissed. She quickly went into the kitchen, grabbed a bottle of wine and a corkscrew, and plopped herself back on the couch just as *Love Story* was beginning. *Oh, great*, she thought, taking a bite of pizza.

Later that night, after almost finishing a bottle of wine and half the extra-large pizza, Connie stumbled to her bedroom. She hadn't slept in her bed in three nights because it reminded her of Walt. She lay face down on a pillow, which smelled like Walt, and she began crying again. *When will this pain end?* Before she knew it, Connie had fallen asleep.

*****

Waking up at noon with a massive hangover, Connie went into the kitchen to re-fill her glass, trying to hydrate herself with water. She stayed in bed the entire day crying, eating the rest of the pizza, and watching sad movies. She tried her best not to think of Walt, but he was constantly on her mind. She wished she could change things, but she knew there was nothing she could do to make him understand or bring him back, nor could she bring back the family she missed more than anything. It was times like these that she wished she could talk to talk to her parents and sister. Her dad would reassure her that she was strongest person in the world and could conquer anything, her mother would hug her and let her cry, and her sister would make a joke about how boys were stupid. She'd laugh, and then they would hop on their bikes and go for ice cream.

She leaned back into her pillows and sighed, and in minutes, after imagining pep-talks from her parents and sister, a revelation came to her. "It's time for a change," she joyfully announced to her cats. Hopping out of bed to retrieve the sack of books she'd bought at the store that she hadn't even looked through, a surge of energy rushed through her. Hours later, after flipping through them, Connie reached for her laptop, ready more than ever to make some serious changes—and this time, she'd go about it in a truthful way and wouldn't stop at anything unless she was genuinely happy. It was time to put her marketing degree to some good use.

Not realizing it was past midnight, she closed her laptop and headed to sleep, feeling confident by the fact that she'd emailed her resume to seven companies about open marketing positions. *Now I wait*, she thought, turning off the lamp on her nightstand. She sighed into a pillow, once again inhaling a whiff of Walt's cologne, and she hugged it, allowing the comforting scent to lull her to sleep.

CHAPTER TWENTY-EIGHT

Khloe

Going home was the last thing Khloe wanted to do because she didn't want time alone to think, sulk, or give any thought to forgiving Derek, so, instead, she decided to go to a spa and make a day of it. After all, with the morning she'd had, she could use a little pampering.

"Please follow me, Ms. Harper," said the attendant at the spa's front desk, inviting Khloe through two sets of double doors and into a room with bathrooms and private showers. After showing Khloe to a locker, a luxurious robe, and a pair of slippers, the woman whispered, "And in our waiting area, we have plain or cucumber and strawberry water, along with our signature lavender Oolong tea."

"Thank you," Khloe said, placing her purse in her locker, wishing the woman would go away because all she wanted to do was relax.

"Oh, and one more thing, Ms. Harper," she said. "Here at The Rogue Spa we request our guests turn off their cell phones."

"Believe me, that won't be a problem," Khloe said, reaching into her purse for her phone, ignoring the two new texts she'd received from Derek. She held down the power button with more force than was necessary, and when she did, she instantly felt free. Though, she was pretty sure it was because of the calming aromas and quiet and relaxing music playing through the speakers.

With a pleasant grin, the woman said, "Enjoy your massage and facial," and disappeared.

After Khloe changed, she took a seat on one of the three plush couches in the waiting area. Opting for the cucumber and strawberry water, she sipped it slowly as she leafed through a magazine. *This is relaxing*, she thought, closing the magazine and leaning her head against the cushions. After a few silent moments, she heard her name being called.

"Ms. Harper?"

Khloe opened her eyes to find a short Asian man dressed in white tennis shoes, white nylon pants, and a white collared staff shirt. "Hello, I'm Anton, and I'll be giving you your massage today."

"Hello, Anton," Khloe said. She placed the magazine back on the table and threw her empty cup in the trashcan.

"This way," he instructed, and Khloe followed him down the length of a beige corridor. He stopped, then opened the door to a small, dimly lit room. "Here we are," he said. He clasped his hands together and asked, "Tell me, where do you feel tension?"

"Everywhere. From my head to my toes—I guess you can just consider me one big mess," she joked, wrapping her hands round the back of her neck. "Though, most of it is in my neck and shoulders."

"Well, I'll do my best to get those kinks out." He patted the massage table. "Please undress and lay face down on the table. I will be back shortly," he told her, before opening the door and walking out of the room.

Once the door was closed, Khloe rolled onto her stomach with her face in a padded doughnut. She was looking down at the floor when Anton returned. After turning on peaceful Zen music, he quietly moved around the table and adjusted the covers just above her bottom. With one hand, he zigzagged her back, placing the other on her left shoulder.

Khloe closed her eyes and allowed herself to relax, trying her best not to let thoughts of Derek creep back into her mind. However, as much as she tried, nothing helped. She re-played every moment they'd shared, every word spoken, and remembered how his lips felt on her. Could she forgive him for lying to her and for not trusting her with the secret about Savannah?

Sighing, with no conclusion in mind about what to do about her and Derek, she decided just to let things work out how they're supposed to—with or without him in her life. *Relax*, she instructed herself. With her eyes still shut, she allowed Anton to work on her major kink, which she'd now refer to as the Derek Situation.

An hour later, her rejuvenating massage was over, and Khloe walked back into the waiting area where she grabbed another cucumber and strawberry water before reclaiming her seat on the comfortable couch. Physically, she felt better than she had in weeks, but still, thoughts of Derek wouldn't escape her. *We really could've been good together.*

While she waited to be called for her facial, she reached for the entertainment section of the daily newspaper. Immediately, she saw the headline in bold letters: JUDGE'S RULING: BROOKE IRELAND'S BROTHER AWARDED CUSTODY OF HER YOUNG DAUGHTER!

"Holy crap," whispered Khloe, not believing her eyes, and she instantly began reading the featured article.

> *(Los Angeles, CA.) Three years after the tragic death of the beloved actress, Brooke Ireland, the grueling custody battle for her six-year-old daughter, Savannah Thomas, is over. Just after noon, Judge Ernie Everwood granted Derek Thomas, the brother of the Oscar-winning actress, full custody of her daughter, Savannah. Since the death of Miss Ireland, Mr. Thomas has been in a constant battle with Savannah's father,*

actor/singer Mick S. Meadows (Mr. Meadows and his girlfriend, Spanish actress Mia Jerez, are currently in London on his I'm Comin' Back *tour, where he is also promoting his upcoming film* A Dangerous Man to Love).

When the winning team exited the front doors, there was media frenzy outside the Los Angeles Courthouse, where a short news conference took place. The attorney for the Thomas family, Hughes Moore, spoke first, saying, "This is a huge victory for Mr. Thomas and his family. I hope they can all live in peace now, knowing that the beloved actress is smiling down from heaven, comforted by the fact that her beautiful daughter is where she belongs. For now, there will be no further questions for Mr. Thomas, or the family. However, I'm now turning this over to Mr. Thomas for a quick comment."

As Derek Thomas took to the podium, Savannah, who wore a hot pink dress and a red bow in her chestnut hair, rested comfortably on his hip, and he gave her a high-five. "First, I'd like to thank Hughes for his unconditional time and focus. Not only are you a great friend, I consider you family. To Judge Everwood, words cannot express how grateful I am to you." Mr. Thomas concluded the press conference when he said to a yawning Savannah, "Thank you everyone for your support, but we're headed home now. My little girl needs some sleep." Quickly, with a swarm of security, they were ushered to a nearby black SUV. Though, as Mr. Thomas was getting in the vehicle, one reporter stopped him in his tracks, when asked about Savannah's father and whether Meadows will be in her life. To that, Mr. Thomas simply replied, "No comment."

Note: This story is currently being updated. Head to our website for the latest details.

It was suddenly clear to Khloe that Derek's lies were ones now that she understood, and he was the man she thought he was all along. She had to get in touch with him and tell him how sorry she was for the way she'd acted, and not understanding where he was coming from. He hadn't cheated, he was only trying to protect his niece. Gnawing at her bottom lip, knowing her heart was on the line, she anxiously bounced her foot up and down. If this was her only chance at love—*real love*—she wasn't going to let it slip by. *It's now or never!*

Finally, within seconds, she raced to the showers to rinse the lavendar massage oil off her body, and then quickly dressed.

As she headed out the double doors, a woman in white, who looked like she worked in a psychiatric hospital, not at a spa, stopped her. "Ms. Harper, I'm Linda, and I'll be doing your facial," she said.

Khloe zoomed past her. "I'm sorry, Linda. I have to get my man back." After paying for the massage, along with a seventy-five dollar facial cancellation fee, Khloe waited for the valet to bring her car while she tried to call Derek's cell again and again, but each time it went to voicemail. Minutes later, filled with anxiety, she handed a tip to the driver who finally brought her car around. Quickly, she got in and peeled out of the parking lot.

*****

Khloe cursed herself for not buying another car charger after her previous one broke. With her phone and purse in hand, she quickly unlocked her door and ran into her home, just as the phone powered itself off. "No, no, no!" she yelled, after rushing to her cell phone charger, anxiously waiting for it to boot up.

With a plan in mind she sat down at her laptop, giving her cell phone time to charge enough to make a call, Khloe did a phone number search and seconds later while holding her breath. She nervously dialed with shaking fingers, once she saw she had enough battery life to make a call.

"Thomas and Associates. How may I help you?"

"Hello," Khloe began, her voice shaky. "Is this Mary Knight?"

"Yes, it is."

"Wonderful. Well, this is Khloe Harper. I was wondering if you could patch me through to Derek."

"That shouldn't be a problem, Khloe."

"Great," Khloe said, with a relieved sigh.

"Oh, while I have you on the phone, I want your opinion. Tell me, what arrangement do you think would be best to send to someone under the weather? Pink and red carnations? Tulips? Maybe an assortment of colorful roses? Also, would it be possible to have them delivered today?"

"Well, any of those would be nice, but I think an assorted arrangement of lilies, roses, and other various flowers would work. What do you think?" Khloe asked, forming the beautiful bouquet in her mind. After Mary exclaimed how perfect that would be, Khloe told Mary she would call it in, for her, though, Khloe's mind was far from work.

"Oh, I'm sorry, dear, what were you originally calling about?"

Khloe took a deep breath and let it out. "I need to talk to Derek."

"Yes, that's right. One moment," she said, but then continued speaking, which began to slightly irritate Khloe. "By the way, Khloe, Derek told me everything, and I have to say, before Derek left for California, I told him he should trust you but he didn't listen to me. When he called me needing me to schedule his short trip back to Dallas, he sounded so happy to be surprising you, but then I heard he finally told you everything and my heart broke for you two. I really hope you can patch everything up."

"That's what I'm trying to do," Khloe said in the nicest tone she could muster, because her patience was running low.

"Glad to hear it. Good luck." And with that, the line faded into on-hold classical music. Within seconds the music stopped, and she heard his sexy voice.

"Hello, this is Derek."

"Hi, Derek, it's me."

CHAPTER TWENTY-NINE

Gabby

When Gabby arrived at the park for Andrew's party, excitement soared within her. She couldn't wait to see Harry and his family. She tucked Andrew's gift under her arm and walked over to where groups of adults and children were gathered. There were bright blue and yellow balloons tied to picnic tables, and kids jumped up and down and laughed in a bounce house. She scanned the crowd and her eyes landed on Harry, who was wearing tennis shoes, dark jeans, and a red pin-striped navy sweater. He held out his arms for her. Gabby smiled and quickened her pace, certain she was in love again.

"Hi, my darling," Harry said, kissing her on the lips and hugging her.

"Hello, Harry." Gabby touched his cheek with the back of her free hand. "I'm so looking forward to today."

"As am I," he told her, taking Andrew's gift from her. "You didn't have to get him anything," he said with a chuckle. "He's already got more than he needs."

Gabby laughed. "Oh, don't be silly. It's just a little something."

"Gabby!" she heard Andrew holler from across the field. She looked behind Harry and saw Andrew running toward her.

She bent down to him and wrapped her arms around him. "Happy Birthday, Andrew!"

"Thank you!" He pointed to a sticker on his teal shirt that read: "Birthday Boy" in big, bold, blue letters. "My daddy gave me this sticker." He reached into his pocket and held a soccer ball sticker out for Gabby. "Here, put this on," he instructed, pointing to his grandfather. "Grandpa has one, too."

She did as she was told. "Thank you."

Seconds later, Andrew's friends called him over to where they were playing. "Well, I gotta go," he said, "but I'll see ya around!"

"Have fun, kid," Harry said, tousling his hair, and then Andrew took off for the bounce house.

"There you are," said Jules, who approached them with Jeff beside her.

"Hello," Gabby said. After hugging them both, she looked around and smiled brightly, admiring the setup for Andrew's party. "Everything looks perfect. You both did a beautiful job."

Jeff slung his arm around Jules, and with a proud smile on his face said, "My beautiful wife is a brilliant party planner."

Jules blushed and planted a kiss on her husband's lips. "Oh, please," she said, waving him off, and then turned to Gabby. "My party planning business recently took off, and this is only my eighth event I've actually planned."

"Congratulations! I can only imagine how much fun you have planning evnts."

"Oh, I do! It can seem like quite a chore, but I wouldn't have it any other way."

"My son's right, Jules. You're an amazing party planner." He then turned to Gabby. "But it's more like twenty she's planned—from birthday parties, anniversary celebrations, and even a few weddings—she does it all."

Gabby's eyes lit up. "I know Khloe's Flower Shop is always willing to help party planners."

"You know, I've heard that. I'll have to try them soon, especially since I'm looking for a reputable florist." Jules replied, before she heard her name being called by Andrew.

Two hours later, the party was winding down and Gabby and Harry sat at one of the picnic tables to finish their shared slice of cake.

"I had a blast today. It was so much fun seeing Andrew play with his friends, but my favorite part was when Andrew encouraged me to get in the bounce house with him. It made me feel like a kid again."

Harry's eyes widened with surprise, and he let out a laugh. "You looked like you were enjoying yourself, but with my bad knees, jumping isn't something this old man should do."

Gabby laughed and patted his hand. "Well, at least we know where you're not handicapped." They roared with laughter, just as Andrew, Jules, and Jeff came to join them.

"What's so funny?" Andrew asked in a serious tone.

"Your grandfather was just telling me a joke." Gabby nudged Harry with her elbow.

"What was it?" he asked his grandfather, clasping his fingers together, transforming to listening mode.

"Which flower talks the most?" Harry asked, without missing a beat.

Andrew twisted his lips as he tried to figure it out. "Okay," he said with a shrug. "I give up."

"Tulips, because they have two lips." Harry smiled and waited for a reaction. Jules, Jeff, and Gabby laughed, and then they all looked at Andrew.

"That's not very funny, Grandpa." He looked up at his parents and asked, "Can I open Gabby's present now?" When they told him he could, he reached for the last unopened gift on the table and started ripping off the red ribbon. After he'd torn the wrapping paper to shreds, he stood up and unfolded the life-sized picture of David

Beckham. His jaw dropped and his eyes widened.

"Do you like it?" Gabby asked, hoping and praying his silence was a good thing.

"I love it!" He ran around the table and threw his arms around her. "Thank you so much." He pointed to the poster and said, "This is going in my room." He hugged her again and then plopped himself down in her lap.

"Gabby, that was really nice of you," said Jules, looking the picture up and down admiringly. "It's such a great gift that I might have to put it in my bedroom," she said and gave Gabby a wink.

Gabby laughed. "Believe me, I thought about keeping it for myself."

Before Jules could reply, Andrew chimed in. "But, Mom, that's my gift." He crossed his arms and started to pout.

Jules kindly smiled at her son and rubbed his head. "I'm only kidding, sweetie."

An hour later, Gabby looked down to see that Andrew's eyes were shut, and he was nuzzled against her chest. She'd never had a child fall asleep in her arms before, but it warmed her heart. "I hate to wake him," she said to Jeff, who reached for his son.

Jeff and Jules looked at each other and then laughed. "He'll be fine. He sleeps through anything," Jeff told her.

After all the gifts were loaded in their car and Andrew had been placed in his car seat, Jules said to Gabby, "Thank you so much for coming today. Having you here truly made Andrew's day, and of course, with the perfect gift." She hugged Gabby.

"I wouldn't have missed celebrating his birthday for anything."

After they let go, it was Jeff's turn to hug Gabby. "Like Jules said, thank you for coming, Gabby." He then turned to his father, adding, "And I'm sure we'll see you soon," giving him a hug as well.

After Jeff, Jules, and Andrew pulled out of the parking lot, Gabby asked Harry, "Would you like to have dinner with me tonight?"

"I was hoping you'd ask," he said with a grin. "But this time, I'll cook." After they let out a chuckle, Harry kissed her.

CHAPTER THIRTY

Connie

Connie was ready for her reinvention. "It's a new day," she said, silencing the alarm on her phone, which she'd set for six-thirty. Since she was jobless she would have preferred sleeping in, but she was determined to stick to her goals. She reached for one of the inspiration books she'd bought and flipped to the daily devotional.

"Just because the past didn't turn out like you wanted it to, doesn't mean your future can't be better than you've imagined." She read the passage twice to ensure she was making a full effort to believe the positive reading and then threw on a pair of sweatpants, a red hoodie and tennis shoes, grabbed her gym bag, and sailed out the door.

She made it there shortly after seven, right when the sun was coming up. She was surprised to see so many people running on the treadmills and spinning on bikes, which made her wonder how people did this every day—especially so early in the morning—but vowed to make it part of her routine.

Connie entered the giant room where lively music boomed through the speakers. Taking in all buzzing the energy, she was ready to get in shape, this time for good. She took off her hoodie and trotted to an available treadmill and was about to get on it before a petite blonde bounded up on the platform and began pressing buttons on the dashboard.

"Um, excuse me," Connie said, but the woman said nothing. "I was just about to use this machine." She looked at the woman, who must have been in her early thirties, wearing a white top and black and pink yoga pants. Still, there was no reply from the woman, and Connie was getting frazzled. Finally, she walked to the front of the machine and tapped on the dashboard.

The woman finally looked up and scrunched her nose. "Uh, yes?" she asked.

"I was here first," Connie said directly, placing her hands on her hips.

"Oh, I'm sorry," the woman replied, sounding anything but apologetic. She glared at Connie and looked her up and down. Then she added, "Maybe you should try the bikes. I hear they're good for those who have a hard time running and *really* need to lose weight."

Connie was appalled at the woman's rudeness. She looked down at herself, wondering just how overweight she looked. Her sweatpants were two sizes too small, her favorite old, black and red CCR concert T-shirt had holes in it and showed her muffin top midriff, which had grown the past week thanks to the damage she'd done to her body to comfort herself over losing Walt. As the pain flooded through her again, Connie did something she never thought she'd do. She gave the woman the finger, not caring what anyone else thought.

The woman responded with a wave and sarcastic smile, which pissed Connie off even more and made her feel hopeless and foolish. "Maybe I can't do this," she mumbled to herself. She was about to run out of the gym when a man at one of the punching bag stations caught her eye. It was Walt.

Confused at what he was doing at her apartment's gym, her heart started to beat quickly, and Connie watched as Walt slammed his fists rapidly and aggressively into the black punching bag. If at all possible, he looked more handsome than she remembered, and she ached to hold him. Part of her wanted to run up to him, but what could she say that would get him to listen? What could she say that hadn't already been said? Then, she saw a woman come up to him and place her hand on his arm, give him a nod, and then she proceeded to punch the bag as well. That was all Connie could take, and feeling more self-conscious than ever, thanks to her outfit and the blond woman's not-so-kind words, she ran out of the gym before anyone could see her cry.

*****

Connie was tempted to go to Dunkin' Donuts, buy a box of two dozen doughnut holes, and find solace in the sugary indulgence. But she didn't. Instead, she headed home.

When she got there, to her surprise, there was an unknown number on her missed call list, and she tapped voicemail button. As it played, Connie's eyes widened and the corners of her lips turned up. She dialed the number back and waited patiently for someone to pick up.

"Eve's Marketing Group. How can I help you?" asked a cheerful woman.

Connie gulped. "I'm Connie Albright, and I'm calling for Eve Vanguard about the job opening," she said nervously, taking a seat at her kitchen table as she eyed the box of quinoa that she was planning to add to her kale salad for lunch.

"Oh, hello, Connie," replied the woman. "This is Eve. Thank you so much for getting back to me so quickly."

"Absolutely!" Connie's knees began to shake as she eagerly awaited to hear what Eve had to say.

"Well, Connie, I've looked over your resume, and while you've got an impressive academic background at the University of Texas, your previous jobs don't mention your ever doing anything with marketing. May I ask why not?"

"I guess I never seemed to dig my way out of what I thought would be a short-lived job," she said with nervous laugh and banged the palm of her hand on her forehead. *What a stupid thing to say*, she thought. To Connie's surprise, Eve began to laugh along with her.

"Believe me, I know what that's like. I also worked in the medical field for a bit, too, and that's when I decided to start my own company. Anyway, if you're still interested, I'd love to interview you. Maybe sometime next week?"

"That would be perfect," Connie replied. They set up a date and time for the interview, and after Connie hung up, she danced around the kitchen.

Connie's life was finally changing, and this time it was all for the best—at least that's what she hoped.

CHAPTER THIRTY-ONE

Khloe

"Khloe?" Derek asked, sounding confused. "What's this about? Mary said this was one of my clients with some kind of emergency."

"This is an emergency!" she replied defensively. "I need to talk to you." She opened her mouth, but Khloe didn't know where to start.

"We can talk when I'm home," he said, his voice monotone.

"I heard you won custody of Savannah. Congratulations!" she said, not wasting any precious time she had. "Look, Derek, I'm truly sorry about everything. I should have—"

Derek cut Khloe off by saying, "I'm sorry, Khloe, but like I said, we'll talk when I'm home."

"Derek, please," she begged as tears filled her eyes. "I'm sorry."

After what seemed to be the longest pause Khloe had ever heard, he said, "I'll call you tonight, and we can talk then. Savannah needs me right now, so I have to go." And with that, he ended the call.

A tear ran down her cheek. Before she called Sharon, Khloe gave herself a moment to calm down.

"So, how's your day off, doll?" Sharon asked.

She told Sharon everything, ending in a sigh. "With all that Derek's going through, I can't believe how badly I treated him. I'm such a horrible person."

"Khloe, you have to stop blaming yourself. It's not like you knew any of it anyway, and it's certainly not your fault. There's nothing you could've done differently. Look, Leonard and I had planned to go out, but if you want me to I can cancel my date night, and we can have a girls' night. I'll even bring the ice cream, full-fat, of course," she said with a giggle.

"You're sweet, Sharon, but I think I'm going to pass. I'm exhausted and emotionally drained. Besides, Derek said he's going to call so we can talk. Also, I need to prepare for my phone meeting with Millicent tomorrow, so I'm going to work on that a bit, and then hopefully, I'll crash early." She then told her about Mary's order, which needed processing and delivered that day.

"Okay, I'll take care of that, but as for tonight, if you change your mind, I'm all yours."

Khloe laughed. "Will do," she said.

"It's a deal."

"Thanks, Sharon," Khloe replied. "You're a great friend, and I'm lucky to have you. I'll talk to you tomorrow."

"Sounds like a plan. Good luck with Derek tonight. Just know that I'm here for you and that you're loved by so many."

Taking the sympathetic gesture to heart, Khloe said a simple, "Thank you," and then hung up, anticipating what she had ahead of her.

Still reeling from her emotions, Khloe busied herself by thumbing through magazines, purchasing more holiday decorations and gifts for the store's inventory, and paying bills for both her store and herself. While watching *The Young and the Restless*, she felt restless herself, making notes for Millicent's wedding and anticipating Derek's call.

It wasn't until the six o'clock evening news was starting that Khloe realized it was so late. "Whew," she said, taking a breath and closing

Millicent's folder, feeling overwhelmed but prepared for the meeting the following morning, hoping she hadn't changed her mind since they last spoke. Having had not eaten all day, famished, she headed for the kitchen and decided to make something easy—spaghetti with a lemon-butter sauce. As she ate at her dining room table, she decided to call and check in with her parents.

"Hello?" answered Linda. At the comforting sound of her mother's voice, Khloe broke down and started crying. "Khloe, what's wrong. Are you hurt?"

As if her mother could see her, Khloe shook her head no. "I messed up big, Mom," she began, and then told her mother about what happened since she'd last told her about Derek, and how she'd managed to screw it all up, no longer caring what her mother would think of him, even if they were to get back together. Right now, she just needed comfort from her mom. "He's supposed to call tonight, but who knows if that will happen."

"Oh, sweetie, I'm so sorry, but you're doing the right thing by following your heart. Do you need me to come for a visit? Just say so, and I'll put the pilot on notice."

Khloe rolled her eyes, amazed at how her mother could always find a way to mention that they had a private jet. "Thanks, Mom, but I think I'll be okay. It just hurts, you know?"

"I do, honey, but when he does call, tell him how you feel and don't leave anything out. You don't want to regret not telling him anything." Khloe knew she was referring to her parents' dating years, when Linda and Kyle got into a disagreement, but after her mother confessed to kissing another man, which was her way of saying a final goodbye to him, knowning she wanted to be with Kyle for the rest of her life—they ended up with their happily ever after.

"I just don't want to disappoint you," Khloe told her mother. "I know how desperate you are that I—"

"Khloe, I know it seems like I'm desperate for you to find a man and to give me and your father grandchildren, but what we really want is for you to be happy, so please don't put any pressure on yourself thinking you have to be with someone to make us happy. We want you to find someone who makes *you* happy."

Khloe reached for her napkin and dabbed her eyes. "Thanks, Mom. I love you."

"I love you, too, Khloe, and if you change your mind, I'll be on the jet the second you tell me you need me there."

Khloe laughed. "I will. Be sure to tell Dad I said hello, and that I'm thinking about him."

"He's out with his golf buddies again, but I will when he gets home. Khloe, sweetie, never forget how much I love you," she heard her mother say before they hung up.

Though her mother was overbearing and meddled in Khloe's love life, she felt better after talking to her. *Everything will be okay*, she told herself, plugging in her cell phone to its charger. She looked down at her plate of uneaten pasta and shook her head, realizing she was too tired to eat. It had been a long couple of days, and she thought it would be best to get her rest because she didn't want to get sick during the holiday season. After sloppily placing her dinner in a plastic container and storing it in the fridge, she headed to her bedroom.

After changing into her pajamas and climbing into bed, she still hadn't heard from Derek, and there was nothing else to do but try to sleep. She turned off the lights, doing the best she could to convince herself she needed sleep more than she needed to hear from Derek. Thirty minutes later, just as Khloe drifted into a soft slumber her phone rang, and with a racing heart, she sat up and reached for her phone. "Hello?"

"Hey, it's me," Derek said in a slow and quiet voice.

"Hey, you," she said, not quite sure how to start their conversation. Apparently, neither did Derek, as indicated by his long pause on the other end of the line. Finally, Khloe took the lead. "Derek, I'm really sorry about everything. I realize now you were only trying to protect Savannah."

"And I should've at least given you the chance to be trusted."

"Please, don't worry about that…it was my own insecurities. So, where do we go from here?" she asked in a timid voice, assuming the worst.

He sighed. "I'd love to see you. Maybe tomorrow you could come by my office? Say four o'clock?"

She smiled, thinking this might be the step they needed to repair what was broken between them. "I'll be there," she said, closing her eyes, feeling grateful to have the chance to see him. "Oh, and Derek?"

"Yes?"

She hesitated, but only for a moment, wanting to tell him how she felt. "I miss you."

"I miss you too, Khloe," he said, then the line went dead.

That night, as tired as Khloe was, all that ran through her head was every possible scenario about the following day. Shortly after two o'clock in the morning, Khloe drifted off to sleep, dreaming of Derek.

CHAPTER THIRTY-TWO

Gabby

Gabby looked down at the cornucopia she'd picked up at Khloe's Flower Shop as she and Harry walked up the steps where Jules, Jeff, and Andrew lived. "I hope they like this arrangement," she said, glancing up at the two-story stone house, which wasn't small, but it wasn't too large, either. On each side of the yard were two massive trees, both of which had swings hanging from their trunks. Along the pathway were vibrant-colored flowers that created a homey feel, and Gabby immediately fell in love with the exterior of the house, picturing Andrew playing soccer in the front yard with the neighborhood kids.

"Darling, Jeff and Jules will love it," Harry said, assuring her and kissing her cheek. "Now come, it's getting cold out here." He gave her backside a little push along the path to the front door, and just as he did, Andrew zoomed out the door toward them.

"Grandpa! Gabby!" he yelled as he leaped into Harry's arms.

"Happy Thanksgiving," Harry said to Andrew, giving him a hug.

"You too, Grandpa." Andrew looked at Gabby. "Happy Thanksgiving, Gabby," he said. He stretched his arms out as far as he could, and put them around her neck.

"Happy Thanksgiving to you, too," she replied, ruffling his hair and trying to balance the heavy arrangement in one hand.

Once Harry put Andrew down, Andrew held out his hand to Gabby. "Come on, I think my mom's punkin pie is almost finished," he said and tugged at her arm.

"Then, let's go," she said, allowing Andrew to pull her into the house, laughing to herself at the adorable way he said "pumpkin." Seeing that the arrangement was wobbling, Harry took it from her, and then she gave him a smile and a wink, then away they went, with Harry following behind them.

"Oh, yay, you're here," Jules said, coming around the counter to hug them.

"Hi," she said, observing the impressive buffet of food. From green bean and squash casseroles, stuffing, three different kinds of rolls, and cherry cream, pecan, and pumpkin pies were scattered around the kitchen, it all looked delicious, and Gabby could hardly wait to eat.

Jeff looked up from carving the turkey and waved. "Happy Thanksgiving, guys." He proceeded to place slices on a large silver platter.

Harry handed Jules the cornucopia. "This is just a little something for you and your family," Gabby said. "Thank you for inviting me, especially today. It means a lot to me." The thought of it being her first Thanksgiving without Charlie weighed on her heart, but she was thankful to be with Harry and his family.

"And it won't be the last," Harry said, sneaking up behind her and giving her a soft kiss on her cheek.

"Really? How do you know that?" she asked, turning around with a sly grin.

"I have a way of knowing things." He gave her a pat on her shoulder and then followed Jeff, who was now carrying the large silver platter of turkey into the dining room.

"What can I do to help?" Gabby asked, then proceeded to help Jules select the wine, a red and a white.

"We have more bottles in our wine fridge at the bar," Jules commented. "After all, it is the holiday season—a time for celebrations. However, I'm sticking to water this year." After they shared a look, Jules quickly added, "I'll just get so tired after all the food, and wine doesn't help."

Gabby laughed. "Yes, indeed, it's definitely a celebration," she said, just as Andrew ran into the kitchen, sensing there was more to Jules's story.

"Mom, is it time to eat yet? I'm starving! I haven't had anything since breakfast," he said.

Jules laughed and nodded. "Yes, honey, it's time." She reached for a basket of rolls. "Here, take these to the table. Gabby and I will be right behind you."

"Yay!" squealed Andrew, as he took the basket and ran into the dining room, and the women laughed.

"Jules, I must say, he's absolutely adorable," she said and noticed Jules swallow hard. "Children that age are so much fun." Something about the sorrowful expression on her face made Gabby wonder if she'd said the wrong thing. "I'm sorry if I said something I shouldn't have…"

Jules held up a hand, then shook her head. "No, you didn't say anything wrong at all, Gabby." After clasping her hands together, she finally spoke in a quiet voice. "Andrew was a twin. He had a sister who died at birth."

Instantly, Gabby's heart broke for the family, but especially Jules. "Oh, Jules, I'm so sorry," she said, placing her hand over her heart.

Jules gave Gabby a weak smile. "It's okay. You had no way of knowing. We had a bedroom for her, too. I decorated it purple and brown—my favorite colors. I always wanted a little girl, but I guess it wasn't meant to be."

Gabby opened her mouth to reply but was silenced when Jules

suddenly fell into her arms, and Gabby had no choice but to comfort her. Holding Jules close, she rubbed her back, not knowing what to say, trying to calm her down the best way she knew how.

When Jules pulled away from Gabby, she wiped under her eyes and said, "I'm so sorry. I don't know what came over me."

"Dear, it's okay. If you ever need me, I'm here for you." And in the moment, Gabby knew that not only did she feel like part of Harry's family, she wanted to be part of it, too.

"I haven't talked about Lilly in so long—that's what Jeff and I named her—and with the holidays, I just get emotional."

"Your feelings are normal," she replied, thinking of Charlie.

Moments later, Jeff stepped in the kitchen and noticed Jules's puffy red eyes. "Honey, are you okay?" he asked, rushing to her side.

She nodded, letting him take her into his arms. "Yeah, I'm good." She kissed him on his cheek.

"I'm going to leave you two alone for a bit," Gabby said. She walked into the dining room and took a seat next to Harry.

"Everything okay?" he asked with a tilt of his head.

"Yes, couldn't be better," she said, patting his arm just as Jules and Jeff came into the room, carrying the two bottles of wine.

After the blessing was said, they all raised their beverages to toast the Thanksgiving holiday.

"Cheers," said Andrew, raising his cup of milk as high as it could go, and then he quickly started eating what Jules had put on his plate.

After Gabby took a bite of the savory squash casserole that Jules had made, she looked around the table. Jules, Jeff, and Harry were laughing, and Andrew was chomping away. Watching the way they all interacted, and how they welcomed her into their lives, made Gabby more thankful than ever. Even though the love of her life might have died, she'd found a new love in Harry, and just the thought of it made her heart melt. Gabby heard a dinging sound, which took her out of her thoughts. She looked over to see Harry smiling at her, and suddenly, her heart started beating fast, feeling pretty sure she knew what was about to happen, but she didn't try to stop it, nor did she want to.

Harry stood up, scooted his chair away, and then got on one knee beside her. Taking her hand in his, he gave it a gentle kiss and gazed up at her. "Gabby, my darling, we haven't known each other that long, but I know I've found love again." He bowed his head and laughed, then looked back up into her eyes. "I'm so in love with you, and I want to tell and show you how much I love you each day, for the rest of our lives." He reached into his pocket, took out a diamond ring, and held it out to her. "Gabriella, will you marry me?"

Instantly, Gabby's eyes filled with tears, and they were soon running down her face. She cupped Harry's chin. "Oh, Harry—" she began, but was interrupted by the sweet sound of Andrew's voice.

"Grandpa, is Gabby going to be my new grandma?" Andrew asked, and everyone laughed. He got up from his chair and started to walk over to Gabby and Harry, but before he could, Jules reached out, catching him with one arm.

"Come here, buddy," she whispered in his ear, and then put her finger over her lips. "Shh, let's just watch."

"Okay, Mommy," Andrew whispered back.

Even with Andrew's little interruption, Gabby's eyes hadn't left Harry's. She was truly in love again and didn't want to let it slip away. She pressed her lips to his, and then finally, she nodded. "I love you, too, Harry, so very much, and yes, I will marry you." Boisterous cheers rose from everyone as Harry slid the engagement ring on her finger. She couldn't have imagined anything more perfect as she looked down at the silver antique band and noticed the round cut diamond was small and dainty, which made for a perfect fit for her delicate hands.

"I look forward to spending the rest of our lives together, Gabby," Harry said, pressing his lips to hers.

"I feel the same way," she replied, as she thought about their past, present, and what their future would be like, which was something Gabby didn't want to miss for anything in the world. She knew her life with Harry wouldn't be like it had been with Charlie, and she was okay with that, because she had a new life.

She felt a little finger tap her on the shoulder, stirring her out of her thoughts, and turned to find Andrew smiling up at her. "Congratulations, Gabby," he said and he jumped into her lap.

"Thank you, Andrew," she said, kissing him on the top of his head.

"*Now*," he began, "does this mean you'll be my new grandma?"

She looked at Harry, who had a twinkle in his eye, and then back at Andrew. "It does, Andrew. Are you okay with that?"

Very eagerly, Andrew nodded. "Yes, and I can't wait to go back to school next week and tell my friends," he said, and everyone burst into laughter.

CHAPTER THIRTY-THREE

Connie

Having spent Thanksgiving alone, Connie continued focusing on herself and her diet, and planned to shop for new clothes the following day. Of course, now that she realized it was a bad choice, thanks to it being Black Friday, with lengthly checkout lines. Since her interview was set for the following Monday, she was determined to find somoething presentable to wear, a task she desperately hated.

As she strolled through a department store at the local indoor mall, she tried on numerous business suits, along with more skirts and tops than she could imagine, but nothing looked good on her. Even now, wearing a gray skirt and white dress shirt, she stared at herself in the three-way mirror. She'd been on her diet for over a week—without having had cheated once—yet she felt like she still looked like a blob of ugliness.

"Knock, knock," said the saleswoman, tapping on the door of Connie's dressing room. "How's everything going?" she asked, but before Connie could answer, the woman had opened the door.

"Just fine," she said, hoping this would satisfy the British-speaking woman, whose name tag read *Arabelle*, and Connie instantly tried to cover her body with her hands and arms, reprimanding herself for not remembering to lock the door to the dressing room.

Arabelle shook her head. "No, it's certainly not, but I think I have something that might work for you," she said, snapping her fingers and then rushed out of the room.

"I have to get out of here," Connie whispered to herself. She quickly continued to undress, put back on the clothes she'd worn that morning, reached for the black pantsuit (the only thing she tried on that looked, at the very least, somewhat suitable), and ran out of the dressing room, hoping she wouldn't be caught. She tried to find an open register, but she was out of luck. Just as she turned, she spotted Arabelle holding what could pass for as a beige onesie for adults.

"Ah, there you are," Arabelle said to Connie as she grabbed her arm and proceeded to drag her back to the dressing room. "This will solve all your problems."

"I think I'm just going to take this," Connie said, holding up the black pantsuit and jerking herself out of Arabelle's grasp.

"Miss," began Arabelle, this time in a forceful tone. "Please, try this on." She took the pantsuit from Connie's hand, only to replace it with the hideous beige contraption.

Fine, Connie thought. "Okay. What is this anyway?" she asked, scrunching her forehead.

"Spanx!" Arabelle exclaimed with a bright grin. "Just be sure you put on the open bust body suit the correct way." She showed Connie where the low cut went, and without another word, pushed Connie back into the dressing room and forcefully closing the door behind her, leaving her alone in the room with the ugliest piece of clothing she'd ever seen.

She leaned against the dressing room wall, watching the seconds pass on her watch. There was no way she was trying that thing on. After five minutes, Connie walked out with the Spanx and headed to the only counter she found, the one Arabelle was working.

"Next," she said as Connie walked up.

"I'm taking the pantsuit, but I will not be needing this." She then draped the Spanx over the edge of the counter, where it almost fell on the floor, but Arabelle caught it.

"No, miss," she said, quickly shaking her head. "You," she said, wiggling her finger, "*need* these. They help smooth out certain…parts."

That last comment came close to bringing Connie to tears. What the hell was so special about these Spanx? "Fine!" She pulled out her credit card, praying that the extra purchase wouldn't break the bank.

Minutes later, Connie zoomed out the mall's door as Arabelle called out, "Good luck with the Spanx!"

*****

That night, after taking another long walk around her neighborhood, Connie sat down at her dining room table, an ahi tuna salad in front of her, and looked through the large document that Eve had sent her about the company. Eve's Marketing Group was a women-only company, made up of eight employees, including Eve, and Connie was determined to make friends with at least one of them.

Connie had to admit there was something about working with all women that made her apprehensive. At her last job, the spiteful women she used to work with, Connie always hoped they didn't meant to be mean, but rather they were bullied and persuaded by Nicola to treat her like the ugly duckling she always thought she was. Shaking her head, Connie decided to put that negative thinking aside and spend more time thinking positively. "I will get this job, and I will be liked," she thought to herself. Smiling, already feeling positive, Connie she whispered, "Love yourself first and everything else falls into line," her favorite quote from Lucille Ball.

By the time Connie got ready for bed, she was a ball of excited nerves. While it was only an interview, she had a good feeling about it. After washing her face, the scale in her bathroom caught her eye. She knew getting on the scale before bed was probably something she shouldn't do because it could possibly lower her self-esteem (she needed all she could get for her interview), but she couldn't help it. After all, the scale was right there, practically challenging her. "Step on me, step on me, step on me." She took off her clothes and slowly crept onto the scale. Cringing, she looked down, seeing she'd lost five pounds.

After she leaped off the scale and did a happy dance into her bedroom, Connie pulled out a brown nightgown from her dresser and pulled it over her body, feeling proud of herself—so much so that she wanted to share the news with someone. Without thinking she reached for her phone, but when she was set to dial, she slumped down on her bed, saddened by the thought that she had no family, friends, or anyone she could talk to. The only person she wanted to share the good news with was Walt, but if she called him, she was pretty certain he wouldn't pick up. Connie brushed away a tear, willing herself not to cry, and forced herself to go to bed before she made another mistake, like dialing Walt's number.

CHAPTER THIRTY-FOUR

Khloe

"So, today's the big day, huh?" Sharon commented. "How are you feeling?"

"I'm okay, but I can't help but be a little nervous," Khloe admitted. "I just want everything to work out, so I'm trying not to get ahead of myself." She lifted her shoulders, adding, "We'll see."

"All you can do is hope for the best," Sharon replied.

"Uh huh." She nodded and they shared a hopeful grin before Khloe headed back to her office, not really into having any sort of conversation about Derek. She plopped down in her chair and ran her hands through her hair. Anxious and exhausted, she knew she should rest before seeing Derek because she didn't want to come off as cranky, which she was known to be when running on little sleep. *Just for a moment,* she told herself as she leaned back and closed her eyes. Within a matter of minutes, she'd drifted off, imagining herself with Derek in Bora Bora, sipping on champagne as they bathed under the bright sun, and at night, making love until the sun came up.

"Khloe. Khloe!" she heard Sharon say, standing in her doorway.

Jolting herself out of her exotic dream, she opened her eyes and turned to Sharon. "Yeah, what is it?" She looked at the clock on her computer, realizing how long she'd slept. *Crap!*

"You have a phone call," she said, sounding unlike her usual self.

"Who is it?" Khloe asked, spinning around and straightening herself in her chair.

"It's um…" she began, and then in one quick breath said, "Josh."

At the sound of his name, knots formed in Khloe's stomach and throat, and she felt her mouth turn dry. A million reasons as to why he'd be calling her ran through her head, but after all the time they'd been apart, she couldn't pinpoint one. "Did he say what he wants?"

Sharon shook her head. "No, but I can take a message, or, hell, I'll even handle it for you." Her lips turned up in a grin.

Khloe shook her head and let out a slight chuckle remembering how Sharon and Josh had never gotten along, and her dislike for him grew after finding out about his being unfaithful to Khloe. "I'll take care of it."

"You're the boss," she said, lifting her hands in the air, and then spun around to go back to the front of the shop.

"Well, well, well, this is certainly a surprise," Khloe said to Josh, after picking up the phone's wireless receiver.

"Hey, darlin'," he said. "Long time no talk. How are you?"

She rolled her eyes at his deep southern accent and how he called her "darlin'." "I'm great, and you?" *Not that I give a damn*, she almost added but bit her tongue.

"I'm glad to hear you're doin' well. Anyway, I'm callin' you because I'm gettin' married, and I thought who better to help with the flowers than you," he said, and then chuckled with delight. "After all, you're the best woman in the business."

Josh's getting married! After it took a moment to sink in that her low-life, cheating ex-boyfriend was engaged, she asked, "Who's the, um…lucky lady?" using the *lucky* term loosely. Quickly, she scribbled on a notepad, tore it off, and then ran into the front of the shop to hold it up to Sharon's face.

After reading the message that Josh was engaged and wanted Khloe's business, Sharon's eyes bugged out, and then she mouthed, "What the hell?"

In agreement, Khloe nodded, and continued listening to Josh talk about his fiancée as she walked back into her office.

"Anyway, that's when I told Eunice I'd be more than happy to handle the flowers."

"And, let me guess, she doesn't even know about our past?" Khloe asked, guessing that Josh hadn't changed a bit.

Josh roared with laughter. "Oh, Khlo-bear, you know me so well." He sighed, before saying, "Look, Khloe, I know I wasn't the best boyfriend, but I'm really sorry."

Nothing about his tone or words were sincere, and Khloe knew it. She'd heard enough, and just talking to a scumbag like Josh, even for what had been only a few minutes, was making her miserable. "Josh, I sincerely appreciate you coming to me for help with your wedding, but I will *not* be creating your wedding flowers. I wish your fiancée the best of luck for putting up with a scumbag like you for the rest of her life. As for yourself, I sincerely hope you go to hell. Have a good day!" She slammed the phone down, hardly believing what just happened. "Take that, asshole," she mumbled, looking at the clock. *Shit!* Khloe brushed on lip gloss, grabbed her purse, and rushed to the front of her store, only to stand by Sharon as she finished with a customer. "Hey, I gotta go," she told her. "I'll call you later." She took two steps before she heard Sharon call after her.

"Wait, what happened with Josh?" Sharon asked.

Khloe turned around and gave her friend a wide grin. "Oh, him? Well, it turns out he's still the same asshole he always was." She gave a quick wave and then headed out the door, doing her best not to be slightly jealous that her ex was engaged, because, at the moment, she had more pressing matters to worry about.

CHAPTER THIRTY-FIVE

Gabby

"Champagne, my darling?" Harry asked, handing a glass to Gabby. After celebrating Thanksgiving and their engagement with Jeff, Jules, and Andrew, they went back to Gabby's house and popped open a bottle to continue the evening.

"Thank you," she said, taking it from him and bringing the bubbly liquid to her lips. "Oh, this is so good."

Harry pressed a button on his phone and seconds later, Frank Sinatra's voice echoed from the dock where his phone was charging. He took a seat next to her on the couch. "I agree," he said, placing an arm around his fiancée. "You know, Gabby, I was nervous about proposing today. I know we both agreed to take things slow, and I didn't want to scare you off, but I know I didn't want to lose you."

Gabby caressed his cheeks and shook her head. "You never will. I've fallen in love with you, Harry, and I can't wait to marry you. Now, all we have to do is start thinking of a date." She couldn't believe the words were coming out of her mouth so easily, but they were real.

"Okay, then how about a Christmas Eve wedding?"

Gabby laughed, but then realized that Harry wasn't joking. "Harry, that's too soon. How on earth will I plan a wedding in three weeks? It's just not possible."

"Well, I happen to know this wonderful party planner. You might know her…um, what's her name? Oh, yes, Jules," he teased her. "Remember, before we left, she said she'd love to help us with anything we need."

"I know. I just don't want to bother her. I mean, a wedding is a big deal. She shouldn't be working, especially during the holidays." Gabby couldn't help but remember what Jules had revealed to her earlier. "Also, Harry, Jules told me about Lilly." When he didn't respond, she looked at him and saw that he was staring off into the distance. "Do you want to talk about it?" she asked, taking his hand in hers.

"I always wanted a granddaughter, Gabby. I dreamed of us sharing ice cream together, playing dolls, and introducing her to good music, like the Rat Pack," he said with a chuckle. "When I heard that she didn't survive my heart broke, but I had my grandson, so I decided to put all my heart and soul into loving him. I guess that's one reason we're so close, but the truth is, I think about her all the time. I have a granddaughter, too, she's just not here." He paused for a moment to catch his breath, adding, "I know it sounds silly," as his eyes welled up with tears, "but I think of her as my guardian angel."

Gabby reached for a tissue and handed it to him. "Harry, that's not silly at all. Actually, I find that very heartwarming." She put her hand on the back of his neck. "I love your family, and if Lilly were anything like Andrew, then I know she'd be the most beautiful little girl in the world, inside and out, because she's part of your family."

"I think you mean part of *our* family," he said, tapping the tip of her nose.

Gabby sighed happily and nodded. "Yes, part of *our* family." After a few moments of silence, Gabby looked at Harry. "Okay, a Christmas Eve wedding it is," she said, kissing him as she sealed the date for her second wedding with the second love of her life.

*****

The next morning, Gabby woke up and a strange but happy feeling rushed over her. *I'm engaged!* Grinning, she held up her hand, the glistening shimmer of the diamond on her finger catching the light and sparkling around the room. It was stunning and she was in awe of it, but it wasn't the ring that mattered to her, it was the man who gave it to her. Then, it hit her. *I need to tell the girls in my Scrabble group.* She was about to get out of bed but stopped when she saw Harry.

"Good morning, my love," said Harry, walking into her bedroom and holding two coffee mugs. He placed them down on her nightstand, took a seat on the bed next to her, and kissed her. "How did you sleep?"

"With you next to me, wonderful," she told him, toying with her engagement ring. She looked at it again. "I still can't believe we're getting married—and on Christmas Eve!" Gabby sat up and adjusted her pillows.

"You'd better get started on planning, and if you want, I'll be right there to help you."

"Thank you, darling." She took a sip of coffee and eyed him, observing his white sneakers, white socks, and red tracksuit. "By the way, you're dressed snazzy this morning."

"Well, I went for a quick run back to my place to get a few things, took a shower, and now I'm here with you."

"Speaking of your place, we really haven't talked about the whole living situation. Do you move in here? Do I move in with you—what should we do?" she mused, looking to Harry for answers, taking another sip.

"Actually, I was thinking about that earlier and I was wondering if you'd like to go look at houses?" he suggested, but when he saw

Gabby's eyes widen, he added, "But we can stay here, too. I just want you to be comfortable, and be anywhere with you."

Gabby wasn't offended by Harry's offer to go look at houses, but after Charlie died, it never occurred to Gabby to ever move out of the house they'd built a life together in. While she'd made her peace with Charlie at the cemetery, she knew it wouldn't be fair to Harry, and part of her would always think of it as her and Charlie's house, and not their house. With a heavy heart, Gabby did the only thing that she thought was right, because if the roles were reversed, she'd feel like a third wheel who was living in someone else's home, even if she was now married to the deceased wife's husband, and said, "I want to start fresh with you, Harry, so I think that looking at houses is a great idea."

He lifted his head in surprise and widened his eyes. "Really?"

Gabby set her coffee on the nightstand and reached for Harry. "I want to grow old with you, but I want to do that in *our* home."

"I like how you think," he said, kissing her.

"Good, now take off that tracksuit."

CHAPTER THIRTY-SIX

Connie

Connie woke up earlier than she expected on the day of the interview. Since she'd be meeting with Eve over lunch, she took her time making breakfast—a spinach and feta egg white omelet, something she was beginning to look forward to each morning—and sipped on her coffee. While she ate, she took another look through the document Eve sent her, preparing herself for any questions that might arise. By ten she'd had three cups of coffee, her brain was full of knowledge of Eve's Marketing Group, and it was time to get ready for the interview.

Connie shaved her legs (something she hadn't done since the last time she'd slept with Walt), waxed her lip, shaped her eyebrows, curled her hair, and carefully applied makeup. The night before she'd laid out her black pantsuit and a red top to go under it. However, that morning, she changed her mind. She wanted to wear a skirt, and she raided her closet, searching for the perfect thing. When she stumbled upon a green skirt that had always been snug, she considered trying it on, hoping that with the weight she'd lost she'd be able to fit in it, and then reached for a white dress shirt. Unfortunately, the ensemble had looked better in her head. That's when she remembered the Spanx. She dashed to the entryway where she'd left it still in the bag. When she pulled out the receipt, she was surprised to see that Arabelle hadn't charged her for it. Confused, she turned it over and found there was a message to her: *I was like you when I was younger and thought I would give you just a little help to get you through your journey in life. Arabelle.*

That woman knows nothing about me, Connie thought, as she crumpled up the receipt, threw it in the trash, and carried the Spanx back to her room. Leaning against her bed, she observed it up and down, front to back, before she placed one foot in the small hole, and then repeated the process with the other foot. As the material tightened its grip, almost suffocating Connie's leg, she she wished they were a little more stretchable. With all her might, she tugged, pulled, and inched her body into the suit, but nothing worked. Determined not to give up, she not-so-gracefully tumbled onto the floor, hoping that maybe it would help if she were lying down. After ten minutes of grunting, pulling, and doing everything she could to get the Spanx up to her waist, then past her stomach, she finally hooked the straps around her shoulders. She stared up at the ceiling, catching her breath, while wondering how famous actresses suffered this torture every single day. That's when Connie realized that she'd somehow ended up on the other side of her room. With a sigh, Connie noticed she'd flopped around her room like a fish out of water, then managed to stand to look at herself in the mirror.

"Fucking great," she said to herself, noticing she'd put the repulsive bodysuit on backward. Connie looked at the clock and saw she had spent most of her time shimmying herself into a contraption that was way too tight for her, and she would be late if she took the thing off, only to attempt to put it on again. To hell with it. She could deal with wearing it for a few hours. Besides, nobody would see her in it, so nobody would know if it were on backward or not. Once she'd put on the skirt and dress top, she slid on black flats and looked at herself in the mirror. "Holy crap," she said, putting her hand to her lips, amazed at the person she saw staring back. Thanks to the Spanx, Connie looked ten pounds lighter, and she had curves—and she observed with excitement that they were in all the right places. Connie could have spent more time ogling herself, but if she did that, she'd be late to her interview. With one last glance, she thought, *Thank you very much, Arabelle.*

*****

"Hello, I'm here to meet Eve Vanguard," Connie informed the hostess at the modest downtown restaurant.

"Please follow me," she said, giving Connie a bright smile.

As Connie trailed behind the woman, she began to give herself a pep talk. *You can do this!*

"Here you go," said the hostess, extending an arm to the booth, then quickly walked away.

Connie looked took a seat across from a woman whose hair was straight, eyes were hunter green, and bright red lips were turned up in a smile. "Hello, I'm Connie Albright," she said, stretching out her hand.

"Hi, Connie. I'm Eve Vanguard. It's a pleasure to meet you." Eve reached for a folder that lay on the table in front of her, pulled out a few pieces of paper, and straightened herself in the booth as a waiter took Connie's drink order. "As we discussed on the phone, you've been working in the medical business for a while, but besides graduating with a marketing degree, do you have any previous experience, even the smallest little bit?"

"While I still worked in the medical industry, in college I interned at four marketing companies on the weekend and during the summers."

"Wonderful," replied Eve as she made a checkmark on the paper.

"Now, have you had a chance to look over the document I sent you?"

Connie nodded. "Yes, over and over." She laughed nervously. "You could quiz me if you'd like," she added, hoping Eve knew she was joking, glad the waiter just placed her tea in front of her, at that exact moment, then she took a sip.

Eve laughed. "There will be no quizzes during the interview, so there's no need to worry. Tell me, are you a people person, and how do you get along with other females?"

On second thought, I'd rather be quizzed, Connie thought, trying to decide how to answer Eve. She took another sip of her tea, trying to find the right words to say. "I'd like to think that I work well with people and create impressive outcomes for whatever the task might be. While I didn't work with a lot of people at my last job, I'm a hard worker, a go-getter, and a person who will step up and lead any business ventures that come my way. Since I'm single my nights are free, which gives me the opportunity to focus on my job." She paused and took a breath before answering the second part of Eve's question. "As for working solely with women, I find it intimidating, only because I'm often judged by my appearance." She looked down at herself, then back up to Eve. "I know I'm not beautiful, but I am smart, and I prefer staying out of office gossip, and out of the way of catty women who are in it for themselves." She thought about retracting the last sentence, but it was the truth, and she didn't want to hide who the real Connie was anymore. "I hope you can respect that." Anxious to see how Eve would respond, Connie nervously chewed on her straw, then locked eyes with Eve, who was staring at her with a wide grin.

"I'm very impressed with you, Connie," she said, as she pointed a finger at her and picked up her menu. "How about let's order lunch, and then we'll keep on talking?"

"Sounds great!" Hearing Eve say that Connie had impressed her was way more than she could have ever expected from a possible boss, and a nice change. Connie followed suit by picking up her menu, but in her mind, she was jumping for joy. *Now, it's time to focus on what to order!* As she scanned the menu, she realized it was the first time she'd eaten out since the start of her diet. While Connie used to be one who celebrated the tiniest things with either an afternoon cheeseburger or large bowl of pasta, it was time for her to learn how to dine out and still be healthy. While it was tempting to order something that was filled with scrumptious calories, Connie settled for the grilled chicken with black beans and a side of salsa. *Protein, protein, protein!* All good choices, she knew, as she handed the menu to the waiter.

"I'm sorry. I never eat like this," Eve told Connie, after ordering a bacon cheeseburger with extra fries. She rubbed her stomach. "Being five months pregnant does crazy things to a woman," she said and they both laughed. Looking at Eve, Connie wouldn't have ever guessed Eve was pregnant.

"Congratulations, and believe me, I'd much rather prefer the burger," replied Connie, then they shared a laugh.

"Now, where were we?" Eve asked, placing her arms on the table, once they quieted down. "Oh, yes, you were impressing me," she said as she tapped the pen on the paper. "Now, I'm going to give you a few marketing scenarios, and I'd like to hear your strategies, opinions, and thoughts."

"Great, let's get started," said Connie eagerly, hoping to wow Eve. And that's just what she was doing when she spotted Walt rise from his chair and wrap his arm around a stunning, older brunette, which made Connie stop talking mid-sentence. Some might even say the woman with Walt could pass as Jane Seymour's double, in her bright red flowy dress which emphasized the tiniest waist Connie had ever seen. Connie's body went numb, her eyes began to water, and her heart beat quickly as she watched Walt escort the woman out of the restaurant. While Connie hadn't been ready to confront him at the gym, she knew it was now or never. "I'm sorry...I have to go do something, but I'll be right back," she promised, giving Eve a pleading glance, making sure to keep one eye on Walt and the model-looking woman he was with.

With tight lips, Eve nodded, raising a hand. "Uh, sure. Whatever you need—"

Before Eve could finish her sentence, Connie bolted out of her seat, leaving her jacket and purse at the table, and ran out of the restaurant.

When she finally spotted him outside, he was starting to get in a black town car. "Walt!" she yelled and ran as fast as she could toward him. "Walt!" she yelled again, this time now only a few feet away. He and the woman he was with turned around as Connie tried to steady her breath. "Hi," was all she could say.

"Would you give us a second?" he asked the woman.

"Of course, honey," she said, patting his shoulder, and then, to Connie's surprise she gave her a genuine smile.

After the woman got in the car and the door was shut, Walt turned back to Connie. "What do you want?"

As pedestrians bustled around them, Connie looked at Walt, who was more handsome than she remembered, and she'd give anything to plant her lips on his. She opened her mouth and was about to apologize again, beg him to let her explain why she'd lied to him, but instead she simply said, "I just wanted to tell you...well, it's good to see you, Walt." He looked happy, and if he was happy with Miss Red Dress, Connie didn't want to ruin it for him, because he deserved the best.

Walt nodded and flashed Connie a charming smile—one that made her melt like chocolate ice cream on a hot Texas summer day.

"You, too," he said. He opened his mouth to say something more, but with a sigh, he opened the car door and got in, leaving Connie standing there to watch it drive away, with the man she loved inside.

Doing everything she could not to cry, Connie sauntered back to the restaurant. Feeling bile about to rise in her throat over seeing Walt with someone else and running out of the interview of a marketing job she desperately needed and wanted was too much for her to handle. She just had to get through the next five minutes, then she could go home and try to forget this day ever happened.

"Connie, are you okay?" asked Eve in a motherly tone, reaching her hand out to Connie when she made her way back to the table.

Connie didn't bother to sit down. She put on her jacket and grabbed her purse. Ashamed of herself and the way she acted, she finally looked at Eve, who was also standing now. "I'm sorry about running out on you," Connie began. "As for the job, while I would love to work for you, I understand that I probably ruined it." She blinked back tears. *Unfortunately, my life is a complete mess and I deserve nothing*, she wanted to add, but decided against it.

"Thank you for your honesty, Connie. I have a few other people to interview, but I'll be calling you within a few days—a week at the most—to let you know about the job."

With a simple nod, Connie replied with, "Thank you for your time," and then walked out of the restaurant, willing herself not to cry until she was in her car.

CHAPTER THIRTY-SEVEN

Khloe

Of all days, why today? With a stressed sigh, Khloe rested her forehead on the steering wheel and then glanced back at the expressway, which had become a parking lot. Khloe could see Derek's high-rise office building but knew it was miles and miles ahead, and that she was going to be late. There was nothing she could do while she sat in congested traffic, so she leaned her head aginst her seat and strummed her fingers anxiously on her pant leg. After about ten minutes, Khloe slowly accelerated past a construction worker who was holding up a sign to let traffic continue, and in an instant, Khloe was back on the open road.

When she finally arrived, she raced to the suite of Thomas and Associates, thankful that his office was on the main floor. Taking a quick second to collect herself, she ran a hand through her hair and smoothed her sweater. *Now I'm ready,* she thought, opening the door.

"Hello, dear," Mary said, sounding as sweet as sugar, and not the least bit surprised to see Khloe.

"Hi, Mary." She smiled, sensing that by Mary's fluttering eyelids, she knew why Khloe was there to see Derek.

"You can go on back," she said, pointing to Derek's office. "He's been waiting for you."

"Thank you," Khloe said, taking a few hesitant, but excited steps.

"You know, I'm still pulling for you two," Mary called after her and gave Khloe a wink as she reached for the ringing phone. "Thomas and Associates, how may I help you?"

Khloe walked to the dark wood door that had a decorative but masculine-looking handle and a plate with Derek's name written in gold. Her heart raced and her mouth was dry as she chewed on her bottom lip. The door was open and she could see him in his charcoal-colored dress pants and forest green sweater. He was an exquisite sight. Finally, like ripping off a Band-Aid, Khloe announced her arrival by knocking. "Hi, Derek," she said, almost in a whisper. They locked eyes, but no words were spoken. Khloe couldn't tell if he was staring or glaring at her, waiting for him to make the next move.

"Please, come in and take a seat." His tone was professional, almost as if their meeting were about business, and suddenly, Khloe's heart began to race, thinking that the outcome of their talk wouldn't be good. In two quick strides, Derek walked past her and peeped his head out the door. "Mary, please hold all my calls." He closed the door, then turned toward Khloe, and in a gentler tone, said, "It's nice to see you," then took a seat in a chair next to the couch where she sat.

"You, too," she replied, clasping her hands, which already felt clammy.

Derek rested his elbows on his knees and leaned in. "Khloe, there's no easy way to start this conversation, so—"

"Derek, if you don't mind, can I go first?" When Derek nodded, she knew it was time for her to save what could be the best thing that ever happened to her, so she had to give it her all. "Let me start off by saying I'm so deeply sorry…about everything. I should've trusted you, but like I told you from past experiences, I only knew one way to be. I want to wipe the slate clean, because the truth is, I've missed you—I've missed you so damn much." A small tear began to streak down her face, but before she had a chance to wipe it away, Derek held out a tissue to her. "Thanks," she said, giving him a weak grin. She waited for him to reply, but when the only thing she heard was the faint ticking sound on her watch, she couldn't take it anymore. "Like I said, you were only trying to do what was best for Savannah, and I should have respected that. You didn't owe me any kind of explanation, and I should've given you the benefit of the doubt."

He crossed his arms, giving her a stern but steady look. "Khloe, I've had some time to think, too. If the roles were reversed, I'd feel betrayed, too."

"You don't have to say that. Truly, it's an honorable thing you've done, and I'm sure your sister would be proud of you." She dried her eyes before adding, "Congratulations, by the way."

"Thanks, that means a lot to me, but I'm the lucky one." They held a glance, and Khloe felt the room turn into a sauna, and for a moment she didn't know if he was lucky because of Savannah, or her.

"So, what do you say? Can we start over?" she asked him as he stood, taking a seat next to her on the couch. Now they were only inches apart and his erotic cologne tickled her nose, and Khloe couldn't hold back any longer, not bothering to wait for an answer. She pulled his face toward hers and was pleasantly surprised when he didn't try to stop her. Magically, when their lips touched, Khloe felt the room begin to spin, smelling his woodsy cologne, along with the sugary taste of his lips. *God, how I've missed this.* Once they parted, Khloe was left breathless.

"Khloe..." he said, letting out a breath and running a hand through her hair. "Dammit, I missed you so much."

"Oh, Derek—" she began, but with his other finger, he stopped her by pressing the tip of his finger to her lips.

"From the first moment I met you, I knew I wanted to get to

know you, and the few times we've spent together are ones I'll never forget, but when you thought that I hurt you and didn't believe me, well, it hurt me, too." He brushed the back of his hand gently across her cheek. "While most of my time was focused on Savannah, my mind couldn't escape you, and it killed me to not be able to tell you everything when I had to leave town the first time." He slowly pressed his lips to her left cheek. "I can't tell you how much I missed you," he added, and then said, "I often wondered how your day was going." And then he kissed her right one. "I wondered what perfume you were wearing that day, and if it was the same one you had on during our first date." He lifted her head and planted a kiss on her neck, just above her collarbone. Then, when their lips were less than an inch apart, he said, "Khloe?"

"Yes, Derek?" she replied, panting, as she anticipated him again pressing his lips on hers, knowing that she was ready—physically and emotionally—for them to make love.

"Do you like pancakes?" His tone was serious, as if he were in business mode.

"Do I like pancakes?" she repeated, then every erotic thought she'd been feeling went out the window, wondering if this was some kind of trick question.

"Come on, it's simple," he said before repeating the question and flashing her a wide grin. He licked his lips and inched closer to her.

"I love them, but why—"

"Good," Derek said, interrupting her, then pressed his lips to hers, wrapping his hands around her waist as they collapsed onto the couch.

When they came up for air, Khloe beamed at Derek, knowing his body and lips had given her the answer she was hoping for; that they were back together.

"You know, it might seem silly, but I was beyond nervous coming here today," she told him, resting her head against his chest.

"Oh, and why is that?" he asked, after he brushed a strand of her hair out of her face.

"I was afraid we wouldn't be where we are now." She reached for his other hand that lay on her leg and squeezed it. "I want you to know that I promise to believe you from now on—"

"Shh, it's okay," he told her, interrupting her and kissing her forehead. "The past is behind us."

She nodded. "Okay," she said as tears began to roll down her cheeks.

"Hey, what's this about?" Derek asked, wiping them away with the back of his thumb.

"I just missed you, that's all." She kissed him, and then asked, "So, why did you ask me if I like pancakes?"

"Oh, that? Well, I was wondering if you'd like to join me and Savannah for breakfast tomorrow."

She wanted to ask him if it was too soon, but Khloe caught herself. While her first instinct may have been to decline because she didn't want to interfere in the time between Derek and Savannah, she let that all go. If she was going to be in Derek's life, she had to trust him. Derek wasn't only thinking of Savannah, he was thinking of her, too. "I'd love to," she said as he pulled her in for another make-out round.

When Khloe woke up that morning she didn't know how the day would turn out, but everything had gone in her favor, and this time she wouldn't mess it up.

CHAPTER THIRTY-EIGHT

Gabby

Two days after Gabby called the girls in her Scrabble group, telling them that Harry proposed, they insisted on throwing her an engagement celebration. Gabby agreed, but on the conditions that it would be an intimate gathering with just the four of them, and that they wouldn't make it out to be anything over the top. When they obliged to Gabby's requests, she agreed to meet them at the Diva Tea Rose Room at noon for lunch.

"Congratulations," Clara, Wilma, and Fern said in unison when Gabby walked in to the Tea Rose Room and made her way to their table, which was decorated with white and silver confetti, in the shapes of wedding bells that spelled out the words *bride* and *groom*.

Gabby clasped her hands under her chin and smiled at her friends, and suddenly, tears welled in her eyes.

"Oh, Gabby, what's wrong, sweetie?" asked Fern, the first of the three of them to comfort her.

Gabby shook her head, keeping her eyes glued to the table, which was also set up with tea sandwiches, a selection of petit fours on a tiered tray, and a miniature white wedding cake on top. "Nothing, nothing at all. Everything is perfect." She was in awe at the display her friends had managed to put together, and while they probably thought it was nothing to them, to her it meant everything. She shook her head and began thanking her friends, and hugged each one before they all took their seats.

"Champagne for the bride-to-be?" asked a waiter, who promptly came up to her holding a bottle of bubbly.

She lifted her hands in the in air, smiled, and then said, "Why not?" As the champagne was being poured, the words *bride-to-be* rang in her head. It had been years since she'd been one, and she couldn't believe she was about to be one again.

After all the champagne flutes were filled they raised their glasses, and Wilma said, "To Gabby, our best friend. We wish you and Harry a lifetime of happiness and love, and may the two of you live a long and beautiful life together," before clinking their glasses.

"So, Gabby, we know how Harry proposed, but have you two set a date yet?" Clara asked, after they all took a sip.

"Believe it or not, we're getting married on Christmas Eve!" she said with enthusiasm, adding in a slight chuckle.

"But that's, like, soon—very soon," Fern commented, sounding surprised.

"I know, and believe me, I didn't think pulling together a wedding in such a short time would be possible, but Harry's daughter-in-law is a party planner, and we're having a meeting later on in the week to discuss all the details." She looked around the table, adding, "We want our wedding to be a small affair, and while I'm sure all of you might be celebrating the holidays with your own family, you're invited."

The three of them looked at each other with blank faces, and Gabby didn't know what to think. *Are they mad? Did I do something?*

Finally, Fern joyfully announced, "We'll be there!"

This caused Gabby to smile and clap her hands. "Thank you, ladies. Truly, this means so much to me, and I want you all to know how special you are to me." She held out her hand and pointed to the assortment of deliciousness that lay in front of them. "You did so much for me, and I don't know what I'd do without your help through the years."

Wilma put a hand on Gabby's shoulder. "We're beyond happy for you, our friend, and we cannot wait to meet the lucky man."

Gabby smiled. "I'd like to think so," she joked, then added, "but the truth is that I feel I'm the one who's blessed." Again, she felt her eyes brim with tears, so much so that she had to dab them with her napkin. "Okay, now can we dig in before I turn into a ball of mush?"

"Absolutely," said Clara with a laugh.

An hour later, as she watched her friends reach for tea sandwiches and sip on champagne, Gabby sat back in her chair observing them, thinking just how fortunate she was to have friends like them in her life.

CHAPTER THIRTY-NINE

Connie

Connie was still mortified by her behavior during her interview with Eve as she waited to hear back about whether she'd gotten the job or not. In the meantime, she turned her focus to her weight loss, applying for other jobs just in case, and started going back to the gym, this time with a brighter outlook.

After buying a few new items of workout gear so she would feel more confident about achieving her fitness goals, Connie was still managing her diet. She created a plan to eat slowly, avoid carbs, drink more water, and only sip on wine, not guzzle it, and to her surprise, she'd made more progress than she'd expected.

While she had no job (yet) and no boyfriend to come home to, Connie seemed to be getting along just fine—even with the recurring nightmares about seeing Walt with the beautiful woman in the red dress. She knew she needed to move on without him, and even considered trying online dating—this time for real—but she wasn't ready yet. However, Connie had made a pact with herself: on January first, she planned to put herself out there once more and try to find love, determined to not spend the rest of her life alone.

Coming home after a half-jog half-walk, Connie's phone rang.

She looked down at the number and took a breath. With a hard swallow, she answered. "Hello?"

"Hi, Connie, it's Eve. How are you?"

"I'm good. Thank you."

"That's good to hear," Eve replied. "Anyway, I wanted to let you know that the job is yours if you'd still like it. Now, I would need to know by—"

Connie didn't allow Eve to finish her sentence. "Yes, I'll take it!" Though they hadn't discussed her salary, she wanted this job no matter what, even if she had to cut back on her expenses, she was okay with that, because she finally had a job that where she could put her passion to work. She took a seat on her couch, grateful that Eve was giving her a chance. "Thank you, thank you, thank you. You have no idea how happy you've made me."

Eve laughed. "You're very welcome. I'm looking forward to working with you, and so are my other employees." She went on to tell Connie that she wouldn't be able to start until the second week of the year but would like for her to come in the following week, so Eve could introduce her to the rest of the staff and show her around the office.

They talked for a few more minutes about minor details, then they hung up, which led to do Connie a happy dance around her living room—something she was getting used to. Once she stopped, she sighed, not realizing how worn out she was from her workout or the little dance, but for the first time in a long time, Connie had something exciting to look forward to.

After making herself a healthy dinner that night, Connie lay in bed. As excited as she was about starting her job, she couldn't stop thinking of Walt. What if she called him just to say hello? She looked at the clock, seeing it was almost midnight, then guessed he was probably distracted by extra-curricular activities with Miss Red

Dress. She closed her eyes, knowing Walt probably would always be the one who got away, and it was all because of her lies.

She lay in bed, trying her best to drift off to sleep, but she couldn't. Feeling curious, she reached for her laptop on her nightstand and opened it up. After it booted up, she opened a browser and signed into her Facebook account. Scrolling through news and entertainment topics, she took notice that she didn't have any "real" friends on the social media site, and that they were merely acquaintances from high school and college. She remembered back to the excitement when she was flooded with Facebook friend requests, but now Connie was wise enough to know that they probably friended her to follow her non-existant exciting life. It was in that moment that she decided to unfriend all of them. Though, when it came to Walt, who sent her a friend request after their first date, she sighed, weighing her options. Before she made any decision on whether to keep him as a friend on Facebook, she clicked on his profile, and instantly, her jaw dropped. When she saw that his profile picture had changed to the one of them in front of the rose bush, with Connie cropped out, except for a small chunk of her hair resting on his shoulder. Blinking back tears, she couldn't believe it, feeling a wave of emotions. While she loved that picture, remembering that day and the love the made, she was hurt because she knew she'd probably never feel for anyone like she felt for Walt. Then, she took a different take on it, thinking Walt put that picture and cut her out to hurt her, knowing she'd see it. *No, he wouldn't do that,* she thought. "He's not evil like I was to him." When she clicked the picture, wanting to see him better, Connie sank lower into her bed, feeling her broken heart melt even more when she saw it read: "One of the best days of my life."

Finally, after staring at his picture long enough, she knew what she had to do, and clicked the unfriend button. If she couldn't have him in real life, then she didn't want to be able to see him on her Facebook feed. "And that, Buttercup and Tillman, is how fairy tales end."

CHAPTER FORTY

Khloe

As Khloe dressed the next morning, she stumbled around her room, trying to find the perfect thing to wear, while rehashing all the juicy details about her and Derek getting back together, holding her phone up to her ear with her shoulder.

"Oh, Khloe, I'm so happy things worked out for you and Derek, and I still can't wait to meet him."

"Well, he's the complete opposite of Josh, so you'll love him." They shared a laugh. "Anyway, I just wanted to catch you up on everything, and tell you how much I appreciate your friendship. Thanks for sticking by me."

"I wouldn't have it any other way. Now, have a wonderful brunch, and we'll talk later," she whispered. "I'm sneaking into Leonard's apartment, hoping to wake him up in the most fun way possible."

And there's my friend I know and love! Khloe couldn't help but laugh. "Okay, well, good luck with that, and enjoy the TARDIS sex."

"I will. Bye!" With a click, the line went dead.

Settling on dark skinny jeans, an orange sweater and brown knee-high boots, Khloe was a ball of nerves as she drove to Derek's house. Since they'd re-connected, giddiness enveloped her. After Khloe left his office—feeling an overwhelming sense of being hot and bothered—that night, they talked late into the night over the phone, and she put all her worries away when their conversation seemed to flow as easily as it had in the past.

Even though she knew they would be having pancakes, she'd stopped at a grocery store for doughnuts to give to Savannah, along with a bottle of champagne and orange juice so she and Derek could make mimosas.

As she reached for the grocery bags in the backseat of her car, just as Derek's front door opened and he walked out to greet her. His purple T-shirt hugged his body, showing off his chiseled chest muscles, while his jeans gave her a great view of the lower-half of his body. *Damn!*

"Hi," he said, taking her groceries with one hand and placing the other around her waist. "You look beautiful."

Khloe fell into his embrace, and she breathed in his sweet yet spicy cologne. "Hey, you," she said, looking up at him. "I brought—" she began to say, but was silenced by his mouth, just as he'd done the day before in his office. When she curled her arms around his neck, Khloe felt a tap on her waist. When she pulled away from him, she noticed a little girl staring up at them.

"Uncle Derek, is this the lady you've been talking on and on about?" she asked, as she placed her hands on her hips.

Derek bent down to her eye level. "Savannah, this is Khloe." He looked up at Khloe. "Khloe, this is Savannah."

Khloe bent down to Savannah's level, too, and said, "Hi, Savannah. It's nice to meet you. I've heard so much about you."

Her green eyes curiously sparkled, and she looked at Derek and then back to Khloe. "Hi," she finally said, shyly.

"I brought you a surprise," Khloe said, hoping it would help ease the introductions between her and Savannah.

"You did?" she shrieked, suddenly leaping toward Khloe, her shyness evaporating in an instant.

"Do you like doughnuts?"

"I do." She giggled. "But only the ones that have colored sprinkles on them."

"Well, that's exactly what I have." Khloe winked at Derek, and Savannah started jumping up and down.

"Go on inside and take your seat at the table," Derek told Savannah, adding, "but first I need to talk to Khloe." He reached into the bag and handed Savannah the box of doughnuts. "We'll be there in a few moments."

Eagerly, she took them and said, "Okay," and then the energetic six-year-old skipped back into the house.

Khloe looked at Derek and her heart fluttered. "She's absolutely precious."

"And you're absolutely stunning," he said, kissing her lips.

Her knees weakened, and his affection warmed her from the chill in the air. "Mmm," she said after Derek pulled away.

Holding the grocery bags in one hand, he said, "I just cannot wait until her quiet time." And he led them to the entrance of his house.

"And what exactly is quiet time?" Khloe asked.

"I give her a healthy snack, and she has a choice between reading any book she wants or watching an educational cartoon," he told her. "And most of the time, she chooses to read."

"I like how she thinks," Khloe commented, already loving how the little girl chose reading. *At least Savannah and I have one thing in common*, she thought.

Derek gave Khloe a grin as they crossed the threshold. "Come on, let's go have brunch."

*****

Khloe had no intention of overstaying past brunch, but she was having so much fun with Savannah and Derek—who stole a few kisses between playing with the little girl. When he asked if she'd like to stay for dinner too, she graciously accepted the offer. "Well, how do you think things are going?" Khloe asked Derek as they sat outside on the patio and watched Savannah swing on a new play-set, which was a gift from Derek's parents.

"I think pretty well," he replied, and then lazily placed his arm around her shoulders, taking a sip of his red wine.

Khloe nodded. "I agree." She looked off into the distance and waved at Savannah, who waved back. Savannah had clung to Khloe like a new best friend the whole day. They sat beside each other at brunch, played dolls while Derek cleaned up, drew pictures of princesses wearing fancy gowns, and Khloe braided Savannah's hair before having an indoor princess picnic. The day had been better than Khloe could've ever imagined.

Derek looked at his watch and hollered, "Just a few more minutes then it's bedtime!"

"Okay," Savannah replied back with a frown, then suddenly her face turned up. "Can Khloe tuck me into bed and read me a story?"

"I'd love to," Khloe told Savannah, who then leaped off the swing and ran toward them.

"Okay, I'll go pick out a book," she said and raced inside.

"Good, and while you're doing that, brush your teeth, too," said Derek, just as Savannah closed the door.

Khloe couldn't help but smile. "She certainly seems comfortable here," observed Khloe, sipping the last bit of her wine.

"Believe me, it wouldn't have been this easy if you weren't here," he said, leaning over and kissing Khloe's lips. "You're a natural with her."

She shrugged her shoulders and grinned. "Hey, I do what I can." She placed her hand on Derek's thigh.

"What's going on in that beautiful head of yours?" Derek asked.

Khloe smiled wide as she stared at the man who sat beside her. "How about I show you instead?" she said, then kissed him twice on the lips.

"You know, I really don't like this being responsible thing. Would it really be so bad if a six-year-old knew that her uncle might have a woman in his room?"

"Take me on a few more dates, and then we might find out together," she said, winking at him flirtatiously.

"You're such a tease," he said, before kissing her quickly on the lips.

"Oh, I know," she replied, standing. Khloe reached for Derek's hand and they headed inside, then Khloe went up to Savannah's room, leaving him downstairs to do the dishes.

Earlier in the evening, Derek told her about how he had Savannah's room painted, with Mary supervising the workers, while he was in California. It was a definitely a girl's room, and Khloe admired the bright pink paint with scattered purple squares covering the walls. After observing Savannah's room, she saw her in her double bed, along with about a dozen stuffed animals and dolls around her, and on her lap was a pile of books. "So, which book do you want me to read?" Khloe asked, taking a seat on the edge of the bed.

"All of them," Savannah replied in a tired voice.

"How about we start with one for now, and we'll see if you're still awake?" Khloe took the book that Savannah handed her, *The Day I Lost My Cupcake*. She turned to the first page and started to read but was immediately interrupted.

"Come sit by me?" Savannah asked, eagerly shoving her stuffed animals and dolls out of the way.

"Oh, of course," Khloe said, without hesitation, taken aback by the little girl's sweet gesture. As she re-positioned herself on

Savannah's bed, she felt Savannah's small head rest against her arm.

"You can start now," Savannah instructed.

After about five minutes of reading, Khloe heard heavy breathing and noticed Savannah was peacefully sleeping. Khloe didn't want to wake Savannah but didn't know how to escape without doing so. Inching away very carefully, Khloe tuned off the light on Savannah's nightsand, twisted her legs to the side of the bed, and watched Savannah unconsciously adjust her head on her pillow. Khloe bent down and gently kissed the little girl on the top of her head, saying, "Good night," and began to walk out of her room, accidently bumping into her dresser. She paused for a moment. When she didn't think she'd woke her, she continued to the door.

"Khloe?" Savannah said in a whisper.

Crap, I woke her! "Yes, Savannah?" she replied in a soft voice, standing at the doorway.

"I'm sorry for getting my uncle in trouble."

"What are you talking about, sweetie?"

"You know, that night when you called, and I was playing games on his phone."

"Savannah, it's not your fault. You didn't do anything wrong."

"You know Uncle Derek likes you, right? He talks about you all the time." She giggled, adding, "I think he's got a crush on you."

Khloe felt herself blush. "And I think I have a crush on him, too," she said to Savannah. "Now, get some sleep, and I'll see you soon. Good night."

"Good night, Khloe," Savannah said.

Once she took one last look at Savannah, Khloe headed downstairs to find Derek waiting for her in the living room.

"So, how'd the reading go?" he asked her, handing her a glass of wine.

"Thank you." She took the glass from him and sat beside him.

"Pretty well, I think, though she did say something about you."

"Oh, she did, huh?" Derek asked, grinning. "And what was that?"

Khloe took a small sip of wine, then put her glass on the table. "Well, let me see if I remember correctly," she said tapping her chin, pretending to mess with him.

Derek laughed and wrapped his arm around her, bringing her closer to him. "Come on, spill it."

"She said something about you having a crush on me," she said, and then her voice got serious. "Do you, Derek?"

He put his glass on the table and traced her cheek with his thumb. "Just a little one," he said, which made Khloe laugh, and he pushed her back on the pillows and placed his lips over hers.

CHAPTER FORTY-ONE

Gabby

"Okay, when we talked on the phone last week, you said you and Harry decided on a small wedding?" Jules asked, confirming what she'd been told.

Gabby eagerly nodded. "Yes, that's correct." She sat back in one of Jules's dining room chairs and casually flipped through options for themes, decorations, and other ideas for her and Harry's wedding and reception, but everything she saw was so elaborate and way over the top for what she and Harry had in mind. "So, Jules..." she began, sliding the book away from her. When Jules looked up from taking notes, Gabby tried to find the words to say what she and Harry discussed the night before. "Today, Harry's going to ask Jeff to be his best man, and Andrew to be his other one."

"Oh, Gabby, that's so sweet! I just know the boys will love standing beside Harry at the altar."

"Well, I was wondering if you would be my Matron of Honor." She held up a hand, adding, "I know we haven't known each other long and if you're not comfortable with it I'll understand—"

To Gabby's excitement and surprise, Jules leaped out of her seat, ran around the table that sat between them, and threw her arms around Gabby's neck. "Yes, I'd be honored to," she replied, hugging her tight.

When they parted, Gabby smiled. "I was hoping you'd accept, and since you did, I have a little something for you." She reached down into her purse, and then handed Jules a box, wrapped with white paper and a silver bow.

"Oh, Gabby, you didn't have to do anything for me," Jules commented, reclaiming her seat across from Gabby, and proceeded to open the box. Holding up the silver heart necklace that Gabby had Jules, Jeff and Andrew's birthstones added to it, Jules dropped her jaw. "This is beautiful," she said. "I don't have anything like this, and I love it." She draped it over her neck, and reached for Gabby's hands. "Thank you for giving me something I'll treasure forever."

"You're very welcome," she said, squeezing Jules's hand. When they parted, Gabby gnawed on her bottom lip before adding, "Also, Harry and I were wondering if we could somehow honor Lilly." She paused and looked at Jules, who had a stone-cold sober expression on her face, though her eyes were blinking, which Gabby could only guess meant she was paying close attention. "We'd love to have our wedding colors be purple and brown. It was Harry's idea, and I loved the suggestion, too. If it's okay, would you mind wearing a purple dress and carrying lilies—"

"I think that would be a beautiful way to honor her," Jules told her, with tears in her eyes. She reached for the napkin, which lay under her cup of hot tea, wiped her eyes, and nodded. "It'll be perfect. Just perfect."

Once the color theme had been chosen, Gabby and Jules continued to sit at the dining room table for hours, working on flowers (they'd put a call into Khloe's Flower Shop, and Khloe assured her she'd love to do the flowers), and Jules had vendors for napkins, caterers, a lighting company, and everything else they would need for the big day, until Jeff, Andrew, and Harry came home from playing golf.

"Hey, honey," Jeff said, bending down to kiss Jules on the lips, then went around the table to hug Gabby. "How's the wedding stuff coming along?" he asked.

"Absolutely wonderful, all thanks to your lovely wife," she said, standing to hug Harry when he came in the room. "Hello, my darling," she said, and then kissed his lips, just before Andrew came in and ran up to her, putting his arms around Gabby's waist.

"Hi, Gabby—um, I mean, Grandma Gabby." He looked at his parents, Harry, and then up at her, as though hoping he hadn't said anything to get him in trouble. "I can call you that now, right?"

"Absolutely, sweetie," she told him, after she bent down and kissed the top of his sweaty head.

"Well, now that we're all together," Jeff began, as he put his hand around his wife's waist. "Jules, Andrew, and I have some news."

Gabby looked at Harry, seeing if he knew what Jeff was talking about and he shook his head, and they gave Jeff and Jules their undivided attention.

"I'm going to be a big brother!" Andrew shouted with his hands in the air, just as Jules opened her mouth to speak, which turned into a smile and then a laugh from all of them. When they quieted down, Andrew said to Gabby and Harry, "Mom and Dad told me and made me promise to not tell you." Then, Andrew turned around and said, "See, I told y'all I could keep a secret."

Jeff high-fived Andrew and said, "Good job, buddy, and just for that, I'll take you to the toy store to get a surprise."

"Yay!" Andrew chanted, clapping his hands and then hugged his dad.

"I was bursting with excitement to tell you all morning," Jules said to Gabby after the two hugged, and then Gabby hugged Jeff, telling him, "Congratulations." She stood back and looked at Jules, Jeff, Andrew, and Harry, thinking how much had changed, along with how fortunate she felt.

"I had a feeling something was up when you weren't drinking at Thanksgiving," Gabby commented, which now made Jules's crying at Thanksgiving and then the excitement about the wedding make more sense.

"Yeah, I could tell you assumed something, but thanks for not asking about it—chances are I would've spilled the beans, and, of course, we wanted to be sure to include this little one," she said, picking Andrew up and kissing his cheek.

After staying another hour, talking about the wedding and the new baby, Gabby and Harry said their goodbyes and walked hand in hand out the door. When Harry reached to open Gabby's passenger side door, she placed her hands on his, stopping him.

"Is everything okay, love?" he asked, looking worried as Gabby's eyes formed with tears.

Without saying a word, Gabby pulled Harry close to her and kissed his lips. "I love you, Harry."

He kissed her back. "Where's all this coming from? You're awfully affectionate today—even this morning," he commented with a wink.

"I just want you to know I appreciate you, and that I'm blessed. I didn't think I'd ever fall in love again, but you proved me wrong, and I'm so looking forward to being your wife."

"That makes two of us," he said, wiggling his brows, which made Gabby laugh. After allowing him to open the door and she quickly got in, Gabby was certain they'd be making love the second they got to her home, which they'd be putting on the market within the next few weeks.

CHAPTER FORTY-TWO

Connie

Dressed in her lime green and orange flannel pajamas, Connie sat on her couch to watch a marathon of Christmas-themed Hallmark made for TV movies. She reached for her new purple journal and started to write her goals and resolutions for the upcoming year.

Connie's New Life!

1. *Tell yourself you're beautiful each day, even when you don't feel like it.*
2. *Get up early and do your hair and make-up—even when all you want to do is go back to bed for another forty-five minutes.*
3. *Don't worry about what other people think.*
4. *Believe in yourself, even when you feel your whole world is crashing down on you.*
5. *You can be like Cinderella and have your happily ever after, too, so get out there and find your prince—a real one—not imaginary!*

Connie looked over the five rules she'd set for herself and liked what she saw—except for the last one. Yes, she'd done a horrible thing by lying to Walt, but she began to think of it as part of her journey and part of her story, on the path to finding the one. She looked up from her journal, just in time to see a commercial of a waving Santa. Connie laughed to herself, thinking that, without any doubt, he'd be putting coal in her stocking this year because she'd been a very naughty girl. "I'll be good next year," she said right as her doorbell rang. She set the journal on the table and got up to answer the door. When she did, nothing could've prepared her more for who was standing in front of her.

"Hi, Connie," Walt said.

"Hi," Connie whispered, reaching her hand out to the doorframe to steady herself. She couldn't believe he was standing in front of her. "What—what are you doing here?" The way he looked in his brown dress shoes, dark jeans, and off-white sweater took her breath away. She also couldn't help but notice he was holding a wrapped gift. *Damn,* she thought, taking in the sexy view in front of her.

"Can I come in?" he asked. "I need to talk to you."

"Sure," she said, extending the door and inviting him in. She followed him to her couch, leaving the middle seat on the couch empty between them. She wanted to ask about Miss Red Dress but resisted the urge. *Whatever he came to say, you can take it, Connie.*

Too afraid to say anything, and even more afraid to hear what he had to say, Connie was too afraid of what he wanted to talk about, deciding to avoid looking at him and stare straight ahead at the TV.

"The first moment I saw your picture online, I thought you were the most beautiful woman I'd ever seen, which is why I replied to you, genuinely looking for a relationship. When we met, you were exactly the woman I'd been waiting for all my life, and I couldn't stop thinking about you." He leaned toward Connie and handed her the present, and she hesitantly took it. "Before you open it, I want you to know that I've done a lot of thinking and need to know one thing, so no matter what the answer is, please answer me honestly." He paused for a moment before he asked, "Were your feelings real, or was I just some joke to you?"

Connie turned toward him, positioned her legs under her, and clasped her hands together as she held the present close to her. "I didn't go searching for someone like you. I only meant to find someone who would make me feel the way you did. So, when I walked into Tequila Taco and saw you, my heart melted. I felt like I was in a dream world. I've never had anyone's touch affect me like yours does. I loved all our conversations, I loved getting to know you, and especially what we shared that day we went to the rose garden." She paused for a moment to remember the way he'd made love to her after they got back to her place. "You were my first, Walt, and that was really special to me. When you told me I was beautiful..." she said, feeling a knot begin to grow in her throat, "that was something I'll never forget. Now, you ask me if everything was real, and my answer to you is yes. Walt, my feelings were and are still very real for you." Though she doubted she'd hear him say it back to her, she wanted to tell him everything, even if that meant ripping her heart into teeny-tiny pieces. Tears welled in her eyes, but she blinked to hold them back.

After what seemed like a lifetime, he nodded, giving Connie no sign of what he was thinking. Finally, he pointed to her lap. "Open the gift."

"Please, just tell me you're going to forgive me for what I did." She looked up at him with confusion and desperation. She needed to know where they stood, and her heart beat faster and faster, waiting for his answer.

"Just open it," he urged, giving her a slight grin from the corner of his lips.

Connie quickly tore the shiny white ribbon off the paper and ripped into the gift. When she saw Walt had bought her an antique edition of *Cinderella*, her body started to shake, not believing what she held in her hands. "You did this...for me?" Tears streamed down her face as she looked up at him. It was the most special gift she'd ever been given, but it didn't mean anything if she didn't have Walt by her side.

"I did," he whispered.

"Why?" she asked, shaking her head.

"Because, even with your lies, I want you in my life, Connie."

In one quick stride, she leaped on him, closing the gap between them, pressing her lips to his. "Oh, Walt, I want to be in your life, too. So, so very much." She looked at him and placed her hands on his face. "Again, I'm so very sorry I hurt you."

"Let's not worry about that anymore." He reached for her and she fell into his arms, allowed him to take the book from her, and set it on the table in front of them. "Now, let me show you how much I missed you." He pushed Connie on her back and began kissing her on her neck and lips, and within seconds he'd lifted her shirt, and soon, she remembered what it felt like to be loved.

*****

After Connie and Walt made love, they lay next to each other, her head resting on his shoulder, and his arm around her.

Connie looked up at him, knowing that it probably wasn't the best time to bring it up, but she needed to know. "I have a question for you."

"Oh, and what would that be?" he asked, his fingertips grazing her back.

"When I saw you the other day, who was that woman in the red dress?" When he didn't respond, she hesitated before asking, "Was she someone you were seeing?"

He roared with laughter. "No, Connie, I wasn't dating her. That was my mother."

Instantly, Connie felt like a fool. "Are you serious?" she asked him, burying her face in her hands. "Wow, okay, then. I guess I have nothing to be jealous of then, do I?" She laughed.

"Nope, not at all," he said, kissing her forehead, himself chuckling as well. "Nor will you ever."

"Well, she's absolutely beautiful."

"I guess my family has good genes, you know, since you find me so attractive," he joked.

Connie laughed. "Okay, one more question, and then I'll stop for the night." She looked at Walt. "How did you get into my gym? I saw you there with another woman…"

"I was at your gym because my trainer—who lives here in your building—had me come over here to work out, because she had conflicting schedules."

"Well, the gym is doing great things for your body," she said, crawling on top of him with full intentions of taking every advantage of him.

Later that night, after they went out to dinner then went back to Connie's, they made love one more time, then Walt fell asleep. As she listened to his soft snore, Connie felt at peace, knowing now that her life had purpose. She had a job she'd be starting soon, a man in her life, and as each day passed her confidence was growing—as her body mass was shrinking. She was now becoming the swan she'd always wanted to be. No longer would she have to fake having someone in her life, or worry about not looking as beautiful as other women. With Walt by her side, she knew she could face anything, even on bad days.

She draped her arm over Walt's naked torso and wanted to whisper, "I love you, my prince charming," but that was something Connie would tell him at a later time.

CHAPTER FORTY-THREE

Khloe

It had been just over a week since she and Derek had gotten back together and from when Khloe met Savannah, and she felt as if she were in the best place she'd been in her life. During the days, she worked at her flower shop, but her nights were spent with Derek and Savannah.

As Khloe hopped out of the shower and dried herself off, she couldn't wait to see the man she was smitten with. Derek told her he had a surprise for her, but when she'd asked him for clues, he simply laughed and said to pack an overnight bag. She and Derek had kept their relationship G-rated for Savannah's sake (PG-13, though, after she went to bed), and they had managed to keep intimacy at bay, but Khloe didn't know how much longer she could hold out. Each night after she read a book to Savannah, she and Derek tempted and teased each other on the couch, forcing her to go home feeling like a boiling volcano—a lot of heat with no eruption.

Wrapping her towel around her body and another around her head, Khloe looked at herself in the mirror. She was grinning hugely, eager to find out what Derek had up his sleeve, as she grabbed her overnight bag from under her bed. In it, she packed tennis shoes, a pair of jeans, a T-shirt, and a red fleece sweater, along with a set of

266

charcoal cotton Cosabella pajamas. She thought about adding in a black babydoll nightgown, too, but she didn't want to get her hopes up.

An hour and a half later Khloe looked in the mirror. Dressed in black tights and an off-white long sweater with a red scarf, she approved of her appearance. After one quick spritz of Eternity perfume, she picked up her things and headed out the door.

As she started pulling out of the driveway, she stopped the car and threw it in park. She ran back into the house and grabbed the nightgown. *Just in case*, she thought, as she raced back to the car and stuffed it into her overnight bag. Now she was ready.

On the way to Derek's, she decided to call Sharon. "Hey, what's up?" Khloe asked, after pressing the speed dial button on her car's speaker phone.

"Hey, yourself," Sharon replied, sounding cheerful. "I'm at Leonard's, watching him build Legos. You know, boys never grow up. Anyway, what's up with you?"

"I'm just on the way to Derek's, and thought I'd call to say hello."

Sharon laughed. "You know, you could do that at the store— since we see each other six days a week."

"Yeah, yeah, we've been so busy lately that we've barely had time to talk. So, I know you probably can't talk about it, but how are you and Leonard doing? Is the TARDIS sex still awesome?" she asked, with a laugh.

"We're good. Actually, we're great..." Sharon began, but then stopped.

"I get it. You can't talk, but I'm sensing a bit of hesitation, or even boredom?"

"You know me so well. Yeah, I guess you could say that. Though, the funny thing is, I'm okay with where we are now. I'm starting to think he really could be the one." The last sentence she said in a whisper.

"Well, if he is, then just enjoy the ride. I'm proud of you, doll, you're growing up so much," she joked. "In the end, I'm sure you two can even find ways to spice it up." If Khloe knew anything about Sharon, it was that she could juice up any relationship—whether it be in the bedroom or not. "Why not take a class together on something that interests him and one on something that interests you?"

"Thanks, Khloe, those are great ideas. I guess I've been putting it off because I hate having conversations like these. You know, the serious ones," she growled into the phone, sounding frustrated. "Anyway, it's your turn. How are you?"

After giving her the quickest summary of events with Derek, she said, "And I swear, if I don't get laid soon, I'm going to go out of my mind."

Sharon chuckled. "Well, if he told you to pack an overnight bag, then I'm sure you'll be getting action tonight? Do you not think so?"

"I doubt it," Khloe said, frowning to her rearview mirror. "Derek's just too responsible to do anything with Savannah in the house, but I see where he's coming from, and I respect that."

"Well, if you don't get any tonight, I know what I'm getting you for Christmas."

Stopped at a light, Khloe rolled her eyes. "That's really sweet of you, Sharon, but I can buy my own sex toys, thank you very much." They shared a giggle, and Khloe ran a hand through her hair in sexual frustration.

"Well, ya gotta do what ya gotta do."

"Believe me, the thought has crossed my mind, but we're trying to be a good influence around her. I'm sure it'll happen when the time's right."

"I hope so—for your sake, because you've been kind of cranky lately."

"Oh, hush," Khloe replied, turning on Derek's street. "Anyway, I'm almost at his place, but I'll talk to you soon."

"Go getcha some!" Sharon cheered.

"Have a good night with Leonoard, and you do the same," she told Sharon, hoping she was able to help her friend with her boredom stage of her relationship with Leonard, but now it was time to focus on Derek.

"You look divine," Derek told Khloe when he came outside to greet her at her car.

"Thank you," she said, eyeing him up and down, taking note of how handsome he could make "causal" look in his jeans and brown pullover. "You do, too," she said, and then gave him a quick kiss on the lips and handed him her bag. "Where's Savannah?" she asked, surprised she wasn't there to meet Khloe like normal.

Derek wrapped his arms around her waist, pulling her close. "Well," he began as he kissed her lightly on her neck. "Earlier today, Savannah and I were out for ice cream, and we ran into one of my close work friends and his daughter. They met a while back and seemed to get along well, so she invited Savannah to her birthday party." He kissed her lips. "I hope it's okay that for now, I'm your only host."

"I think I can manage being alone with you for a few hours," she said, putting her arms around his neck and letting Derek continue kissing her, each kiss getting more and more intsense by the second. "Hey, Casanova, how about we have dinner first?"

Derek stopped but kept his lips on her neck. "Okay, but we will continue this," he said, and then kissed her once more. "Come on, dinner's almost ready." He took her hand in his, leading her into the kitchen as sweet and spicy aromas floated in the air.

After a scrumptious candle-lit dinner and dessert, they sat on Derek's couch, cuddling. "Dinner was amazing," she said and sipped the last drop of wine in her glass.

"I'm glad you enjoyed it. Lasagna is one of my favorite dishes, but Savannah doesn't like it. Right now, she's all about chicken tenders and SpaghettiOs," he said with a laugh.

Khloe watched Derek as he talked about Savannah. It was easy to see that he was easily taking over as a father figure in her life. "Well, feel free to make it again for me anytime you'd like," she said, before kissing his cheek. Whether it was all the red wine, delicious food, or the fact that Savannah wasn't there, Khloe felt ready to let Derek know she wanted to be with him.

Derek stared into her eyes as he brushed her hair out of her face. "God, you're sexy," he whispered.

Take me now! She bowed her head, feeling the blush creep to her cheeks. "Thank you," she said in a sultry voice that made her seem like she was some low-budget porn star.

Derek leaned toward her and teased her skin with his tongue, making her crave to have him inside her.

The slightest sensation of his delicate kisses almost sent Khloe over the edge. When he kissed the nape of her neck, Khloe whimpered and dug her nails into the back of his shirt. While his kisses had turned her on before, she'd never felt so ready to have him. "Um, Derek," she said, hating to break the mood—even for a second.

"Uh huh," he said, slowing his pace, but still nuzzling the side of her neck as the tips of his fingers ran along the band of her pants. He looked down at her, and their eyes locked, but he didn't stop. Very slowly, his hand slipped under her pants, and a smile crossed his face.

"You like that, don't you?" she asked him, almost breathless, loving the fact that she caught him by surprise going commando, instead of trying to stop him to take their actions upstairs.

"Don't you?" he said, kissing her hard on the mouth as his hand slid up between her legs.

When she felt him enter her, Khloe's eyes rolled back and her neck fell against the cushions. "Derek...I—I think we should take this upstairs." *Anymore of this is bed-worthy.*

On cue, Derek stood up, reached for her hand, and said, "Well, come this way, my lady," he said, and she more than willingly followed behind him.

After an hour of gentle—yet, very erotic—lovemaking, Khloe lay sprawled on top of Derek's bed, perspiration glistening on her forehead. She was in heaven. *Now I know what TARDIS sex feels like,* she thought, giggling to herself.

Derek propped himself up on one arm. "What's so funny?"

"I just haven't felt like this before," she told him, thinking it would be for the best if she kept the orgasm comment to herself—at least for the time being. She kissed Derek on his lips, inching closer to him. "You, Derek, are an extraordinary lover, and I cannot wait until next time." She tossed the covers off and started to get out of bed, thinking that Savannah would be home soon, but Derek stopped her with a hand on her back.

"Derek, but what about Savannah?" She crossed her arms over her waist, suddenly feeling shy in front of him, even though he'd just sucked, toyed, and tantalized her body to her heart's desire.

"Well, do you want to know the rest of your surprise?" he asked her, flashing a seductive grin, turning on his side to face her.

Khloe cocked her head. "There's more?" she asked cheerfully, arching an eye at him.

Derek nodded, patting the spot beside him, and said, "I'll tell you if you come here."

She lay back down next to him and Derek began kissing her lips, neck, and shoulders.

"Derek, you have to stop," Khloe repeated, this time more forcefully.

"Sweetie, Savannah's not coming tonight." Khloe tilted her head and frowned in confusion, then allowed him to continue. "Oh, did I forget to tell you it's a slumber party?" Derek asked playfully. Khloe's eyes widened and as she grabbed a pillow behind her and threw it at him, but he stopped her, pulling her in for a kiss, which, this time, she didn't try to stop.

EPILOGUE

Springtime was almost over, and Khloe wasn't looking forward to summer, only because of the scorching Texas heat. After all the April showers, Khloe was smiling at the May flowers that popped up everywhere on her drive to her shop.

When she entered her store, Sharon was busy with a customer, so she picked up the ringing phone. "Khloe's Flower Shop, how may I help you?"

"Khloe, it's Millicent!"

"Millicent, it's so good to hear from you. What can I do for you?" she asked. She thought back to Millicent's wedding day and how beautiful it turned out. Khloe was a bit surprised and very thankful to have received a ten-thousand-dollar paycheck from the governor to her business, along with a separate check filled out to her personally, with a special thank you note expressing how she and her flower shop had exceeded Millicent's expectations. Even Mrs. Pluma made a personal call to Khloe the Monday after the wedding to compliment Khloe on what a beautiful job she'd done, which made Khloe try to offer a percentage to her, but she still wouldn't have it.

She giggled. "Well, newlywed bliss is amazing. Actually, so much so that I'm expecting!" she shrieked into the phone. "I just found out this last week!"

"Oh, wow, congratulations," Khloe said, surprised by Millicent's revelation. "That's great news."

"Thank you. We're very excited. Anyway, I was wondering if you would do the flowers for the baby shower. We're planning it for the middle of August—I'm sure you've seen the news that Daddy bought a new piece of property and built a special place for me and my hubby, and, of course, our bundle-of-joy-to-be, so that'll be where the shower will be held."

While wedding season was a busy time for her shop, after getting to know Millicent, she knew she could handle a simple baby shower—or so she hoped. "Of course, I'd be happy to help." After Khloe reassured her she still had her contact information, she promised to call her later on in the week to schedule a time for a meeting.

"Thank you so much, Khloe! You're the best!" They hung up. Minutes later, she said, "Good morning," to Sharon.

"You're a little too perky for the morning," Sharon said with a yawn. "What's up?"

"Oh, please, I've been giddy since Derek and I got back together. I guess it's just the way he makes me feel."

"Derek only gets more handsome and Savannah gets cuter and cuter. You're one lucky lady." Over the past few weeks, Khloe, Deerek, Savannah, Sharon and Leonard had gone out for brunch and dinners on several occasions, and after each one, Sharon gave Khloe a nod, meaning Derek was the man for her. "Oh, okay, so, this reminds me, I received an email from your mother this morning, telling me to start talking marriage with you."

Khloe rolled her eyes. A month after Derek and Khloe got back together, Khloe introduced Derek and Savannah to her parents, via FaceTime. Leading up to the moment, she was nervous, but much to her relief, everything went better than imagined. Khloe, her mother, and Savannah planned to go shopping and Derek and her dad were going to play golf the next time they came in town. "Oh, my gosh, I'm so sorry. You know how my mom is," she said to Sharon, wishing she'd never given her mother Sharon's email address because she didn't need her mother hounding her friends about her daughter's love life.

"Hey, I don't mind, and to be honest, it seems like you're the happiest you've ever been, so why not marry him—or at least think about it?"

"Because, like you and Lenoard, Derek and I are happy where we are in our relationship, and I don't want to rush anything." The past few weeks she'd spent with Derek and Savannah had been wonderful. Whether it was going to Derek's to help them make dinner, attending Savannah's dance recitals, helping her braid her hair and paint her nails, Khloe enjoyed all of it. Though, when social media caught wind of where Savannah was now living, Derek hadn't questioned Khloe's loyalty, and thanks to security guards Derek hired, Savannah was even more protected. On most nights, after Savannah was put to bed, Khloe relished in the precious, quiet moments she had with Derek. Though Khloe never slept over, Derek had recently brought up the subject of their moving in together, but Khloe thought it was way too soon. "While I'm not there yet, I fall for him more each day. He's the most amazing man I've ever met." She shook her head and then said, "As for my mother, it's like she's died and gone to heaven. We FaceTime with them all the time, and she's started sending gifts to Savannah, along with wine for us."

"Well, we know your mother's in love," Sharon joked.

"Yeah, no kidding. I've also talked to her about getting Savannah involved when it's too early to see where this might go. I mean, it's not even been a year yet."

"Well, I'm glad to know you've handled it." She slipped her purple apron over her head, ready to get to work. "Well, I'm going to get to work. Holler if you need me," she said, then disappeared into the workroom.

"Will do," she replied, then reached for a pen before Khloe sat down and started writing messages.

Darling,

I love having you as my wife!

Yours always,

Harry

Khloe thought of how much she learned about watching Gabriella and Harry through their passing of the cards she'd written for their arrangements, and she was even more ecstatic for Gabby when she found out she was engaged. Not only had Khloe's Flower Shop created flowers for the wedding, she was surprised when she'd received an invitation, with the option of bringing a guest, which Khloe did, and Gabby was more than thrilled to meet Derek. In the past few weeks, Gabby had also been coming into the shop more often, mostly with Jules, and thanks to them, Khloe had gained several more customers.

Her next card, which was to Connie from Walt, made her beam, thinking about how far Connie had come. Now, she was a confident, self-assured woman who was in a relationship with the love of her life. Last week, Khloe received a call from Walt, requesting that a large bouquet of roses be sent to Connie at work, "just because." Today's message:

You're the most beautiful woman in the world! I love you!

Walt

Hours later, Sharon observed as she locked the cash register and handed Khloe a stack of receipts. "Well, it looks like things are picking up, and just before wedding season starts, which means we'll be busy, busy, busy."

"Tell me about it." Khloe looked down at the large pile Sharon handed her. Khloe's Flower Shop was now blossoming, she was looking forward to spending the summer with Derek and Savannah and taking a vacation to Napa to visit her parents. Sharon gave Khloe a wide grin. "What?" Khloe asked.

"Just go home to the man you love," she said. "I'll finish up here." She reached back for the receipts, but Khloe didn't budge.

As much as she desperately wanted to, she shook her head. "Believe me, I'm fine. I'll see Derek and Savannah later tonight."

"Okay, but I'm sure you'd rather be doing something else," Sharon said with a giggle.

There's nothing better in this world than an orgasm from Derek. Khloe felt herself blush. "Oh, yes, most definitely. Like I told you after the first time I slept with Derek, I love TARDIS sex—" Before she could continue, Sharon started jumping up and down.

"Ha, ha!" she said, clapping her hands. Then she reached for Khloe's arm and grasped it. "Isn't it the most amazing feeling in the world? I swear, Leonard really is a TARDIS god, if there is one."

"Speaking of him, how are things going?"

"So, so good!" She beamed. "Thank you for encouraging me to talk to him. We've been trying new things each month, and tomorrow night, he's taking me for a hot air balloon ride!" She squealed. "Though I'm afraid of heights, I'm so excited about crossing this off my bucket list."

"I'm glad to hear things are working out, and how cool about the balloon ride!" Khloe shook her head, smiling. "You're braver than I am, and I'm not afraid of heights." They shared a small chuckle, and then Khloe added, "Isn't it funny how life has a way of working itself out?" Sharon nodded and wiped a tear away.

"It sure is," she agreed.

Deciding to take Sharon's advice, Khloe gathered her personal items and went to Derek's, but before she did that, she stopped at the grocery store, where she hoped to wow him with her culinary skills by making him chicken picccata. When Derek walked in he was more than delighted to see Khloe, but was even more surprised to see Khloe in his kitchen making them dinner, which turned out to be such a success, especially when Savannah announced it was the best meal she'd ever had.

After dinner, and Khloe had read and put Savannah to sleep, she and Derek relaxed with a second bottle of wine and talked about their day, and that night, for the first time, Khloe spent the night at Derek's.

*****

The next day, after writing all the messages, Khloe went in the back and gave them to Sharon, who was working away. When she came back to the front of the shop, Derek was standing at the counter waiting for her. "Hey, you, this is a surprise," she said and threw her arms around him. "What are you doing here?"

"Oh, I just came to say hello, and to give you something," he kissed before kissing her.

Khloe got weak in the knees when she tasted mint on his lips. "I could get used to that," she said as he pulled her close to him.

"So, there's no way you can get off early, huh?" He winked.

"As much as I want to, I can't," she said, pointing to the back where Sharon was working. "We have a lot of new orders today, and I think it's better if I stay and help Sharon."

"Not even for a surprise?" he asked, pulling a key out of his pocket and handing it to her.

"Is this what I think it is?" she asked, smiling at him as she took the silver key from him.

He nodded. "Khloe, I know it's soon, but I'm falling in love with you, and Savannah is crazy about you." He held up his finger. "Oh, I almost forgot." From his shirt pocket, he pulled out a folded piece of paper, then handed it to Khloe.

She unfolded the paper to find a drawing from Savannah. It was of a house that looked just like Derek's, and above it, written in clouds were the words, *Move in with us!* When she placed a hand over her heart, her lips turned upward, and she looked at Derek. "There's no way I could ever say no to the two of you," she told him, before jumping in his arms and tears forming in her eyes.

After spinning her around a few times with joy, he sat her down on a stool behind the counter and brushed a strand of hair back from her face. "You make me so happy, Khloe," he said, closing his mouth on hers.

Breathless, she held up a finger. "You know what, I'll be right back." She rushed to the workroom to look for Sharon. "Hey, how's it coming?" she asked her, trying to sound breezy, like she wasn't investigating how much work Sharon still had left to do.

Sharon laughed, waving Khloe away. "I saw him walk in, so just go have fun with Derek," she said with a grin, knowing it would make Khloe happy, and Khloe leaped around the table and hugged her tight.

"He just asked me to move in with him!" Khloe bounced up and down, clapping her heands in excitement, and soon, Sharon stopped what she was working on and joined in on Khloe's news.

"Well, what did you say?" Sharon asked, knowing she was hesitant.

"I said yes, and while I know it's soon—like I told you—it just feels right."

"Then go, go celebrate!"

"You're the best," Khloe told her friend, giving her another hug, and then quickly went to her office, grabbed her purse, and put on her sunglasses. "On second thought, I think Sharon can do without me today," Khloe said to Derek only moments later, standing in front of him.

Derek reached for Khloe's hand, and they headed for their home, where they popped a bottle of champagne he'd had waiting for them, and spent part of the day in bed, until it was time to they went to pick Savannah up from school.

THE END

Acknowledgments

To the readers, this book has been in the making for a long time, but due to vertigo challenges and my brother's tragic death, it got pushed aside. In advance, I thank you for your patience, love and understanding for the delay in sharing Khloe's, Gabby's and Connie's story with you. I hope you enjoy reading it as much as I enjoyed writing it.

Tom IV (my Clayton), thank you for being the best "twin" brother a sister could have. Not only did you teach me about motivation, but you also you inspired me to be the best I can be. I miss you every single day, but now you're my guardian angel watching over me. "I'll be there for you…and lightswitch!" R.I.P., little bro.

Evan, you're my greatest love and best motivator. From the start to finish of this book, you've picked me up when I needed it, and have been by my side every step of the way. You say you love me, but the truth is, I love you more.

Dad, I don't know how you do it, but through all the ups and downs, you've continued to be my rock. Thank you for reading my books, even though they're not in your genre, and I hope my characters never let you down because you've never done that to me—especially during the hard times. You will *never know how much I love you*.

To my long list of extended family and friends who have continuously cheered me on through all the highs and lows—I am truly blessed to have you all in my life. To Michelle and Ryan, thank you for your unconditional friendship, love, and support, because it means so much to me.

Finally, to all my author friends on Facebook and Twitter, and the Chick Lit Goddess and ChickLitChatHQ groups; without all your helpful advice, I would've given up long ago. To my beta readers, thank you for loving Connie, relating to Gabby, and for helping Khloe find her way. Thank you to my editors and copyeditors, Samantha Stroh Bailey, Francine LaSala, Wendy Janes, and Samantha March—without you all, this book would be nothing.

Scarlett Rugers, thank you for my beautiful cover—it's just as I imagined. You're brilliant! Also, thank you, Polgarus Studio, for the amazing formatting job.

ABOUT THE AUTHOR

Isabella grew up with a book in her hand, and to this day nothing has changed. She focuses her time on featuring other writers on her blog, Chick Lit Goddess, along with organizing Goddess Book Tours, and is a member of the Romance Writers of America.

She lives in Dallas with her husband, enjoys spicy Mexican food, margaritas, gin on the rocks (with a splash of lime). She loves spending time with family and friends, and cheering on the Texas Rangers. Not only is Isabella an author, she's also a Scentsy consultant and hoarder.

Isabella's short story, "Meet Me Under the Mistletoe," was featured in Simon & Fig's Christmas anthology, *Merry & Bright*, in November 2013. *The Right Design* is her first novel, and she's currently working on her next release.

OTHER BOOKS BY THE AUTHOR

"Meet Me Under the Mistletoe" featured in
Merry & Bright: Six Tales of Christmas Cheer

The Right Design